Don't Be Late in the Morning

KAREN ETTE

Published by Goldcrest Books International Ltd
www.goldcrestbooks.com
publish@goldcrestbooks.com

ISBN: 978-1-911505-61-7
eISBN: 978-1-911505-62-4

For David

He certainly had no wish to die, and now that he had got what he wanted, a dust-and-ashes feeling had come. He neither hated the Germans nor loved the Belgians; the only possible motive for going was 'heroism in the abstract', and that didn't seem a very logical reason for risking one's life.

Roland Leighton, in Brittain, V,
Testament of Youth

Contents

Prologue

The stretcher-bearers moved down the congested underground room. They passed a doctor, who was sitting beside a makeshift operating table holding his head in his hands, desperately in need of sleep. The air was fetid, and they hacked and wheezed as the heavy stench filled their lungs. They approached a nurse who was finishing-off retying a dressing around an ambulant soldier's face.

'This one?' a bearer asked, pointing to an unconscious soldier who was lying on a broken stretcher behind her.

The nurse turned and bent down. She pulled a torn tunic upwards to cover the shattered man and shook her head. Picking up a blood-spattered water bottle, which lay empty beside the soldier, she followed the stretcher-bearers out of the cellar.

She never looked back.

PART ONE

FORESHADOWING OF YOUTH

Chapter 1

Thursday, 1st September 1904

Tripe

'No!' David cried out when he heard the school bell sounding its call over the rooftops and through the narrow streets. 'No, no, no, no, no.' A can full of tripe swung from his clenched hand; it was his final delivery of the morning and he needed get to school before the bell stopped ringing, although he knew that was now impossible.

Standing on the freshly scrubbed step, he hammered on the vicarage's front door.

'Come on, come on, come on,' he whispered under his breath. But no one came. He pounded on the door until his knuckles hurt. Still no one came. There was nothing else for it – he left the can of tripe on the doorstep and ran back down the drive, across High Street, and just as he was making his way along School Street the bell gave two elongated peels and then fell silent. His shoulders drooped and he slunk into school.[1]

---

1. See photograph 1, page 319

David pulled off his cap and crept into the classroom, which was silent; forty heads bowed as the headmaster read from the Book of Common Prayer. He didn't stop reading but his dark eyes glared at the noisy latecomer who sidled into his place at the end of a long bench at the back of the classroom. After prayers, the boys in the infant class stood up to leave and head into their own room, but the headmaster raised his hand to tell them to stay where they were. He intertwined his fingers in a slow, thoughtful movement and glowered towards the nine-year-old who had arrived late. David's mouth was as dry as sawdust and he swallowed hard.

'Adcock!'

'Yes, sir.'

'Stand up, boy, when you are spoken to.'

David scrambled to his feet.

'Yes, sir.'

'Come out to the front and tell the class why you are late, again!'

David lowered his head and walked slowly to the front. He could feel his face burning, not only from running but also from embarrassment.

'Well?'

'I'm sorry, sir, but I had to deliver the tripe this morning and there were a lot of orders today.' He shuffled, finding it difficult to stand still with everyone staring at him. He saw the headmaster's eyes narrow and thought the teacher's facial expression would fit well on the outer wall of a church.

'That is no excuse for being late, boy. Hold out your left hand.'

David's stomach tightened. He felt sick, but there was no chance of avoiding the punishment. He held his hand in front of him.

'Further than that! Stretch out, boy. And turn it over, palm upwards.'

David did as he was told and closed his eyes. He heard a swish as the thin cane cut through the air, and then a pain, worse than a bee sting, worse than a dog bite, cut across his flesh.

'Oww!' he howled.

'Be quiet, boy, and hold your hand still.'

Swish, thwack, swish, thwack, swish, thwack. Then it stopped.

David wanted to cry, but he knew he couldn't. He'd get another lashing if he did, and besides, boys of his age didn't cry. Crying was for babies.

'Sit down, boy. Let that be a lesson.'

David hurried back to his seat. He heard a few sniggers as he passed the others in his class, but paid no heed.

All morning the throbbing in his hand pulsated like a Church Lads' Brigade drum, and he began to tap his foot in time with each spasm, until the headmaster slammed a ruler down on the pitted dark wood of his desk.

At playtime the boys spilled from their classrooms into the schoolyard.

'Let's look at yer 'and,' Harry Hamson said. David held out his swollen palm and a group gathered around.

'Did it 'urt much?' George Partridge asked, his ears glowing almost as red as David's palm.

'Nah.' David shrugged – it did.

'Hey, Adcock, show us your war wound.' Bobby Swann poked at David with a piece of wood.

'Clear off,' David said, and pushed the boy with ripped shorts and dark eyes away. Bobby ran across the playground to annoy some of the younger boys with his stick.

'Mam'll kill yer,' David's brother Charlie said.

'So don't tell her. It's all right for you, you get to feed the chickens – I have to deliver the tripe.'

'Remember when Whattoff used to come home with thick red lines across his legs when he'd been late to school?'

'That were through deliverin' tripe an' all,' David said.

'Yes, but he delivered it for Dad, when he were alive.'

'Mr Wakelin's all right. He gives Mam some tripe and chitlins, and a tanner, for me deliverin' it round the village.'

'Hey, David, do you want a game of football after school?' Ernest Wade was grinning; he had an inflated pig's bladder in his hands.

'Yes, we'll go down to The Green,' David said as the bell rang to call them back into their classes once more.

By the end of the school day the pain in David's hand hadn't eased much, and after the boys had all sung 'Lord, Dismiss Us, with Thy Blessing' he went outside and waited for Ernest beside the school gate. The other boys poured out like a swarm of bees leaving their hive and headed off to their homes.

'Hello.'

David looked up. A pretty girl in a dark dress and white pinafore smiled at him.

'Hello, Emily. I'm waiting for your Ernest.'

'Oh, what have you done to your hand?' Emily Jane Wade stared at David's puffed-up palm.

'I had to fight off a tiger on the way to school and it scratched me.'

'Don't be a fat head,' Emily told him. 'It looks like a caning to me.'

David shrugged and began to chuckle. Emily laughed too, and they were both helpless when Ernest arrived, inflated pig's bladder tucked under his arm.

'What do you want, Jane?' Ernest asked his sister. He had always called her Jane, not Emily, from the moment he could talk.

'We've got to go home,' she answered.

'But I'm playing football,' Ernest moaned.

'No, Ernest. We must go home.'

'Can't I come after football?'

'No you can't.' Emily looked cross. 'Mother is very ill and I've to take you home.'

'Mother's been ill for ages,' Ernest grumbled.

'Father said we have to go straight home. Now come on.' She grabbed his hand and pulled him along. David watched them until they turned the corner towards Albion Street. He then set off to face his mother; he knew he would get another clip when she saw his hand. Whattoff would probably laugh when he arrived home from the shoe factory.

A wonderful smell greeted David when he pushed open the back door. September meant Mam would do lots of baking, especially wake cakes for when the Wakes came to Syston and they could ride in the swing boats and try their luck on the hoopla. He could just eat a slab of spicy fruitcake.

Adam Wakelin was sitting at the kitchen table and David's mother was standing beside the range, her dark hair fluffed up from the heat of the oven. The kitchen felt sultry and David pulled his cap off.

'Here he is,' Mary Adcock said. 'Where have you been till now?'

'I was going to play football with Ernest Wade, but he had to go home. His mam's really bad.'

'David.' Adam Wakelin spoke; his soft voice had a slightly rough edge. David jerked his head upwards and smiled at the tripe dresser who had taken over his father's business after he'd died.

'Yes, sir.'

'Why didn't you deliver the tripe to the vicar this morning?'

'But I did.'

'Well, the vicar's wife had to come to the shop to buy some. She said she hadn't received her delivery.'

'But I did deliver it. I left it on the doorstep.'

'Why didn't you wait for someone to take it in?'

'Because the school bell was ringing and I was late.'

Mary grabbed his hand and turned it over.

'For goodness' sake! Your brother had enough canings for being late. I thought you would be different.' She raised her hand to clip his ear, but David dodged and ran out through the back door and into the street. He raced along Paddock Row and onto High Street, which he crossed and then ran up the vicarage's drive. His shoulders slumped when he saw that there was no can on the doorstep. He glanced around but couldn't see it anywhere.

'Death's head on a mop-stick,' he cursed. Someone else must have visited and decided to help themselves to the vicar's tripe. As he turned to go he heard the sound of something tapping against the ground. He moved towards some rhododendron bushes that flanked the left-hand side of the driveway, and listened.

Tap, tap, tap.

The big oak front door to the vicarage swung open and the Reverend Avery stepped outside.

'Hello, young man. What can I do for you?'

'I'm sorry, sir, but Mrs Avery thought I didn't deliver your tripe this morning. Well, I did, but it's gone.'

The vicar looked puzzled.

'I left it there.' David pointed to doorstep, now smeared with something unpleasant and far from the freshly scrubbed sill of that morning.

The tapping had begun again.

'What's that?' David asked.

Without answering the clergyman strode towards the rhododendrons. David followed him.

'Ah, there you are.' The vicar spoke to a black dog that seemed to be in some difficulty; it had its nose inside the narrow neck of a tripe can and was trying to free itself by dragging it along the ground. The vicar took the canister, gently, in his hand and pulled it from the dog's nose. He held it out to David, who could see slobbered-on tripe in the churn's lower chamber. His hand flew to his mouth and he looked up at Reverend Avery, his blue eyes bright.

'The dog tried to eat your tripe, sir!'

'It would appear so, and I think he has succeeded in reaching the top pieces.'

'Sorry, sir.'

Try as he might, the vicar couldn't control his lips, and David noticed that they'd spread into a smile.

'Well, he won't need feeding today,' he said. The dog was licking its lips. 'But you will, so run along home and take this with you, please.' He held out the tripe tin, which was wet with dog slobber.

'Thank you, sir,' David said and took the can. He ran back along the streets of Syston towards home.

Adam Wakelin was leaving as David arrived. He was about to explain what had happened to the morning's delivery at the vicarage when there was a knock on the door. Mrs Walker-Holmes strode into the kitchen.

'Ah.' She sounded triumphant. 'It's quite fortuitous that you are here too, Mr Wakelin.'

David looked at the woman; he noticed how the feather on her hat quivered when she spoke.

'Good day, Mrs Walker-Holmes. How may I help you?' Adam Wakelin enquired.

The woman, who was around the same age as David's mother but looked older, pointed to David.

'He didn't deliver my tripe today. You need to take him in hand, Mrs Adcock, and you need to get a more reliable delivery boy, Mr Wakelin. If this happens again I shall take my business elsewhere. When can I expect my tripe to be delivered?'

David noticed that the eyes on the fox stole she wore looked crossed.

'But your delivery isn't until tomor—' Before Mr Wakelin could finish, David held out the metal churn he had brought back from the vicarage.

'It's here. Sorry it's late.'

Mrs Walker-Holmes's mouth moved into a lopsided pout and she looked from his mother to Mr Wakelin. They were both staring at David. She snatched the tripe churn from his outstretched hand.

'I shall thank you not to be late next week,' she said, turned on her heels, and left.

'Where did you get that from?' David's mother asked.

'The vicarage.'

'But you didn't deliver to the vicarage.' Adam Wakelin looked puzzled.

'Oh, I did, sir, and I went round to show the vicar where I'd left it.'

'Why did you bring it back then?'

David grinned.

'The vicar didn't want it.'

Chapter 2

Wednesday, 7th September 1904

Emily Jane

Through the slightly open door, Emily could hear the mutterings of grown-ups who were standing around the stout elm coffin that balanced on slender wooden trestles in their front room. They had been there for ages, crowding in on the family's misery. She bit down hard on her bottom lip in an effort to stop any tears from brimming over onto her cheeks. She was scared of forgetting what Mam looked like, sounded like, smelled like. Earlier she had sneaked a drop of lavender water onto her black lace handkerchief, and when she dabbed at her nose, the sweet, memory-laden scent drifted gently into her nostrils. She screwed up her eyes and pushed with all her strength at the heavy door in her mind, which had slammed against the past. Wanting to remember her mother playing with her in the garden, showing her how to press flowers and bake bread, all she could bring to mind was a gaunt figure struggling to walk and eventually struggling to breathe, until Mam could no longer draw breath and gave in.

Emily pulled on the high collar of her black pinafore. It was stiff and scratchy, making her neck sore. Aunt Eliza said she would have to wear it until next September. As she was contemplating the eternal discomfort she felt a hand take hers and she opened her eyes to see Ernest standing in front of her. She held him close until he squirmed and pushed her away.

'Jane,' he said, as a frown crossed his face, 'when will they go?'

'In a little while,' she told him quietly, gently pushing a piece of blonde hair across his forehead.

'But, Jane, I really want Mam.' He looked up, his blue eyes rheumy and sore.

'I know,' she said, 'so do I.'

He pulled away and ran through to the kitchen.

A thin shaft of afternoon sunlight sliced between the heavy curtains, which had been drawn together but didn't quite meet. Tiny dust particles danced in its beam as it pierced the gloom and fell across Emily's foot. She looked down and concentrated on the illuminated space where a missing button should have been on her polished black boot. Hot tears were threatening to escape from her eyelids again and she screwed them shut.

'Ouch!' Emily jumped as she felt a sharp pain stab the inside of her arm just above her elbow.

'You'll be all right,' Alfred, her elder brother, whispered into her ear.

'What did you do that for?' She frowned at him.

'It helps to stop you crying,' he answered. 'I learnt that from Tommy Smith when his dad died.'

'Am I being sent away?' Emily asked in a quiet voice that trembled almost uncontrollably. She could ask Alfred the question she hadn't dared to ask her father; the question to which she dreaded hearing the answer.

'I think you're going with Aunt Eliza.' She thought that Alfred was trying hard to sound cheerful. 'Don't worry, it ain't that far away.'

Emily's heart sank. 'But I won't see you all.'

Before Alfred could answer, the sound of subdued voices in the front room swelled, and a sea of black-clothed figures washed into the living room, accompanied by the smell of mothballs. The women hid their faces behind veils and black fans. The mourners mostly ignored the two children, who wrinkled their noses against the smell. Only Aunt Eliza spoke to them: 'Come on, it's time to go,' she said. 'Put your cap on straight, Alfred. No bawling now, Emily.' She strode into the kitchen and quickly returned with Sydney and Henry, gripping their small hands in her large black-gloved ones. Ernest ran to Emily's side and Aunt Eliza shepherded them all towards the front door. In the doorway, Emily turned to look for her father. She saw him bend over and kiss her lifeless mother, before the undertaker placed the lid onto the coffin. He then covered it with a purple cloth. The sob, which rose up and caught in her throat, made a noise louder than she had wanted it to. Aunt Eliza narrowed her eyes and threw her a stern look.

They stepped out of the gloom into bright sunlight and Emily felt the firm pressing of her aunt's hand between her shoulder blades as she was guided down the path and into the street. A glass-sided hearse, decorated in gold and silver with a canopy of black ostrich feathers, was waiting to take Annie Wade on her final journey. Two shiny black horses with black feather plumes on their heads stood waiting: one to pull the hearse, the other the mourning coach that followed. Emily noticed that there were only two coachmen, their black top hats trimmed with black silk.

She glanced up and down the road and saw that all the neighbours' curtains were respectfully drawn. The strong arms of her Uncle George lifted first Emily, then the three younger boys, into the coach. Alfred was able to scramble up unaided. When the five children in their stiff black clothes were all on board, her father climbed in and sat beside Emily and opposite Aunt Eliza and her husband.

The coach began to move slowly down Albion Street and on to the Barkby Road, heading into the village and towards the church. At a sedate pace, a procession of family members and close friends followed. Ernest clung to Emily, and she wiped his eyes and nose on the lavender-scented handkerchief.

'You can't afford this, Alf,' Eliza hissed at her brother-in-law. Alf didn't speak.

Emily looked up at her father and saw a spot of blood behind his ear where the barber's razor had caught his flesh. She noticed that the thick, dark curls, which normally brushed his collar, had been cut back. The white skin of his neck was exposed beneath the straight cut, as if a ruler had been used. His jaws were twitching behind pursed lips. Emily clenched her teeth and released them slightly, then did it over and over again, feeling her cheeks twitch, just as her father's were. She slipped her hand into his and he looked down. She saw a snail's trail glide from the corner of his eye down to his jaw.

'Have you thought about how you are going to pay for this?' Eliza appeared not to notice his misery. 'Well, have you?'

'Not now.' Alf finally answered her. 'We'll be fine. Now leave it alone, woman.'

Emily shuddered when, as they approached the church, a solemn bell tolled. The hearse pulled up beside the lychgate and their carriage stopped behind it. The bell continued to ring sombrely. Reverend Avery was standing under the canopy preparing to begin the service as soon as the coffin was lifted out. Emily watched as it was pulled from behind the glass panels and lifted onto the shoulders of the pallbearers. She started when her aunt called out:

'Alf!' Eliza was trying to stop him as he pushed forward and strode towards the now elevated coffin, but he moved in behind the leading pallbearer and slid his right shoulder under the oak casket. The bearer moved aside. George followed and took his sister's weight onto his left shoulder. The five children followed like abandoned chicks as the vicar led the procession into the church.

The funeral service seemed to go on forever. Eventually the coffin was once again lifted and carried towards the south door. As they reached the centre of the transept, the church bell gave two quick rings announcing that the deceased was female and that the funeral party were about to leave the church. Henry clapped his hands over his ears, and Sydney burst into tears.

'Come along.' Eliza took Sydney's hand and pulled Henry's away from his ear. 'The carriage is waiting. Look lively.'

The hammer-rope tolled the bell again and Emily began counting.

'Nine, ten...' She watched the coffin being slid back behind the glass.

'Why do they call it a bier?' Alfred asked. Emily turned to face him and pushed his dark curls back under his cap.

'Eleven. I don't know.'

'I thought you drank beer.' He shrugged and clambered up into the carriage.

'Come on then, you next.' Alf lifted his daughter and she smiled to see the same dark curls escaping from her father's hat too.

'Sixteen. Move over, Ernest, Father needs to get in.'

'Folks are wondering why you've brought children to a funeral,' Eliza said to Alf as he settled himself opposite her once more.

'Twenty-two,' Emily whispered. Ernest looked at her and frowned. She held her finger to her lips before he could open his mouth.

'Give it a rest, will ya,' George told his wife. The horses snorted and the carriage wobbled. They watched the bier pull away.

'Twenty-eight.'

'Where's Mamma?' Henry asked.

'Twenty-nine.'

'Gone to heaven,' Eliza told him. He pursed his lips and looked down at his shoes.

'Thirty-three.' The wheels crunched on the cobbles.

'Sit down, Alfred,' Eliza scolded.

'Thirty-seven.' Alfred dropped onto the seat and craned his neck to look down the serpent of followers.

'Thirty-eight.'

'Will she come back when she's better?' Henry looked at his father, who lifted him onto his lap.

'No, son,' Alf told him, 'she won't.'

'Thirty-eight!' Emily announced. 'The bell stopped at thirty-eight.'

'So young.' George spoke softly, but Emily heard. She hadn't known how old her mother had been. When Emily had asked she'd always said: 'I'm as old as me tongue and a little bit older than me teeth.' Now she knew; the bell had given her secret away.

'If you don't want that, I'll have it.' Alfred was looking longingly at the piece of bread and butter that Emily still had on her plate. A transformation had taken place in their front room. Emily was sitting at the table, which had been covered with Annie's best cloth, and she traced her fingers over the embroidered stitches that her mother had deftly sewn into it. The black-clad figures had all enjoyed a feast of cold ham, fresh bread and butter, cheese and fruitcake, even Sydney, who had tasted butter for the first time.

Emily pulled the bread in two, gave one piece to Alfred and pushed the other into her mouth. She stared at the plate that was decorated with pretty violet flowers, and tried to remember her mother lovingly polishing the china after Sunday tea. She closed her eyes tightly, but the only image that came to mind was that of the coffin being lowered into the ground. Thoughts of the committal crowded in: she had looked down into the deep hole where her mother lay inside the oak coffin and thought about how damp the soil would be thrown back in on top of her. Small trickles of water were running down the clay walls, as though the whole of the earth was crying. Then she remembered seeing a mound of earth become visible a few feet away when the black halo of mourners around the grave began to disperse. Ernest had been standing on it, waving. Then Emily laughed. She couldn't help herself. The short, chubby sexton was chasing Ernest whilst trying to hold on to his hat with one hand and shaking his stick with the other. His foot slid on the freshly dug earth and he fell with a splat, his squidgy bottom landing on the soft earth with a loud squelch. Ernest scrambled over the top of the mound and ran through the mud, easily avoiding the sexton's attempts to seize him.

'You can wipe that smile off your face, girl,' Aunt Eliza told her. 'Take these dirty cups through to be washed.'

'Yes, Aunt Eliza.' Emily's eyes snapped open and she blinked. The room seemed less dark as most people had gone home, and Emily began to work her way around the table collecting dirty crockery. She carried the cups and saucers into their tiny kitchen and looked around for somewhere to put them.

'I'll take those, ma duck,' the woman washing dishes told her. 'You're a good girl.' She smiled. Emily smiled back. The woman had a kind face and her auburn hair was swept up into an elegant pleat. 'Off you pop then. There ain't enough room for both of us in here.' Mary Adcock turned back to the sink and Emily returned to the room where her father was standing by the fireplace talking to a stout woman with rosy cheeks.

'Eeh, Alf, it were a grand do.' Betsy Walker laid her hand on his arm. 'You gen 'er a good send-off.'

Alf nodded.

'I did me best,' he told her, 'no more than she deserved, God rest her.'

'What'll you do now?'

'We'll manage.'

'But the children, Alf. How will you look after them?'

'We'll manage.'

'Well, you know where I am if you need owt.' Emily watched Betsy Walker, dismissed by Alf's silence, turn and waddle across the room. She scooped up Sydney and he wriggled when she planted a kiss on his forehead. 'Eeh, lad, I don't know what's to become of you,' she told him, and lowered him back down to the floor. Without a backward glance the woman walked down the path and heaved herself into a waiting trap beside her husband, who slapped the reins against the chestnut pony's back, and they headed off down the street and out of sight.

'Jane.' Ernest was pulling at Emily's pinafore. She picked up the last cup and saucer and turned to her brother, who was holding a black feather.

'Where have you had that from?'

'The horseman gave it to me.'

'What are you going to do with it?'

'It's for when I die; you can put it on my horse.'

'Don't be daft, you ain't goin' to die.'

'But they were all sayin' Mam was in heaven, and she was restin' in peace. Heaven must be nice if you rest in peace. Can I have some more cake?' Emily took his hand and guided him to the table. She glanced quickly over her shoulder and, satisfied no one was watching, she took the last piece of cake and handed it to Ernest. He began stuffing it into his mouth and Emily smiled to see him enjoying the tasty treat. Then, without warning, her father's voice made her jump:

'Go and get your things, Emily. Aunt Eliza's ready to go.'

Chapter 3

Wednesday, 7th September 1904

Grief

His knee was burning where loose gravel had grated the skin away when David fell flat in the road outside Alf Wade's cottage. He picked himself up, brushed grit from his hands and limped over to Mr Wade's back door. Ernest and Alfred carried on kicking their ball about, unconcerned, so David pushed the door open and tumbled into the small scullery where his mother was standing beside a slate sink washing teacups.

'Look out!' Mary Adcock scolded her son, who sat down on the flagstone floor. Blood trickled from a wound the size of a florin on his right knee and ran down his shin. It seeped into the top of his grey sock, colouring it a deep crimson.

'Stay there,' his mother instructed. 'I'll go and get the dog to lick it clean.'

'Ernest pushed me,' David wailed. His mother didn't answer, but she walked over to the door and called to Alf Wade's dog. The black-and-white terrier soon appeared and she brought it into the kitchen and pushed its nose towards David's bloody knee. The dog licked at the wound and David giggled as its rough tongue slurped across his leg. He sat on the cold flagstones and watched his mother lift a pile of plates from the table in Mr Wade's front room and bring them back through to the kitchen.

'Where's Emily?' David asked. His mother smiled and ruffled his hair.

'She went with her Aunt Eliza after she'd brought me the cups in to wash.' Then he just heard her whisper, '...pity the child.'

'Why?' David asked as the dog continued to lick his leg.

'She has to live with her aunt.'

'But Adelaide didn't leave us when Father died.'

'That was different. Now go and sit on the stairs and wait until I've finished here.'

'Can't I go back outside?'

'No. Ernest didn't push you, so you can sit on the stairs for telling fibs.'

The dog gave a final flick of its tongue and his mother pushed it outside again. David limped to the foot of the stairs and sat down. He'd slipped a piece of bread from a plate that was next to the sink and began to chew on it whilst watching his mother from his seat behind the thick drawn-back curtain.

When she had finished the last of the washing-up, his mother took the white china plates, edged with violet flowers, through to the living room and put them away in the sideboard. She then spoke to Emily's father as she pulled her pinafore from around her slim waist, revealing a dress that wasn't black but a blueish-grey.

'Well, that's me done, Mr Wade. Everything's put away, and I've swept the kitchen floor. The boys are playing outside. Would you like me to make you a nice cup of tea before I go?'

'Aye, that'd be grand. Thank you.' David thought Mr Wade looked weary. 'Will sixpence be enough for today, Mrs Adcock?'

'I don't want your money, Mr Wade.' His mother tilted her head and gave Mr Wade a sympathetic smile. 'I know what it's like to lose a loved one, and believe you me, you'll need to take all the help that's offered.'

'I shall pay my way,' Alf Wade said, and he sat down with a thump in the threadbare armchair beside the fire. David picked at the loose skin on his hands. His mother turned and went back to the tiny kitchen where the kettle was beginning to splutter and emit a shrill whine as the steam built. She lifted it from the stove, cutting short its crescendo. As she poured boiling water onto tea leaves in a brown teapot, she looked back into the living room. David followed her gaze; Alf Wade was sitting, head bowed, staring at his hands. After waiting silently for a few minutes whilst the tea infused, she poured out a strong-looking brew.

'Here you are, nice and sweet.'

Alf Wade took the steaming cup of tea and held it in front of him, still staring at his large, rough hands. Then he took a deep breath and blew onto his drink a few times before taking a sip.

'Thank you,' he said, 'but I must pay you for today.'

'Very well then,' she conceded. 'There's no hurry, you've a funeral to pay for.'

'I have enough for that,' he told her.

David pushed the last of the dry crust into his mouth and tried to get comfy on the stair whilst he waited, listening to his mother and Mr Wade; he could see them quite well if he pulled the curtain further to one side. His mother wasn't saying anything. She sat down on a hard-backed chair by the table rather than in the armchair opposite Mr Wade, the chair where his wife must have spent her evenings for the past eleven years.

'You see,' he continued, 'Annie and me had some money put by for our children's funerals, if any of them had died. I suppose we were lucky that none did. Eliza thinks I'll end up in the debtors' prison, but I don't tell her all my business.'

'You've just told me though.' His mother was looking intently at the broken man. 'Don't worry, I won't say owt,' she reassured him.

Mr Wade smiled in what looked like gratitude and took another sip of his tea.

'You see, two of our children died, and we had to have them buried in with someone else,' she told him.

David sat up straight and listened; he hadn't known about any of his brothers, or sisters, dying.

Mr Wade's brow furrowed and he seemed to be thinking about what she had just told him.

'But I thought you had a couple of strapping lads,' he said.

'Three actually, and a fine lass.'

'But you said two had died.' Mr Wade looked as puzzled as David felt.

'Oh, so I did. That was years ago though, and they were nowt but babies. That's why Mr Gamble said to bury them like that – to save money. Lay them in the coffin of someone who had lived to a good age. The young and the old together.'

Mr Wade sighed. 'Aye, I've him to pay too. It shouldn't be much as we only had the hearse and one carriage, and just one horse each to do the pulling. Eliza said we should have walked, but I wanted better than that for my Annie. I reckon it'll be about five guineas.' They sat for a while without speaking. The heavy pendulum of the long-case clock ticked and tocked, and in the stillness of the room

David could see tears streaking down Mr Wade's cheeks, leaving a glistening trail on his weather-beaten face. His mother was looking down, probably to save Mr Wade's embarrassment. The silence was broken when Alf Wade pulled out his handkerchief and gave a loud blow to clear his nose.

'I'd best be off then.' David's mother stood up.

'Aye,' Mr Wade said, and she took his empty cup to the kitchen. David watched her lift her bonnet and shawl from the hook on the back of the door. She beckoned him from the stairs.

'I'll send the boys in, shall I?' she asked.

'Aye.'

'I'm charring up at the big house tomorrow, and for the Wakelins on Saturday morning. I can come and do you next week if you want.'

'No, thank you. We'll manage.'

'Well you know where I'll be if you need any help, and mark my words, you will. No doubt you'll be paid a visit by "Pantry" North afore long, so don't leave any money where he can find it, and make sure you haven't got much in your cupboards. You know what he's like.' She opened the door to leave and David shivered as the night air stole in. She pulled her shawl around her slender shoulders and moved to take her leave. Mr Wade rose from his chair, manners intact, spirit broken.

'Emily will be fine, Mr Wade.' His mother was again offering reassurance. Alf Wade looked up, his face carrying a surprised expression. 'She's a lovely girl, and Mrs Tomblin will look after her, I'm sure.'

'I expect so,' Alf Wade agreed. 'Eliza's heart's in the right place even if her tongue's too sharp sometimes. She wanted me to send the lads away for a bit too, until I get some better-paid work. I told her we can't all have George's gift, and there's nowt wrong wi' a bit of hard graft.'

David tugged at his mother's skirts and she swatted his hand away.

'I'd better go,' she said again. She looked embarrassed that Alf Wade had confided in her once more. Mr Wade nodded, and she pushed David in front of her and out through the door, calling back over her shoulder: 'Goodnight then, Mr Wade.'

'Goodnight, Mrs Adcock.'

David's mother took his grazed hand in hers and called to Ernest and Alfred to go indoors. As they ran past, Ernest stuck out his tongue to David, who did the same back, knowing they would be friends again in the morning. David and his mother made their way home, walking beside the brook towards Paddock Row.

'Who's Pantry North, Mam?' David asked. She chuckled. David looked up at her, eyes wide.

'It's Mr North to you.'

'Why do you call him Pantry then? What does he do? Does he bring you stuff?'

'Quite the opposite. When someone dies, like Mrs Wade, Mr North will pay a visit to see how much the family can afford and decide if they can live off the parish, or not.'

'Did he visit us when Father died?'

'Oh yes, indeed he did.'

Chapter 4

Wednesday, 7th September 1904

Annie

'You can sleep with Annie,' Eliza told Emily, pointing to a high bed next to the wall. She looked up at her aunt and then back to the bed. She'd never slept with anyone before, except for when she had been poorly and Mam had allowed her to sleep with her, but that was different.

'Won't Annie mind?'

'She'll do as she's told,' Eliza said. 'Put your belongings away and get to bed.'

The sun was going down, and a burnt orange glow coloured the dark room. Emily looked from the large, high bed to a smaller one against the opposite wall. Ted was already fast asleep, and even though it was warm, Emily could only see the top of his head above the blanket, his ginger hair sticking up like a cock's comb. Without a 'goodnight, sleep tight' that her mother had always bid her, Aunt Eliza turned and walked out. Emily heard her aunt's feet tapping down the stairs and then the door at their foot slammed shut. She looked again at Ted's head and turned her back to him. Lifting her cardboard case onto the bed, she flicked the locks open and took out her nightdress and her favourite rag doll, Margaret. Hugging the doll close, she twisted her fingers into its dark curls that were made from horsehair and whispered, 'Well, Margaret, this is our new home.' She pushed the doll under the blanket and began to undress. It was quite a relief to take off her starched pinafore and black dress. She pulled the lavender-scented handkerchief from its sleeve and, closing her eyes, pressed it to her nose and held it there in the quiet of the room.

Outside, a bird was singing, its chant a fast succession of high, low and rich notes.

'There's a nightingale singing outside,' she told Margaret. 'Perhaps that means we shall be happy here.' Then Emily frowned. Her dad said they only sang until July and flew away in September. Or was that cuckoos? No, she was sure it was nightingales. Ernest would know. He probably had one of their eggs in his collection. Or maybe it was really Mam singing her a goodnight song.

'Annie!' Aunt Eliza's piercing cry from downstairs penetrated the dusky air and made Emily jump. She pushed the handkerchief underneath Margaret, slipped her nightdress over her head and reached into the case for her hairbrush. Mam used to brush her hair every night, until she became too ill, then Emily had learnt to brush it herself. One hundred strokes before bed. She untied the black ribbon and let her hair fall down past her shoulders then picked up the brush and began to stroke it through her waist-length curls. She wished she had blonde hair like Ernest or dark like Alfred, but she had been blessed with mousey-brown, a sort of nondescript colour. Her father still called it her crowning glory. It smelt soapy and sweet from the morning's bath they had all been given, even though it was Wednesday. Emily thought about the Sunday afternoons when she had been allowed to have her bath after her mother, before the boys climbed into the tin tub; Alfred first, then Ernest, and after he had bathed she had helped her mother to wash the two younger boys, who splashed each other and laughed until they hiccupped. She doubted there would be any bath-time fun with Aunt Eliza.

'Get yourself up to bed, young lady.' Aunt Eliza's tone was harsh, and even though Emily knew she was talking to Annie, she scrambled up onto the iron bedstead and slipped under the blanket. It felt rough and scratchy on her bare legs, and smelt funny. She wrinkled her nose at the odour of camphor and reached for the handkerchief. Her mind drifted back to their front room that afternoon and the people crowding into it; the same smell had hung around them too. She closed her eyes, and thoughts about leaving her lovely home earlier came tumbling into her mind. It felt like ages ago since they had walked down the lavender-lined garden path and onto their street where all the blinds were still drawn for Mam. Emily had noticed curtains twitching as they walked past, and Aunt Eliza had gently pushed her on until they'd reached the end of the road. Emily had turned and looked back down the row of houses that flanked Albion Street. She could see Sydney's hobbyhorse by their front door and next to it a small figure waving a black feather. She had lifted her arm to wave back, but her aunt had grasped it and pulled her along towards the stiles where she pushed Emily up and over the first one, then lifted her black crepe skirt so she could easily mount the wooden step and follow her. Emily had hoped the stile would break, but it was far too sturdy to act as the architect of her aunt's downfall. Eventually they had reached her aunt and uncle's home in Brookfield Street where she was now to share a bed with her cousin. Under the blanket, Emily rubbed her hands together. There was a sore ridge across her palm where her soft skin was chafed. The brown cardboard case had felt heavy and its handle unforgiving. She had kept on having to swap sides as her arms ached, even though there were few clothes inside.

The door opened and Annie entered the bedroom. Emily watched as she walked over to Ted's bed and looked over at him. Seeming satisfied that he was fast asleep, she bent down and tied his bootlaces together. She turned to Emily and placed her forefinger to her lips. Emily stifled a giggle and pulled the blanket over her head. She could hear Annie pulling her clothes off and opening and closing drawers. She could also hear the bird singing.

'Move over.' Emily felt Annie pushing gently against her as she slipped into bed.

'Sorry,' Emily whispered, and slid across until her back was touching the cold wall.

'And if you tell Ted that it were me that tied his laces, I'll cut yer hair off.'

'Oh!' Emily felt a ripple of apprehension mixed with distaste run down her spine. She shrank further back against the wall.

'Shall we play a game?' Annie whispered.

'What like? Won't we get into trouble?'

'Not if they don't hear us. You choose.'

'What about *I spy*?' Emily suggested.

'But it's dark, I can't spy anything, you duffer. Now it's my turn to choose.' Annie was quiet for a moment then said, 'You've got to take one of Ted's socks and hide it.'

'But that's not a game.'

'If you don't, I win and you have to sleep on the floor.' Emily didn't want to sleep on the floor where spiders might crawl into her hair or, worse still, her ears. Annie had given her no choice, so she slid from under the blanket and crept over to Ted's bed, her bare feet picking out the ridges of the rough floorboards. She looked all around, beside his shoes, under his bed, but couldn't see any socks.

'I can't find them!'

'Of course you can't, you dunce. They're on his feet.'

'But I can't get them off his feet, he'll wake up.'

'Then you lose.'

'All right, I'll try.' Emily lifted Ted's blanket and felt for his feet. One was bare and he kicked out as she touched him. She waited and then fumbled around again; she found a soft lump at the foot of the bed.

'Time's nearly up,' Annie hissed.

Making sure Annie wasn't looking, Emily took Ted's sock and pushed it inside Annie's boot.

'Done it.'

'I don't believe you.'

'Well I have and it's hidden well.'

'You can still sleep on the floor,' Annie said, and threw Margaret at Emily. 'And take this ugly thing with you.'

Emily felt tears welling up and her throat constricted. She didn't want to cry, but felt helpless. She sat down on the floor between the two beds and hugged Margaret.

'What's all this noise?' The door flew open and Aunt Eliza strode into the room.

'Emily won't come to bed,' Annie said.

'Get into bed now, girl, and no more nonsense.' Aunt Eliza was glaring at Emily, who stood up and slunk over to Annie's bed, head hung low.

'Go on then,' her aunt commanded, and Emily climbed under the coarse blanket and once again pressed her back against the wall.

'Now go to sleep,' Eliza said as she left the room. Ted hadn't stirred.

Annie didn't say anything for a while and then whispered: 'What's it like?'

'What do you mean?'

'For your mother to die?'

Emily pulled Margaret close. 'I don't know,' she murmured.

'You must know. Your mam's just died.'

'It's horrible, and it hurts.'

'Folks are saying it were a blessing.'

'What does that mean?' Emily felt the tears beginning to swell.

'I don't know, perhaps because she was poorly and now she ain't, or perhaps they just wanted rid of her.' Emily couldn't stop her tears and she began to cry.

'Well, you've got me now,' Annie said. Emily wasn't sure if it was meant to be a comfort or a threat. 'I've got the same name as your mam. I think I were named after 'er.'

Emily's sobs swelled, and her small body began to shake uncontrollably.

'Oh shut up, I can't sleep,' Annie grumbled.

Eventually, Emily's sobs subsided and she began to fall asleep, exhausted.

Outside, the bird was still singing.

Chapter 5

Thursday, 8th September 1904

Eggs

Emily pressed her nose against the glass cabinet, which stood on a small table in the corner of the kitchen. It felt warm. She began to count brown eggs that were lined up in rows behind the glass.

'They should hatch out tomorrow.' Uncle George took off his cap and scratched his head as he bent to peer into the incubator alongside her. He tapped the water bottle, which was fixed to it, and nodded his approval.

'Can I watch?' Emily asked.

'If you've done your chores.' Her aunt's stern voice carried in from outside and heralded her return from fetching the morning's milk. Her skirts rustled as she entered the kitchen carrying a small churn and a basket of eggs.

'These will be your jobs from now on,' she told Emily. 'Milk cart comes at seven, so you need to be out there waiting, and eggs need collecting twice a day. You can start this afternoon.'

'Yes, Aunt Eliza,' Emily said, wondering what else she would be given to do for her chores. The door to the stairs flew open and Ted tumbled into the kitchen, his hair still standing to attention. He put his boots down by the back door and climbed onto a chair. He stuck his tongue out at Annie, who was standing in front of the range toasting stale bread. She did the same in return whilst her mother's back was turned and placed a plate of toast onto the kitchen table.

'Come on then, girl, get to the table,' Aunt Eliza ordered, and Emily hurried over to sit down next to Ted. On her plate was a shiny fried egg, the melted dripping forming a warm, greasy pool around it. Taking her cue from Ted and Annie, she reached for a piece of toast after her aunt and uncle had taken theirs.

'You'll not be going to school today,' her aunt told her.

'What about me?' asked Ted.

'You and Annie will go. Emily needs to help me.' Ted shrugged and pushed a piece of toast into his mouth.

'I heard a nightingale singing outside the bedroom window last night,' Emily said.

'It weren't a nightingale,' Ted scoffed.

'Oh.' Emily was taken aback. 'I thought it was. Its song was beautiful.'

'Nah,' Ted said. 'It were a robin. I've got a robin's egg, but I ain't got a nightingale's. I've got loads: blackbird's, starlin's, thrush's, blue tit's, even a magpie's.'

'Be quiet and eat your breakfast,' Aunt Eliza chided. The children fell silent and lowered their heads. Emily was enjoying her toast with the fried egg, even though her head still felt fuzzy from crying so much, when she suddenly let out a yelp. Everyone stared at her and she felt a warm flush creeping up her neck and flooding her face. She thought she would start to cry again and pinched the inside of her arm to stop the tears, just as Alfred had shown her.

'What was that for?' her aunt snapped.

'I, err, I, summat ran over my foot,' Emily said, her voice trembling. Annie bent down and looked under the table.

'It's only a mouse,' she said, and sat back up.

'I've set traps,' George said and frowned. He put down his tin mug and wiped his mouth with the back of his hand. 'Little beggars need catching. Fetch the cat, boy.' Ted slid from his chair and ran outside, calling: 'Tripey, come on, Tripey.'

'Why do you call him Stripey? Does he look like a tiger?' Emily asked.

'It ain't Stripey, it's *Tripey*,' Annie told her.

'That's a funny name for a cat.'

'It's coz it were found round the back of the tripe shop. And it's a she, not a he.'

'Be quiet!' Aunt Eliza scolded. 'You'll speak when you're spoken to.' The back door swung open and Ted struggled in carrying a fat tabby cat, which he dropped as soon as he could and pushed the door to behind him. The cat resembled an over-stuffed cushion, its sides distended over short legs as it ambled under the table, sniffing the floor.

'Watch it doesn't get out of the kitchen,' Aunt Eliza told them, and she closed the door to the stairs. 'It'll want somewhere to have its kittens, and I don't want them in the house. Now get this table cleared. You can wash up, Emily.'

Still not speaking, Annie and Emily cleared the plates away, taking care not to trip over Tripey as the cat waddled over and crouched by the sink. Emily watched Ted as he tried to pull his boots on. When he realised they were tied together he shot Annie a loathsome look. She smiled back insolently without showing her teeth and placed the last of the plates into the stone sink.

'It weren't me, it were Emily,' Annie told her brother. Before Emily could defend herself her aunt called out:

'Hurry up, that's the school bell – you'll be late. Now get gone.' Ted put his cap on, Annie her bonnet, and they headed towards the back door.

'There it is!' Emily couldn't help herself and shouted out. Her aunt narrowed her gaze and her cousins spun round. The cat pounced. The mouse gave a pathetic squeak and then fell silent. Emily covered her eyes. Ted clapped. George opened the door and put his boot behind the cat as it scurried out with breakfast clamped in its jaws. Without further comment, Eliza pulled out a half-full sack from under the sink and lifted it onto the table for the morning's bread making. A white trail followed it across the flagstone floor as flour trickled out through the ragged hole in its base.

Emily was hot from kneading dough, but she carried on silently as she watched, and listened, to her aunt and uncle.

'I'll be off then,' George told Eliza. 'Don't be too hard on the girl.'

'I won't,' Eliza answered, 'but she needs to get some backbone and not be a crybaby. I'm sorry she's lost her mother, and you a sister, Annie was a good woman, but Emily will have a hard life now. She has to understand that we've given her a home until she's twelve – old enough to leave school and go into service.' She spoke as though Emily wasn't in the room. George leaned across and kissed his wife on the cheek.

'Where will you be working today?' Eliza asked.

'Over in Rearsby.'

'Manor Farm?'

'Aye. It'll be a good day's work. Only an hour to get there, and they should have around a couple of hundred chickens ready for me by now. You should see their incubators; five times the size o' mine.'

'It's a good knack you have,' Eliza told her husband.

'Aah, there's few as can sex a chicken round these parts.'

'What'll they do with the cock birds?'

'Dunno till I'm there. They might keep some for fattenin' up a bit, or they may just ask me to neck 'em and leave a coop full of pullets – should see me right for about ten bob.' Emily watched Eliza rub her hands together at the thought of so much money coming into the house. George mirrored her gesture and rubbed his hands together too, probably at the thought of the ale he would drink in The Bell on his way home, Emily supposed.

Having made dough for the day's bread, peeled potatoes, washed cabbage leaves that she had fetched from the garden and swept the bedroom floors after she had emptied the chamber pots, Emily was taken down the garden to the hen house.

'Woe betide you if you ever leave this gate or hen house door unlatched,' Aunt Eliza told her and held out a straw-lined basket. 'Now, collect the eggs and be quick about it,' she ordered. Turning on her heels, she strode away and back towards the house. When she was out of sight, Emily walked down to the hedge that bordered the bottom of the garden. She ran along its length, feeling a sense of freedom; it felt good not to be watched. There was a wooden gate in the corner that led into a lane. She lifted the latch and stepped onto the dirt track that wound down to the brook. She cocked her head on one side and listened. Yes, she could hear the stream as it meandered through the village and made its way to join the River Wreake.

'Shouldn't you be collectin' the eggs?' Annie was leaning on the gate, swinging the empty basket.

'Oh, you made me jump, Annie. Yes I had better attend to that.' Emily walked back to the gate and made to push it open.

'Password,' Annie demanded.

'What? I don't know it.' Emily frowned.

'Then you can't come back.'

'Please, Annie. I need to collect the eggs.'

'Not until you give the password.'

'But that isn't fair. I don't know it.'

Annie's mouth curled up at one side.

'Please?' Emily said.

'No.'

Emily was trying hard to think of a password when Annie stumbled backwards and sat down on the grass. Emily quickly pushed the gate open and ran into the garden where Annie was sitting, rubbing her head. An inflated pig's bladder was rolling along the ground away from her. She looked round and her eyes flashed when she heard another voice.

'Can I have my ball back?' David had walked through the open gate into the Tomblin's garden. Emily began to giggle and watched David scoop up his 'ball' and walk back towards her.

'Go away, you ruffian,' Annie screamed at him, 'or I'll tell my father.' David winked at Emily and slipped back through the gate and into the lane.

'What a horrid boy,' Annie grumbled, and brushed off her skirts. Emily was thinking that she rather liked Ernest's friend David, and she smiled as she listened to a series of thumps followed by the pat-pat-pat of the pig's bladder being kicked along the lane, which grew quieter as they became more distant. Emily picked up the basket and made her way to the hen house to complete her chores before teatime.

'Where have you been?' Mary asked David as he ran into the kitchen and over to the stone sink where he picked up a tin mug and plunged it into a bucket of fresh well water. He gulped down the cold liquid and replaced the mug.

'Just down to see if Ernest wanted to play football.' David's face was red-hot from running and beads of sweat trickled down from his forehead.

'For goodness' sake,' Mary admonished, 'his mother has only just died. Leave the family be for a while. Now sit quietly and wait for your brothers to come home.'

'I saw Emily Wade this afternoon.'

'Oh,' Mary said, 'where?'

'She were at the Tomblin's on Brookfield.'

'Poor lass,' Mary said under her breath, and David watched as she began to slice a freshly baked loaf.

'How did my father die?' David asked.

'He had an accident,' Mary replied, and put the knife down.

'What kind of accident?' David persisted. 'Why won't you ever tell me?'

'You were too young to understand,' Mary said, and she fetched plates to the scrubbed kitchen table.

'I'm old enough now. Whattoff says he were drunk. Was he, Mam? Is that what killed him?'

'It's a long story.'

'Is that why Pantry North came to our house?'

Before his mother could answer, the back door swung open, and Charlie, followed by Whattoff, came in. Mary placed a dish of boiled eggs onto the table and sliced more bread. David knew that his mother wouldn't tell him any more now that his brothers were home.

Chapter 6

Wednesday, 1st March 1905

Slaughter

The daily chore Emily enjoyed most was collecting eggs; even Annie couldn't intimidate her when she was with the hens – Annie was scared of them. The hens had lice – 'little black things' Annie called them – and the lice would get inside Annie's clothes if she ever entered the large wooden hut, and she would be bitten, mercilessly, until she was covered in hives and had to take all her clothes off and shake them outside. The lice never bothered Emily. Every afternoon when she arrived home from school she would collect the egg basket from the kitchen and skip along the path that led to the hen house. The winter had been harsh and she'd trudged through snow in the gloom of shortened days, usually accompanied by the cat that was once again rounded with unborn kittens. The days were gradually lengthening and Emily was able to undertake her collection in daylight; March's watery sunshine even felt warm on her back. February fill-dyke had soaked the ground and the path was claggy with soft mud, which stuck to her boots.

As she made her way along it, she trod carefully so that she didn't slip. She felt a dampness creep through the worn-out soles of her boots, soaking her stockings, that wouldn't dry out before bedtime. Her chilblains itched and she wriggled her heels against the worn leather to alleviate the irritation. On reaching the hen house she lifted the latch and entered. The acrid smell of hen muck that lay thick on a flat bench under a wooden perch stung her nose and throat. A row of nest-boxes hung on the hut's far wall. She went over to them and pushed her hand under a sitting hen in the first one.

'Ow!' Emily jumped back and rubbed her fingers over the spot where the hen's beak had pecked her wrist. She stared at the white wyandotte, and it stared back, its beady eyes defying her to try again. The next nest-box had two brown eggs in it, and the layer had moved on, making a loud crowing noise as it left the coop. Emily placed the still-warm eggs into her basket and searched the other boxes, leaving the wyandotte sitting comfortably on its nest. She took her time looking in the grass around the hen house, as her aunt had told her to, just in case any of the hens were 'going broody' and had decided to lay their eggs outside. A black-and-white cockerel strutted along in front of her, stopping every so often to scratch around in its search for food. The cockerel performed a strange dance, moving from one foot to the other as it foraged, its comb falling lopsidedly onto its shiny black head. Emily gave it a wide berth; she had already been on the receiving end of its aggression. She was delighted to have collected eleven eggs and hoped her aunt would be pleased with her too, even though it was one short of a dozen. She wondered if she should go back and challenge the Wyandotte again to see if it would allow her to take its egg. Looking at the red mark on her hand she instead quickened her step and went through the gate, carefully latching it behind her. She walked towards the house, swinging the basket as she went, but stopped when she saw her aunt standing close by the pump in the yard. There was a tin bucket in front of Aunt Eliza, which she was plunging something into. After a few moments she threw a dark, limp object onto the grass and plunged again. As Emily drew closer, she saw Tripey pacing up and down close by; her mewing sounded pitiful. Almost at the pump herself, Emily saw a tiny kitten being thrust into the bucket and her aunt holding it under the water. Two wet, lifeless bodies lay on the grass. Emily dropped the basket and covered her nose and mouth with her hands, horrified at what she had seen. Eliza looked up.

'You careless child!' she shouted, and strode over to the upturned basket. All but three of the eggs were broken, and the ground beneath was taking on a bright yellow veneer. Emily felt the air whistle before the blow landed at the side of her head. The next caught her across the cheek and stung worse than a hundred nettles. She reeled and fell backwards, landing awkwardly on the damp grass.

'Get up and clear this mess away,' her aunt blustered, 'and when you've done that you can take them and throw 'em on the muck-heap.' She pointed to the tiny corpses, their lives snuffed out before they had even opened their eyes. Eliza picked up the three unbroken eggs and marched back to the house. Emily touched her hot cheek and scrambled to her feet. Her throat constricted and she sniffed, trying to control the flow of tears that trickled down her face as she scraped up the shells. Something pushed against her leg. Tripey licked at the slimy yellow pool and Emily bent and stroked the cat's back.

'Oh, Tripey,' she sobbed, 'you poor thing. Your poor, poor babies.' She looked across at the dead kittens and cried even harder. The cat rubbed around her legs and then went back to licking up the eggs. Emily took the broken shells to the muck-heap and threw them onto the stinking pile.

'How can I throw the kittens on here?' she said out loud, and looked around for an alternative. A piece of rusty metal was sticking up from the ground close by, and she pulled until it became free. It was a strange shape, but to Emily it was an improvised spade. She dug a short trench under a shrub near the fence and then went to collect the kittens, still carrying the piece of metal. She placed them carefully onto her makeshift spade and took them to the tiny grave she had dug for them. She laid them side by side in the ground; one was black and white and one was tabby, like their mother. 'Our Father, who art in heaven,' she whispered as she covered them with earth. She made a cross from twigs and laid it on the little grave, then brushed the earth from her skirt and began to make her way back to the house. The bucket was still beside the pump; her heart sank. The third kitten would still be in it, and she would have to take that one to the grave too. Tripey had gone, and the yellow pool was hardly visible. At least the cat had enjoyed a tasty meal. Emily screwed her eyes shut as she reached the grey bucket, then warily opened one, then both – wide. She peered into the pail. Puzzled, she lifted it and threw the water away. She looked all around her, in the grass and on the path, but there was no third body. She began to shake, knowing how much trouble she would be in if all the dead kittens weren't dealt with. She looked again behind the pump. Nothing. Too afraid to go back into the cottage, she made her way back towards the hen house. Something was moving along the chicken wire that fenced the birds in, and hoping it wasn't a fox, she crept over to the gate to make sure it was closed. Satisfied that the hens were secure, she walked down to the bottom of the garden. Beside the gate she saw Tripey with a kitten in her mouth. Emily approached the cat and knelt down on the damp grass close by. Tripey waddled over and dropped the kitten beside her. It wriggled and opened its mouth and the cat nudged it in close so that it could suckle.

The sound of running came from the lane and then a thump followed by a plop. Emily stood up and, without disturbing the cat, walked over to the gate.

'Ay-up, Emily,' David called out.

'Sssh.' Emily placed a finger to her lips.

'Why, what's up?' David asked. Emily beckoned him over and they both stood watching the kitten suckling on its mother. Emily told David what had happened to the other kittens.

'Phew.' David blew his cheeks out and shook his head.

'Will you take her?' Emily asked.

'What?'

'Please, take them both, just until the kitten is old enough to look after itself. She's a good mouser.' Emily pulled a broken wooden box from under the hedge.

'Here, we can put them both in this and you can take them home.'

'Emily! Hurry up, tea's ready.' Aunt Eliza was calling from the back doorstep.

'Come on, quickly,' Emily told David, and lifted first Tripey, then the kitten into the box and pushed him towards the gate. She watched David stagger along the lane with his heavy load and then turned to go indoors. The sun was setting as she passed the pump; a robin landed on it and began to sing. She could still hear birdsong as she pushed open the back door to face her aunt.

Chapter 7

Monday, 13th March 1905

Lice

The school bell rang to signal the end of afternoon playtime and Emily joined the line, behind Beatie Souter, waiting to go inside. She looked up at the whitewashed lintel, which had *ELEMENTARY GIRLS' SCHOOL 1882* etched into it; beyond was a cloudless blue sky. She wondered if Mam was looking down on her and gave a little wave, just in case she was. A whistle blew, and the girls moved forward into their classroom. In front of her, Beatie was scratching her head. Emily felt hers itch too. She scratched, her reaction reflective of her classmate's. She did wonder if a flea or something had bitten her when she was collecting eggs that morning.

'Come along, settle down.' Hilda North clapped her hands and stood in front of the class. Emily slid into her desk next to Beatie and the room quickly fell silent. Miss North clasped her hands together in front of her and looked over her girls. Satisfied they were all present she walked purposefully over to the classroom door and pulled it open.

A lady entered wearing a pale-grey dress with a high white collar. A starched white apron protected the dress, and she had an equally starched white cap over her scraped-back hair.

'Oh no,' whispered Beatie, 'it's the nit nurse.'

'Be quiet!' Miss North instructed, as a ripple of realisation ran through the room. 'Come along, line up. Edith Austin to the front and the rest of you form a line behind her in alphabetical order.' Emily knew she would be last in line and waited patiently, trying not to scratch. She looked at her fingernails; they were chipped and more or less clean, at least she didn't bite them like her brother, Ernest. Mam had painted bitter aloes on his to try to stop him, but it hadn't worked. There was no one to do that now, so he would probably bite them down to the quick.

'Get that neck washed before you come back to school tomorrow, you dirty girl,' the nurse was telling Maud Preston. Emily stood on tiptoes and saw Maud's hand fly to her neck over the mark, which, as far as Emily could remember, had always been there. Maybe she didn't wash properly, as there were nine of them crammed into their little house on Bath Street. They shuffled forward and then it was Beatie's turn. Emily pursed her lips and waited. She desperately wanted to scratch but daren't move. She could hear the nurse tutting as she pushed Beatie over to Miss North. A faint gasp fanned the room and Beatie was marched to the door. Finally, Emily's hands were pulled forward, palms upwards, and then turned over. The nurse tapped the little finger on her right hand where the remains of a chilblain lingered but said nothing. She then pushed Emily's head down and poked her bony fingers over her scalp, parting the hair as she went along. Then it was all over and Emily breathed out and turned to go back to her seat.

'Not so fast, young lady,' the nurse snapped. 'Come here, girl.' Emily felt her stomach churn, and she looked across at Miss North, who was beckoning her with a curly index finger. In her other hand was a letter. She walked Emily to the door and gave her the note.

'Take this home and do not return until you are clean,' Miss North instructed, and pushed Emily, humiliated, out of the classroom. The door closed, leaving her standing in the corridor scratching her head. On the other side of the heavy oak door she could hear Miss North preparing the girls for their afternoon lessons. The spring sunshine outside was inviting, and Emily ran down the corridor and out into the playground. She went through the gate into Cramp Street then turned towards Brookside and wondered how Aunt Eliza would react when she gave her the note. She stopped, spun around, and rather than going straight home, she headed instead towards High Street. She desperately wanted to go to her real home, to her father and brothers, but knew no one would be there and that she would probably get a good hiding if she did. At the end of the street she looked up at the church clock. The sun lit the dial and the numerals looked like real gold. There was still half an hour before lessons finished for the day. Emily made her way past a row of red-brick buildings to a high gated porch. She looked up at the letters that had been painted onto the wooden gable: *SYSTON HIGH STREET PAROCHIAL SCHOOLS*. Pressing herself tightly against the school's perimeter wall next to a stout cast-iron drainpipe, she waited. Eventually chairs could be heard scraping on wooden floors and the boys sang their dismissal song. Mr Boden, the headmaster, could then be heard telling them: 'Goodnight, gentlemen, don't be late in the morning.'

'Goodnight, Mr Boden,' the boys responded. The tower bell rang three times and a torrent of pounding, booted feet grew louder as the gate swung open and around fifty boys spilled out into the street.

'Ernest!' Emily shouted when she saw her brother as he squeezed through the gate. Ernest stopped and looked around. 'Over here,' she called again.

'Jane!' Ernest cried out when he saw his sister, and he ran to her. They both jumped when they heard the headmaster shouting at one of his pupils:

'Adcock, put that collar straight before you leave.' Emily saw David Adcock run to join a group who were kicking a football down the street, his dishevelled collar more or less straightened.

'What you doin' 'ere?' Ernest asked.

'We were let out early,' Emily lied, 'and I wanted to see you, it's been ages. I don't half miss you.'

'You'll cop it if you're late home,' he warned.

'You've grown.' She laughed and ignored his caution. 'You'll soon be as tall as me.'

'I've got to go.' Ernest looked sad for a moment. 'I've got Lads' Brigade tonight.'

'Lads' Brigade?' Emily held both his hands and straightened her arms. 'Since when?'

'Last month. I'm learnin' the cornet. I've got me uniform an' all. We'll be marchin' on Empire Day in May and at The Feast in July, so I've got to practice.' His face had brightened, and he pulled his hands away.

'Bye, Ernest,' Emily said. A tear trickled down her cheek and plopped onto her hand.

'Bye, Jane. I'll tell Father I've seen you.'

'No, don't,' she told him, 'or we'll both be in bother.' He nodded, and they turned away from each other, heading home in opposite directions.

Emily ran back down High Street and into Chapel Street. Her side was hurting so she stopped and bent over.

'You got a stitch?' a boy, now kicking a tin can along instead of a football, asked.

'Oh, it's you, David,' she said, puffing. 'Yes, I have, and I'm late home.'

'Take bigger breaths then.'

Emily stood upright and breathed deeply. Gradually the pain subsided, and she smiled. David grinned back; his collar was askew once more.

'I heard the headmaster telling you to straighten your collar.' Emily felt better and smiled at David.

'Oh.' David frowned and pulled his collar straight, but he didn't ask why she had been up at the boys' school.

'How is the kitten?'

'It's growin', and Mam were cross when I turned up with it, but then the cat caught a mouse she had been after for ages, so she let them stay.

'What have you called it?'

'Lucky,' David answered, 'because it's lucky to be alive.' Emily laughed and scratched her itchy scalp.

'I'd better go or else I'll be in trouble,' she said. He shrugged and turned to make his way home, giving the can a hefty kick as he went.

Emily ran as fast as she could and had a face like a ripe tomato when she arrived at the back door. She took a deep breath and went into the kitchen.

Her aunt was slicing bread for tea. Without looking up, she said: 'Hurry up and collect the eggs, girl. The hens won't wait for you.' Emily didn't pick up the egg basket immediately, instead she put her hand into her apron pocket and pulled out the envelope Miss North had given to her. She held it out and Aunt Eliza put her knife down, and then she snatched the letter from her. Emily watched a crimson mask creep up her aunt's neck and cover her face. Aunt Eliza's mouth formed a hard, straight line and her eyes narrowed.

'You stupid girl,' she screeched, and raised her hand as she stepped closer. The blow caught Emily across her shoulders, and she yelped. Aunt Eliza gripped her wrist and pulled her from the kitchen into the yard and then to the washhouse.

'Sit there.' Aunt Eliza pointed to a stool and Emily sat. She watched her aunt as she strode over to an old chest of drawers and pulled open the top one. She took out a large pair of scissors and slammed the drawer to. Emily felt a sharp pain as her black ribbon was pulled from her hair and thrown to the floor.

'Sit still, girl,' her aunt growled, and she took a length of wavy hair and cut it just below Emily's ear.

'Please, Aunt Eliza,' Emily begged, 'please...'

'Be quiet and stay still.'

Snip.

'You don't bring dirty head lice into my house, do you hear?'

Snip.

'And don't go anywhere near Annie or Ted or I'll give you a good hiding.' With each tug and cut, Emily felt a sharp pain, as if her aunt was pulling the hair out by its roots. With a final snip the last length of hair fell to the ground. Emily was sobbing. Her crowning glory lay on the washhouse's mud floor. Her breath caught in her throat causing her to make strange whooping noises. Aunt Eliza swept up the hair and threw it onto the fire beneath the copper, which was still glowing from earlier that morning. The flames crackled and spat, and every so often there was a popping noise as lice and eggs perished in the flames.

'Come here,' her aunt instructed. Emily stood up and walked over to the granite sink where her aunt was standing. 'Lean over and close your eyes.' Emily obeyed, trying hard not to cry. She thought she was going to have her hair washed in cold water and waited for the first icy jugful to douse her. Aunt Eliza, however, took the glass shade and wick from a paraffin lamp and began to pour the fuel over the now quite short hair. Emily gagged as the fumes hit the back of her throat. 'Oh dear Lord,' she thought, 'she's going to set fire to me.' Bony fingers prodded and rubbed at her scalp until it was sore.

'That will have to do. Now go and get the eggs.' Aunt Eliza pulled her upright and pushed her towards the door. Emily ran to get the basket, her face swathed in tears and paraffin. She stumbled around the hen house, collecting freshly laid eggs and taking great care not to break any. She was about to take a look in the grass outside when she heard her aunt calling. Not wishing to be in any more trouble, she ran back to the house with the ten eggs that she had collected. In the kitchen Annie was filling the kettle from a jug. She almost dropped it when she saw Emily. Aunt Eliza took the basket and pushed Emily forward.

'Stay away,' she told Annie, 'and you, get in there.' She pointed to a cupboard under the stairs. Emily didn't move; her legs wouldn't work and she looked pleadingly at her aunt, who ignored her and pushed her forward again towards the cupboard. Emily peered into the dark cubbyhole. 'Go on, and you can stay there until you're clean.' Aunt Eliza pushed her in and closed the door. The darkness was almost solid, but gradually her eyes became more accustomed to it, and the light, which glimmered under the door at the side where it didn't quite fit its frame, helped her to understand her surroundings. She fell to her knees; she was a prisoner, a dirty prisoner with no food or water. She rubbed her sore head and cried softly when she felt the ends of her hair just above her ears. Exhausted, she sank to the floor and curled up, hugging her knees to her chest, and rocked herself into a misery-soaked sleep.

Someone was being strangled. Emily woke with a start and thought she must have been dreaming. Then she heard it again: screaming and screeching. Her blood ran cold and she began to shake. Above her there was thunderous pounding and she thought the roof would collapse. The shrieks were spine-chilling, and she clapped her hands over her ears. She heard the back door being flung open, then her uncle shouting from somewhere outside. His gun spat and crackled as he fired it. The terrified cries fell silent. The light under the door to the cubbyhole had rekindled, and Emily heard movement. She drew her knees to her chest and wrapped her still-shaking arms around them. After a while, the back door closed and she could hear her aunt and uncle in the kitchen, talking.

'How many did it take?' Aunt Eliza asked.

'It's killed all but two, the bastard. Bit their heads off and left 'em lying there. Blood and feathers everywhere. I'll clean it up in the mornin'.'

'How did it get in? Is there a hole in the wire?'

'Naw, bloody gate were open. It just walked in and took its pick.'

'We won't have many eggs for a while then,' Aunt Eliza grumbled. 'Can any of the dead 'uns be plucked and gutted?'

'Maybe, I'll look tomorra.'

'At least we have yesterday's eggs,' Aunt Eliza said. Then the realisation must have hit her at the same time as it did Emily, and it hit harder than any of her aunt's blows had.

'She's got to go.' Aunt Eliza declared.

'What?' Emily's uncle sounded puzzled.

'Emily. It was her who left the gate open. She's been nowt but trouble since the day she came. Then she brings dirty head lice into this house and leaves the gate open for the fox. I've had enough of her.'

'Steady on, love. I'm sure you'll feel better in the morning.' Uncle George was trying to appease his wife's fury, but Emily was doubtful that he would succeed.

'Your Annie were a good woman. Goodness knows where Emily gets it from,' she told him.

'She can't go back to Alf,' Uncle George said. 'Not with all them boys there... and besides, Alf can't afford it.'

'He shouldn't have spent all his money on that damned fancy funeral; he'll be in the debtors' prison afore long,' Aunt Eliza countered, 'you mark my words.'

Chapter 8

Tuesday, 14th March 1905

Thurnby

Emily rubbed her eyes; they still felt sore and were stinging. A shaft of pale light had sliced into the closet and fallen across her face, waking her. She uncurled her body and sat up. Her nostrils twitched, and she wrinkled her nose against the dreadful smell that was all around her, filling the cubbyhole's every nook and cranny. Her hand flew to her scalp and the oiliness she felt brought the memory of her aunt's remedy for purging nits to a sickening realisation of her predicament.

'Time to get up.' Annie's voice from the open doorway heightened Emily's awareness.

'Can I come out now?' Emily's words were quiet and fearful. Annie nodded, but Emily didn't see – her inflamed eyes were still adjusting to the light – then she heard her aunt's indomitable footfalls approaching.

'Come on, girl, get up. You can go and empty your chamber pot into the lavvy when you've put your boots on. And hurry up.'

'Yes, Aunt Eliza,' Emily called, and pulled on her boots. As she had slept in her clothes, she quickly smoothed her skirt and pinafore and then lifted the small pot before making her way through the kitchen and outside to the lavatory at the bottom of the garden. She couldn't remember ever feeling as miserable this, not even after Mam had died. Outside the hen house she stopped abruptly, as if she had hit an invisible wall. The carnage in the run was sickening – headless chickens littered the ground. A severed head, its beady eyes still open and staring, looked accusingly at her. She dropped the chamber pot and her hands flew to cover her mouth. She heaved and wretched at the sight of the lifeless bodies who only yesterday had granted her such generous bounty. White feathers drifted across the run as the March wind lifted them, swirling them in its grip and leaving little piles scattered on the ground. Emily picked up the pot, turned it upside-down and shook the dregs from it. As she turned to make her way back to the house her foot touched something solid but soft. She looked down and a surge of bile filled her mouth when she saw the cockerel's body, ripped open at the craw with its gizzard hanging against shiny black feathers and nearly touching the ground. His head was still attached to his body by the windpipe, and his eyes, unlike the ones in the separated head, were closed.

'I'm sorry,' Emily whimpered. 'I'm so sorry.' She bent and stroked the cockerel's back; it felt sticky and she snatched her hand away. There were dark red streaks along her fingers and palm. Her ears buzzed and blackness swirled around her as she pitched forward onto the unforgiving ground.

At first, when she came to, Emily thought she was in her bed, then distant voices invaded her consciousness and she shivered. Her dress was wet and she pushed herself up, remembering why she was on the ground. She felt dizzy and stayed sitting on the damp grass whilst her head cleared.

'Where has that girl got to?' She heard her Aunt Eliza's rough voice. 'Go and look for her, Annie, but don't get too close as she's lousy.'

Emily watched Annie coming down the path towards her, but before Annie reached her, Emily noticed a pony and trap stop by the front gate and a young man jump down and walk towards the house. Annie continued, but after only a few more steps she stood still and shouted, 'Emily! Get up!' The young man stopped and looked over, and then started to run along the path. He passed Annie and came to Emily, where he knelt down beside her and effortlessly scooped her up as if she were made from eider down. He carried her back to the house, kicking open the kitchen door when he arrived there.

'What in the name of glory is going on?' Aunt Eliza sounded shocked.

'Perhaps you'd like to tell me,' Frank Wade said, and sat down, still holding Emily.

'That girl has been nowt but trouble since she came 'ere,' Aunt Eliza said. 'And last night she left the hen house gate open and the fox got in and killed the lot of 'em. She has to go.' Frank didn't answer. Emily had started to cough and struggled to sit up. Annie was peeping around the back door, and when Aunt Eliza saw her, she shouted:

'Go and get your father, and hurry up about it.' Annie turned and ran to find Uncle George. Aunt Eliza moved as if to grasp Emily's arm, but Frank put his large, rough hand between them and then gently slid Emily from his lap, still supporting her so that she could stand close by him.

'And what in God's name has happened to you?' he asked Emily, who didn't speak but hung her head. He turned to Aunt Eliza. 'Well? Who did this?' Frank pointed to Emily's hair.

'She's lousy,' Aunt Eliza snapped. 'I don't want lice in my house or infestin' anyone in my family.' Frank shook his head but said nothing. The back door opened and Uncle George came in, followed by Annie.

'Ah, Frank lad. Glad you've come.'

'Alf said it were urgent, so I came in the trap.'

'Will you tek 'er then?' Uncle George nodded towards Emily.

'I will,' Frank told him.

'Go and get your things, girl,' Aunt Eliza told Emily, who didn't need telling twice; she ran up the stairs to fill her little cardboard case with the few belongings she had. Margaret was already in there, away from Annie, who had threatened to burn the doll. It only took her a moment to pack; she made sure she had her hairbrush, and Mam's lavender water and handkerchief were in, and closed the lid. Without a backward glance, she ran down the stairs, snatching her coat and hat from the back of the bedroom door on the way. She pushed open the door at the foot of the stairs and was relieved to see her Uncle Frank was still there, waiting for her.

'I'll help you clear up if you like,' Frank Wade offered.

'Your lot can pay us for the fowls we lost,' Aunt Eliza retorted.

'Then I'll do that,' Frank said, and pulled out a handful of coins. 'How much?'

'They're three and six each and we lost all nineteen, so that's three pounds, six shillings and six pence.' Aunt Eliza held her hand out.

'Two pounds, nineteen and six,' Uncle George contradicted his wife. 'I told you, two survived.'

'And another five bob for the cockerel, so that's three pounds, four and six.' Aunt Eliza made her final demand. Frank took a half-crown and a florin and placed them on the table, then pulled three pound notes from his inside pocket and laid them beside the coins.

'Come on, Emily Jane, you're coming with me.' Frank took her hand and she felt his large calloused fingers gently hold hers. 'I'll bid you good day,' he said to her Uncle George and Aunt Eliza, tapped the peak of his cap and left with Emily at his side. Emily turned and looked over her shoulder; Annie was standing on the doorstep, grinning. Emily stuck her tongue out, safe in the knowledge that Annie couldn't hurt her now, or ever again.

Dark blue clouds gathered as the pony and trap travelled out of the village. The trees were still bare, new leaves not yet managing to burst their way out to decorate the dull branches.

'Better put your coat on, lass.' Frank was smiling. 'I think it's goin' to rain.'

'Uncle Frank?' Emily looked up at the man who was a younger version of her father. 'Am I going home?'

'No, you're coming with me.'

'To Thurnby?'

'Yes, to Thurnby.' Frank slapped the long reins on the pony's back so that it went a little faster. 'Your father sent a message with young Alfred first thing this morning, afore the sun were up, and told me that you weren't wanted at the Tomblin's any more. He asked if you could come to the Walker's wi' me. You'll like Mrs Walker; she reminds me of yer mam in some ways. She's kind, like Annie was, and a good Methodist.'

Emily nodded, not really knowing what a good Methodist was and if, indeed, there were any bad Methodists. They made their way across country in a light drizzle driven by a cold north wind. Frank pulled a packet from his pocket and offered it to Emily, who was shivering and had pulled her coat around her as tight as she possibly could.

'Is that your lunch?' she asked.

'We can share it,' Frank said, and he smiled as she tucked into the bread as if she hadn't eaten for a week.

'Uncle Frank?'

'Yes, child.'

'You shouldn't have given that money to Aunt Eliza.'

'Don't you worry your little head about that,' Frank said in reassurance.

'It's just that Uncle George doesn't pay for any of his hens.'

'Well, he'll have to buy some point of lay pullets now if they want any eggs.'

'No, he won't,' Emily continued. Frank looked down on her, a puzzled look etched into his face. 'You see, when he goes to the farms and tells them whether their chicks are hens or cock birds, he sometimes tells them that there are more cockerels than there really are and says he'll get rid of them for the farmer. Then he brings them home and they ain't cock birds at all, they're hen birds.'

'Well I never.' Frank shook his head and then said: 'The crafty old beggar. Still, it's on his conscience, and all the chicken shit from sexing 'em is on his trousers.' Emily giggled and Frank slapped the reins on the pony's croup again to hurry it along.

It was raining steadily when the pony and trap pulled up outside the Rose and Crown Cottages in Thurnby. Frank climbed down and tended the pony. He gave it a small wizened apple, which it took and crunched with obvious pleasure, rattling its bit as it ate. Frank twisted the reins around the gatepost to prevent it from wandering and patted its neck.

'Well done, Tilly old girl,' Frank told the mare, and she flicked her tail and lowered her head, pulling at some long grass that was growing in front of a nearby wooden fence.

Tilly's coat, which had been chestnut when they left Syston, was a rain-soaked mahogany, and Emily wished her hair was the same colour as the pony's and that it wasn't so short and didn't stink like an old stove. At least the rain had washed the soreness from her eyes. Frank lifted her from the trap's wooden seat and swung her to the ground. He took the little suitcase and handed it to her. 'Come on then, Emily Jane,' he told her. 'Mrs Walker's waiting.'

As they walked up the path, the front door to the cottage opened and a lady with a round, red face stood on the step. Emily recognised her from being at Mam's funeral and felt relieved, but she wished it had been the lady doing the washing-up that day.

'Hello, young lady,' Mrs Walker greeted her. 'Let's get you inside, and you can dry your clothes in front of the fire.' Emily stepped into a small, dark room with a fire blazing in the cast-iron grate. Frank said goodbye and headed off to work. The chimney belched out smoke when the door was closed after him and Emily coughed and blinked. Mrs Walker chuckled. 'Chimney wants sweepin',' she said. 'Tek yer coat off and put it over the back of that chair to dry.' She pointed to a hard-backed chair in the inglenook and went into the kitchen, leaving Emily to absorb her surroundings. The room gave her a comforting feeling with its small windows and low leather couch. She stood in front of the grate and held her hands towards the flames; she looked at her fingers and they reminded her of the pink sausages Mam used to get from Wakelin's. A whimpering, which quickly swelled to a howling, made her spin round. She hadn't noticed the pram in the corner earlier, and it was rocking as the baby's wailing grew louder and louder. Emily went over and lifted the tiny child, talking and soothing it as she rocked it in her arms.

'What's to do?' Mrs Walker bustled back and then stopped and grinned when she saw Emily settling her youngest. Emily smiled back. 'Well if you can calm our Lizzie down like that, you can stop 'ere as long as you like,' Mrs Walker chortled. 'You wait till Alfred gets going, then we shall have our hands full.'

'Alfred?' Emily asked.

'Yes, Alfred, he's three, then there's Arthur, he's at school. I'll take you tomorra, and Agnes is at the big school, but she'll leave next birthday and go into service.'

'My father is called Alfred and so is my brother,' Emily told the woman she was to live with, for now.

'I know, it's a good name. Now, let's get her fed, and take your hat off whilst you're indoors.' Emily hung her head and pulled her bonnet away. 'What in heaven's name has happened to you?' Emily saw the look of horror on Betsy Walker's face when she set eyes on her hair, which was sticking to her head in uneven tufts, still thick with paraffin.

'I had nits,' Emily said, and burst into tears.

'It's blowing a blizzard out there.' Frank Wade blustered into the cottage and slammed the front door behind him just as the back door, too, slammed against the weather.

'That'll be Mr Walker home.' Mrs Walker rose from her chair. 'And don't leave all that ice 'n snow in here,' she scolded Frank. 'Go through and take your wet things off and I'll put you something nice and hot on the table.' Frank winked at Emily, who was sitting on a brass log-box near the fire clutching a cup of steaming Bovril. She had taken a bath, even though it was midweek. Mrs Walker had washed the paraffin from her hair, and then taken her scissors to neaten it so that it resembled a pony's tail-bob. She watched her Uncle Frank shrug the coat from his back and lift his cap, shaking the snow from its crown and hanging both on the rail near the back door.

'That's better,' he sighed, sitting down to untie his boots. 'Snow's made it twice as heavy, and I fear I may need it again afore long; the sheep'll start lambing any day now.'

'Bloody weather,' John Walker growled, and dropped a sack of coal down beside the kitchen range. 'We shall have to dig the tracks out afore we can work on 'em tomorra.'

'Had a good day then?' Frank nodded to the sack.

'Ah, there were a load of coal on the tracks today, spilled off a carriage wi' too much on it, so the pickings were good afore the snow set in.'

Betsy put two bowls of steaming broth on the table and cut up a fresh loaf of bread. She gave Emily a slice for dipping into her hot Bovril whilst the two men ate in silence; just the clanking of cutlery against their dishes punctuated their meal. Emily watched them intently.

'Thank you, Mrs Walker, that were grand.' Her Uncle Frank took a pipe from his jacket pocket and began to fill it with tobacco from a pouch that he'd pulled from his other pocket. 'And thank you for taking Emily Jane in – our Alf will be relieved.'

'She can stop as long as she wants; that girl needs a good home until she goes into service.' Betsy smiled at Emily and then passed an old copy of *The Times* to her husband, who took it and settled further into his chair to read about world affairs, even if they had happened a few days earlier. The room was quiet except for the deep ticking of a long-case clock and the occasional, triumphant cry of 'snap', as one of the children placed their card onto the hearthrug.

Emily jumped when John Walker dropped the paper to the floor. He rubbed his eyes, stretched and said:

'Well, I'd better go and stoke the boiler, otherwise the school'll be freezin' in the mornin'. I won't be long.' She watched him pull on his coat, scarf, cap and top-boots and then turn to Frank. 'Read that piece about the Russo-Japanese war,' he muttered through his muffler. Frank picked up the discarded *Times* and began to leaf through it. Emily could hear John Walker whistling the Londonderry Air as he stepped outside. It reminded her of when Mam used to sing it to her – she'd always like that tune. Emily pulled back the curtain and watched Mr Walker through the window. She could see that a blizzard was whipping up deep drifts along the lane. She shivered and turned back to listen to her Uncle Frank who let out a low whistle.

'Strewth! The Russians have lost a hundred thousand men in three days and had to retreat from Mukden,' he said. 'What an awful waste of life.'

Betsy Walker was wiping her hands on her pinafore.

'And all them poor widows and heartbroken mothers,' Mrs Walker said, and she went over to make up the fire.

'Come along, upstairs to bed now,' Mrs Walker told the three children who were still playing cards on the hearthrug. 'Get your coat, Emily, it will be dry now. You'll all need your coats on in bed tonight; it's going to be a cold one. Keep your stockings on too.'

They trooped up the stairs, Mrs Walker carrying a paraffin lamp to show the way. 'Come on, lass, it's too cold to wait around, go and get into bed.'

Emily saw her little case on a small bed to her right. Agnes jumped into the other bed, which was on the left-hand side of the room. She pulled the blankets over her until just the top of her head could be seen. Emily started to walk over to Agnes's bed.

'Where the blazes are you going?' Mrs Walker asked, pulling her shawl more tightly around her shoulders. Emily stopped and looked at her. 'For the love of God, child, jump into bed,' Mrs Walker told her, and put the case onto the floor. She pulled back the blankets of the smaller bed and indicated for Emily to jump in by nodding in its direction.

'But isn't this Arthur's bed?' Emily asked.

'No, it's yours. Arthur sleeps with Alfred.'

'Thank you,' Emily whispered as she was being tucked into the welcoming blankets.

'Eee lass, what a to-do.' Mrs Walker sighed. 'And tomorrow we'll see what Agnes can give you to wear. You've been wearing black for long enough.'

Chapter 9

Saturday, 24th June 1905

Worms

'Do you wanna go down the Wreake this afternoon?' Ernest asked David as they made their way home along School Street.

'Yes, it's too hot for football.' David could feel his shirt sticking to him, the sun was high and it was burning the back of his neck; the thought of a swim in the River Wreake was definitely tempting.

'Father's in the tripe shop. I'll tell him where we're off to, come on.' Ernest pointed to Wakelin's shop and both boys ran across the road. The smell of tripe, warming up in the mid-summer sun, caused David's nose to wrinkle in disgust. He stood in the doorway whilst Ernest went inside to speak with his father, who was waiting at the counter to buy his weekend tripe.

'That boy's got worms.' David recognised his mother's voice; it did not befit the harsh sentiment it delivered. He peered inside the shop and saw Alf Wade turn around and look at his mother, who was also waiting to be served. She smiled, and David watched as Ernest's father returned the greeting and then looked away.

'Mr Wade, I mean your boy... there, look at him.'

Ernest's brother, Henry, was scratching his bottom and squirming as he moved his weight from one leg to the other.

'He's alus doin' that,' Alf Wade told her. 'It's just a habit.'

'Mr Wade,' David's mother spoke again, 'I think you will find the child has worms.'

David stifled a giggle as Mr Wade ignored her and gave his order.

'A pound please,' Alf told Adam Wakelin, and pointed to the leaf-tripe, which was showing the cheapest price. Adam winked at David, who, despite the smell, had moved inside the shop where it was cooler. Adam weighed the white offal and wrapped it.

'Anything else, Alf?'

'No thank you.'

'That'll need plenty of long, slow boiling and a good helping of onions,' Mary Adcock said to Alf Wade.

David felt a tapping on his head as his mother spoke – so she had seen him.

'I do know how to cook tripe, Mrs Adcock,' Alf Wade replied, his lips beginning to curl into a smile. David nudged Ernest and fought back a chuckle.

'Really? Oh, sorry, I thought that you being, well, you know...'

'No, I don't know.' David could see that Mr Wade was trying hard not to laugh at her embarrassment from having made such an insinuation.

'Well, you don't have a woman to cook and clean for you.' She sounded contrite without losing too much composure.

'We manage,' Alf Wade said over his shoulder, and he handed three pennies to Adam Wakelin. 'Good day, Mrs Adcock.' He doffed his cap and left the shop, gently pulling Henry's hand away from his bottom to stop him from scratching. Ernest ran after him and David turned to his mother.

'I'm going down the Wreake, Mam,' he told her.

'Not afore you've had summat to eat.'

'But I'll get cramp and drown if I swim after eatin',' David protested.

'Then you must wait until your dinner's gone down. Now come along.' She left the shop with her tripe and strode out in Alf Wade's wake. Before they reached the end of the street, David heard Ernest having a similar conversation about swimming after eating with his father.

'Mr Wade,' Mary Adcock's voice called out and he stopped and turned. She hurried towards him, one hand holding her bonnet, the other her basket. David was sweating in the heat. He watched his mother talking to Alf Wade, the late-morning sun catching the green and purple stones in her necklace and causing them to wink at Mr Wade from the surrounding white pearls that lay against her smooth neckline. 'Mr Wade,' she repeated, 'I don't mean to interfere, but I do think your son has worms and you'll all get them if you don't see to him.'

'I don't want worms,' Ernest said. 'The fish'll come after me when I'm in the river.'

'See to him?' Alf Wade had raised his eyebrows.

'I have some black walnut and wormwood tincture at home from when my Charlie had them. I'll send our David round later with it if you would like me to?' she offered.

'But I'm goin' down the Wreake,' David muttered. He looked at Mr Wade who was obviously thinking. David's mother had cast her eyes down as if she was embarrassed.

'I'll tell you what' – Alf Wade settled his answer – 'why don't you bring it round yer 'sen?'

'Oh, I, er, yes I could do.' His mother stumbled over her words, then, on regaining her composure she pulled herself upright and looked him in the eye. 'About four o'clock this afternoon?' she asked.

'Make it five,' Alf Wade countered. 'I'll be back from work around then.'

'Very well, I shall come at five o'clock,' she agreed. 'Good day, Mr Wade.'

'Good day.' He tapped the peak of his cap and David could see that he was trying hard not to laugh.

'See you at the river down by the Gate Hangs Well,' Ernest called to David, and he ran after his father and Henry, who was still scratching his bottom.

David pulled his shirt off and put it with his shorts on the riverbank, which was strewn with similar piles of clothes. Ernest waved from the green river where he was splashing around with three other lads. David slid down the grassy bank and into the water. The reeds tickled his legs and squidgy mud squeezed between his toes. He was so hot from running he thought steam might rise up around him when he flopped into the cold water. He swam across to the others and saw that Harry Hamson from next door and the Oswin brothers were racing towards him from the broken-down tree that spanned a narrow part of the river. Another boy was diving under the water and David felt something grab his ankle and pull his feet from under him; he was being dragged under. He kicked and flayed his arms until both lads broke the surface once more. David had swallowed what seemed to him like a gallon of river water, and he spluttered and coughed, spitting out bits of broken-off weeds. Bobby Swann was swimming away and laughing.

'Bastard.' David spat again.

'He did that to me earlier,' Ernest said, swimming in a circle around David.

'I'll get him back,' David promised.

'How you gonna do that?' Ernest carried on swimming. 'He's bigger than us.'

'Not much,' David said.

They swam up and down the river until their fingertips became wrinkled in the cool water. When he was tired of swimming, David pretended to have cramp and stayed close by the broken-down tree whilst the others swam back towards the Gate Hangs Well public house. He looked around to make sure all the boys were facing in the opposite direction and then swam underneath the sagging bough so that it was between him and them. He then scrambled up the riverbank. Keeping low, he made his way back to where the piles of clothes were. He hid his and Ernest's under a bush, then lifted Bobby's, the only ones stiff with paint stains from Mr Swann's decorating business, and, still keeping low, took them back to beyond the broken-down tree. He thought about tossing them into the river, but instead he coaxed over a friendly bullock that was chewing its cud and watching him. He pulled some fresh grass and offered it to the black-and-white beast, and whilst it ate he carefully tied Bobby's shirt and trousers around its neck. After giving the animal a friendly pat, he slid into the river and swam back upstream. When he reached the place that was used for dipping sheep, and where Ernest was, he swam past him and said: 'Come on, Ernest, time to go home or we'll be in trouble.' Ernest frowned and was about to speak, but David shot him a look and cocked his head to tell him to 'be quiet and come on'. David led the way to the bush where their shorts, shirts and boots were hidden.

'Why do we have to leave?' Ernest asked as they climbed the bank.

'Shut up and put your clothes on,' David told him.

'But why?'

'I'll tell you when you're dressed. Now hurry up.'

When they were clothed, they pulled on their boots. Ernest stood up from tying his shoelaces.

'Well, what's the rush?' he asked.

David grinned and draped his arm across Ernest's shoulders, his index finger pointing to the bullock wearing Swanny's clothes. Ernest started to shake with laughter and David pushed him towards the five-barred gate. The boys waved to the others, who were just about to set off on another race, and made their way out of the field and into the lane.

'You'll get a leathering,' Ernest panted as the two boys ran back to the village as fast as their legs would carry them. David knew he would be in for a thrashing on Monday, but wished he could be a fly on the bullock's back when Bobby saw his clothes around its neck.

Mary looked into the mirror on her dressing table; the forty-year-old woman who stared back reminded her of her mother.

'This won't do,' she said aloud, and pulled her hair back into the pleat from which it was threatening to escape; the grey hairs would soon outnumber the auburn ones, then she *would* look like her mother. Securing the last tendril with a hairpin, she dabbed a little lavender water on the inside of her wrists and buttoned her clean blouse. She heard the back door open and then slam to again.

'Is that you, David?' she called.

'Yes, Mam,' came the reply from their small scullery. She fastened her necklace of green, white and violet stones in place, and after checking her reflection one last time she went down the stairs, her skirts swishing as she descended.

'Are you going to church, Mam?' David asked.

'No, I'm going to take this tincture to Mr Wade; his lad's got worms, remember?' She picked up a bottle of black walnut and wormwood tincture and waved it in the air in front of David. 'We can have our tea later when Whattoff and Charlie get in from work; I hope Charlie brings some vegetables from Mr Turner's, or some fruit would be nice if there are any leftovers to bring home.'

'We? Am I coming?' David asked.

'Of course you're coming,' Mary said. 'I'm not leaving you here on your own. You can have a game of football with Ernest.' She pushed David in front of her and out into Paddock Row.

They walked past the brook and through the village, heading towards Alf Wade's house. As they crossed the Barkby Road, they could see the new cemetery, which was beginning to be peppered with a few tombstones. Before turning into Albion Street, Mary stopped at the gates. She hadn't intended to visit her late husband's grave today, but she felt he was pulling her close once more. She lifted the heavy chain that held the large iron gates together and pushed one open.

'Are we going to visit Father?' David asked. Mary nodded and they crunched their way along the gravel path until they arrived at her late husband's final resting place. She touched the wooden cross, which marked where he lay.

'Hello, my love,' she said softly. 'I'm sure you didn't expect us today; we're on our way to see Alf Wade. He's a lovely man, quite handsome, just like you.'

Before she said any more she felt David slip his hand into hers.

'How did Father die?' David asked. 'Please tell me. Whattoff won't – he says you'll tell me when I'm old enough.'

Mary sat down on the grass beside the grave and patted the ground indicating for David to sit down beside her.

'Your father was a good man,' she told him, 'but he did like a drink or two, especially when he was playing cards with your uncles. It had been a really hot day and he'd been to the Wolf and Lamb. When he got home it was dark and he couldn't see to take his boots off.'

'Where were you?' David asked.

'I'd gone to bed, but I came down when he called to me. He was sitting on the bottom stair still trying to pull off his boots. I tried to coax him upstairs but he said it was too dark and to fetch a paraffin lamp from the kitchen, which I did. He told me to go upstairs first and he would hold the lamp so that he could see where he was going.' She felt a tear slide down her cheek and quickly wiped it away. 'He looked up at me and told me I was beautiful, and then he stumbled forward. I held out my hand to him and when he reached out to take it his foot slipped' – her voice fell to a whisper – 'and he fell backwards.' She closed her eyes as if trying to hide the image, but it just became more intense.

'Is that why he died?' David asked. 'Coz he fell?'

'Not exactly.' Mary swallowed hard and continued. 'The lamp he was carrying crashed against the wall and paraffin soaked his clothes. He was alight and fell to the bottom of the stairs, flames spreading all over him.'

'What did you do?' David asked. 'Why didn't you save him?'

'I couldn't.' Mary's voice caught in her throat. 'I dragged him outside into the yard and tried to put the flames out. Whattoff helped me – pumping water, filling buckets and throwing it over your father.'

'Where was I?'

'You were fast asleep in bed, and so was Charlie. You weren't even two years old.'

'Did he die out there, in the yard?'

'No, he died two weeks later. I really thought he would pull through, but it wasn't to be.'

Mary wiped another tear away and they sat in silence until the church bells chimed five o'clock.

'Come along,' Mary said, and brushed dry grass from her skirts. They hurried back onto Barkby Road and turned right into Albion Street. She paused for a moment to catch her breath then walked up to Alf Wade's front door and gave three sharp knocks on the hard wood. The door swung open almost immediately, and Alf stood before her. She smiled to herself when she noticed that he, too, had changed into a clean shirt, and he had shaved. She held out the tincture, but he didn't take it.

'Come in,' he said instead, and stood back to let her and David enter. Mary brushed past him, and he closed the door behind them. 'Ernest's out the back, David,' he said, 'and Henry's in here,' he told Mary. David ran towards the back door and Mary entered a bright room, which smelled of beeswax and tobacco; very different from how she remembered it when she had made tea for him after Annie's funeral, when it had been dark and cheerless.

'Hello, Henry,' she greeted the boy playing with wooden animals under the table. He looked up and then went back to his animals.

'Speak when you are spoken to, lad,' his father admonished, and Henry crawled out and stood before Mary.

'Hello,' he said quietly, and his hand shot to his bottom and he began to scratch.

'I've brought you some medicine to make that go away.' Mary smiled and showed him the bottle. 'May I have a spoon, please, Mr Wade?'

'They're in the kitchen drawer,' Alf replied.

'Of course.' Mary went through to the small kitchen.

'Put the kettle on whilst you're there,' Alf called. Mary reached for a water jug, filled the kettle and lit the paraffin heater beneath.

'You will stay for a cup of tea?' Mary felt Alf's breath on the back of her neck, and the closeness of his voice startled her. She turned to face him and held a small spoon up.

'Yes, thank you,' she answered, 'but let me give Henry his medicine first.' He stepped aside, but she still needed to squeeze past, and her arm brushed his. She was surprised when a small bird, seemingly trapped in her stomach, fluttered its wings; a feeling she had long forgotten existed.

'Please may I have my animals back?' Henry asked Mary, who had taken them to scrub clean after finishing her tea.

'Let me wash your hands, and nails too so that you won't make them dirty again,' she told him, and led him through to the kitchen. 'I think you should all take a dose of the tincture,' Mary called to Alf, 'just to be sure.'

Mary dried her hands and followed Henry, who was clutching his animals, back into the room.

Alf had pulled the stopper from the bottle and was sniffing its contents.

'It doesn't taste too bad,' Mary said. 'It's sort of nutty and woody.'

'It smells a bit flowery to me,' Alf said, and put the stopper back. 'I'll give the lads some tonight, then I'll return it to you when he stops scratchin'.'

A moment's uncomfortable silence fell between them. Then, not really wanting to leave, but knowing she must, Mary said:

'I'll be off now then. I've washed the cups and emptied the teapot. Send David home in half an hour would you?'

'I will. Thank you, Mrs Adcock.' Alf rose from his chair.

'Please, call me Mary.'

'Very well, thank you, Mary.'

'Would you like me to post that for you?' Mary pointed to a postcard, which was propped on the mantelpiece, 'I'm passing the pillar box. It won't go until Monday now though.'

'Ah, yes, that would be kind of you,' Alf said. 'It's Emily's birthday next week. I don't normally send cards, but Ernest wanted to.'

'How old will she be?' Mary asked.

'Ten.' Then he changed the subject of their parting conversation. 'Shall you be going to The Feast next month, Mary?'

'Yes, I expect so.'

'Would you allow me to escort you?' Before answering, Mary stepped out into the street, and the late afternoon sun glinted on her necklace. 'I'm sorry,' he said, faltering, 'I shouldn't have been so forward.' Mary tossed her head back and laughed, the green, white and purple stones dancing just above her neckline.

'Of course, I would love for you to escort me.' She smiled and, clutching the postcard, began to walk home. 'Good night, Mr Wade,' she called over her shoulder.

'Alf,' he called back. 'It's Alf.'

Chapter 10

Saturday, 1st July 1905

Feast

'Emily Jane, there's a postcard for you.'

Emily dropped her hairbrush and rushed down the stairs and into the kitchen. 'Happy birthday, love.' Mrs Walker handed the card, with a picture of a watermill on the front, to her.

'Thank you.' Emily took the card and turned it over. 'It's from Father!' She looked up at the smiling older woman who had welcomed Emily into her family.

'I'm pleased your father has remembered to send you a birthday greeting,' Mrs Walker said.

'Ernest has signed it too!' She clutched it to her chest for a moment then looked again at the cursive writing on its back. The green halfpenny stamp had a heavy black ink circle telling her that the card had been posted in Syston a few days earlier.

'And one more,' Mrs Walker said, holding a blue card, decorated with a picture of bright yellow daisies, out to her. She took it and turned it over. The address said simply 'Miss

Wade, Thurnby, Nr Leicester' and the black circle, which read 'Thurnby, AP 27', hardly covered the stamp.

'Thank you,' Emily replied, and Mrs Walker placed the cards side by side on the mantelshelf.

Emily pushed the last piece of cake into her mouth and closed her eyes, soaking up the pleasure it had given her. She swallowed and then took a last sip of her tea. Arthur and Alfred had also enjoyed cake for tea, and even little Lizzie had managed a small piece.

'Oh, I almost forgot, another card came for you in the second post,' Mrs Walker said, and she handed a third postcard to Emily. This one was green and had poppies in the centre and a verse written above them:

Happier may this birthday be, than any yet that dawned for thee;

May all the years that lie before, increase in blessing more and more. A H H[2]

'I don't think I could ever be happier,' Emily said. 'I wonder who AHH is.' She turned the card over and saw it was from Agnes, who was now in service at a big house in Leicester. She placed it on the mantelshelf beside the other two and began to clear the table.

'The nit nurse came to school today,' Arthur told his mother, who looked at Emily and raised her eyebrows.

Emily stroked her hair, which had grown and was tumbling onto her shoulders. She grinned and said: 'But they didn't find any on us, did they, Alfred?' And she patted the younger boy's head.

2. See postcard 1, page 322

After she had washed all the pots and put them away, Emily took Lizzie upstairs. The little girl had moved into Agnes's bed and Emily told her a story and let her cuddle Margaret before she went to sleep. She heard the back door open and Mr Walker call to his wife to help him get his boots off. Satisfied that Lizzie was sleeping, Emily went downstairs again where John Walker was sitting at the kitchen table.

'Run across the road, Emily, and fetch a jug of ale,' he told her, and pulled two pennies and a halfpenny from his pocket. He laid them on the table. 'And then I've a little job for you when you get back.' Emily scooped up the coins and took a large stone ewer from the cupboard. The door opened, and Frank Wade came in as Emily was going out.

'She's off to get us some ale,' John Walker told Frank, who winked at Emily and sat down opposite Mr Walker.

Emily knocked on a small window just inside the entrance to the Rose and Crown. She saw a man's outline through the frosted glass and the window opened.

'Hello, Emily.' William Murrell smiled at her.

'Good evening, Mr Murrell. May I have a jug of ale please?'

'Give your jar over, lass.' He reached through the window and took the three coins, which Emily had placed on the wooden sill, and lifted the jug, which he took to the tap and filled. 'Mind you don't drop it,' he joked as he handed the flagon back. Emily wrinkled her nose at the smell and said goodnight. She heard the window close as she carefully descended the steps and headed back to the cottage, where she placed the ale on the table between Mr Walker and her Uncle Frank.

After the men had eaten and finished drinking, John Walker called through to Emily, who was playing snakes and ladders with Arthur: 'Come on, lass, I'll show you that job I want you to do at the school.'

Saturday, 15th July 1905

Alf straightened his tie and walked along Paddock Row. Just before he reached Mary's house he began to wonder if he should have brought something – a gift, flowers maybe – but that may have seemed presumptuous, and besides, he had the black walnut and wormwood tincture to return, what was left of it. They had all experienced stomach cramps and numerous dashes to the lavatory after they had taken it, but Henry had stopped scratching, and Sydney, who he had checked with a torch after dark just like Mary had told him to, was totally worm-free. He pulled the bottle from his pocket and knocked on the door. He could hear the villagers gathering on the field; the sound of their excited voices carried on the light breeze. He knocked again. He didn't want to be late and miss Ernest playing with the band. The door flew open and David, clutching a cornet, ran past him.

'Would you please excuse David?' Mary called from inside. 'He's playing with the band and he should be there by now. Are you coming in?' Alf stepped inside the bright, airy cottage and closed the door behind him. He could smell fresh baking. He felt his jaws tingle and licked his lips. Mary stood before him wearing a summer bonnet and a high-necked dress with a full skirt. She had pinned a corsage of purple and white flowers with green asparagus fern just below her left shoulder.

'You look beautiful, if I may say so.' Alf's voice cracked, and he felt a warm surge of what he could only think was passion run through his body.

'Thank you,' Mary said, and she stepped closer. He could smell the soap on her face and hair; he wanted to kiss her. He caught his breath and leaned in towards her, placing his hand on her slender waist.

'Cooee. Are you ready, Mrs Adcock?' Mrs Walker-Holmes pushed open the front door. Mary was smiling at the unwelcome woman and they swiftly pulled apart.

'Coming,' she called, and then said quietly, 'You go on, Alf, I'll catch you up.'

'No, it's all right, I'll wait.'

'Sorry,' Mary whispered to him, and she scooped up a heavily laden basket from the table.

'Let me carry that for you,' Alf offered, and they made their way to the front door, where Mrs Walker-Holmes was waiting, dressed in a similar fashion to Mary, but without the corsage, and carrying a smaller basket of freshly baked pastries.

'Oh, I didn't know you had company.' Alf thought he detected a sneer.

'Mrs Walker-Holmes, this is Mr Wade. He was returning something he had borrowed and is also on his way to The Feast.'

Alf detected disapproval shadowing the face of the slightly older woman, who quickened her step, leaving Mary trailing. 'Well I hope this one isn't a drunkard like your last one,' Alf heard her mutter, probably thinking Mary wouldn't hear her scathing remark, but she obviously had.

The field was full of activity; large tents had been erected where the traditional duck-and-pea dishes would be served to as many as could sit at the tables inside. Mary took her basket to the tent where the sweet pies and pastries would be distributed and removed the still-warm pies and tarts. The sun was beating down on the canvas roof, making the tent uncomfortably hot. She lifted her empty basket and went back outside. She looked around at the different tents, which were dedicated to the village shops and filled with displays from green-grocery to the blacksmith's anvil and forge. She walked across the grass and found Alf in a marquee with a large white swan painted onto a blackboard; he had a small glass in his hand filled with amber liquid.

'The band will be striking up soon, shall we go and see?' Mary asked, and they walked together towards the makeshift bandstand to watch their sons play. Mary heard a thud and Alf pitched forward; a thump had landed between his shoulder blades and his whisky almost left the glass, causing Mary to step aside and listen, at a distance, to the banter.

'How are you, Alf?' Frank asked his brother.

'Frank! What are you doing here?'

'It's *The Feast* ain't it?' Frank was laughing.

'How did you get here?'

'In the trap. I've left it over there under yon tree so the pony can have some shade. Are your lads here?' Frank looked around for his nephews.

'Young Alfred is helping in Turner's tent and Ernest is playing with the band. The other two are with Mrs Cook over there.'

Mary squinted to see where Alf was pointing and saw a lady surrounded by young children.

'You haven't asked about Emily Jane,' Mary heard Frank admonishing.

'Is she all right?' Alf asked.

Mary remembered the child being dragged off to the Tomblin's on the day of Annie Wade's funeral.

'She's over there, with Ernest.' Frank pointed to the bandstand, and among the boys in their uniforms stood a slender young girl with shoulder-length curls. She turned as if she'd felt her father's eyes watching her, and when she saw him, she waved and jumped from the stand. She ran over the grass, deftly manoeuvring between the villagers, to where they were standing. Alf bent and held her close, and Mary moved a little further away and into the shade of an old oak tree. The band began to play and Alf hadn't let go of his daughter throughout their repertoire. The sun bounced from one silver instrument to the next, glinting and flashing as if sending a secret code across the land.

Applause rang out over the field and Mary turned to Alf, still clapping.

A young woman was running towards them, and Mary thought she looked panic-stricken.

'Mr Wade,' the woman called out, 'Mr Wade, come quickly, please.' She looked as if she was going to faint: splashes of blood decorated her white dress and her hands were shaking.

'Mrs Cook.' Alf looked shocked by her appearance and released Emily from his hold. 'Whatever's the matter?'

'It's Henry, please come quickly.' Mary and Emily followed Alf and Mrs Cook as they ran across the field towards the ironmonger's tent. When they got closer, Mary heard a child screaming and quickened her pace. She caught up with Alf just as he reached the tent. They rushed inside and pushed their way through a small crowd that had gathered around Alf's son, who was sitting on the floor holding a blood-soaked cloth to his face, howling and crying. Alf dropped to his knees and held Henry close until the boy's cries grew quieter. He lifted the cloth from Henry's face, and Mary's stomach lurched when she saw the gouged eye through a veil of blood.

'What in God's name has happened?' Alf demanded.

'It were your young 'un,' William Meadows, who was holding a pitchfork with a broken handle, told him. 'This were over the back – it needs a new stave, see. Well, your lad picked it up and threw it at his brother. Spike went in his eye.' Henry began to cry again, and Alf lifted him from the ground. Frank was beside him, and Mary was holding Sydney, who had started to cry in unison with his brother.

'Will you take us to the infirmary in the trap, Frank?' Alf asked.

'Of course, but what about Emily Jane and the boys?'

'They can all come home with me,' Mary told him, 'and they can stay until you get back. Now go.'

'Thank you.' Alf spoke in almost a whisper and the two brothers ran to the pony and trap. From what Mary had seen beneath the bloodstained cloth, she knew that Alf's son would never see out of that eye again.

Chapter 11

Sunday, 5th November 1905

Tiger

'It's nine o'clock, Emily,' John Walker called from the kitchen.

'Put your coat on.' Betsy Walker looked up from her knitting. 'There's a cold wind blowing tonight. You'll need your scarf and gloves too.' Emily put down her book and went into the kitchen. She pulled on her boots, which used to belong to Agnes, and lifted her coat from its hook by the door.

'What's that you're readin'?' Mr Walker blew a stream of blue tobacco smoke across the room.

'It's *The Second Jungle Book,*' Emily answered. 'It's really good. I've only read the first story, where Hathi the elephant tells how tigers got their stripes.'

'That Kipling fella can spin a good yarn,' Mr Walker puffed. 'Off you go then, the stove'll need stokin' up well tonight.'

Emily stepped out into the night and the cold air wrapped around her. She ran the short distance from the cottages to St Luke's school, racing against Jack Frost as he spread his icy fingers through the lanes. The moon was high in the cloudless sky, and it lit her way better than the spluttering gas lamps, of which there were few along her short nightly journey. She slipped through the gates and ran towards the tall brick building with intricate black-brick patterning along its face. An owl screeched, and Emily looked up at the tall triangular gable. The moonlight was so bright she could see the shield on its front and even the wording, *AD 1865*, was clearly visible. She thrust her gloved hand into her coat pocket and felt for the large key, which was beginning to wear the lining away. The click of it turning in the lock echoed through the playground and Emily pushed open the heavy door, slipped inside and closed it again, shutting out the cold. She hardly needed to light the lamp, which was on its stand just inside the porch; the moonlight streamed in through the high mullion windows as if it were daytime. She glanced at the lamp and picked up the box of Swan Vestas lying next to it. Taking out a match, she struck it and held it to the wick. A steady flame leapt up and she twisted a small wheel, which controlled the wick's height, until the flame settled. After securing the glass chimney over the flame, Emily carried the light in front of her. At the end of the long corridor and down a short flight of stone steps was the coalhouse door. She lifted the latch and pulled it open. A waft of coal dust drifted out and she sneezed as it tickled inside her nostrils. She set down the lamp, slipped off her coat and set to work, filling a small bucket, the same one she used each night, with lumps of coal. When it was full, she heaved it up and made her way back down the corridor to the school's single classroom. The moon lit her way as she walked past rows of desks to the front of the room where the old tortoise stove stood in the centre of the long wall, its stovepipe rising to, and through, the ceiling. She pulled a chair across and placed it close by the hot cast-iron heater then climbed onto it and pulled a heavy metal implement, which looked like a chisel with two ugly bumps on its edge, from a hook on the wall. Taking care not to overbalance, she placed the bumps into corresponding holes in the stove's round lid and prised it open. A blast of searing heat streamed out and continued to flow upwards as she propped open the lid and rehung the metal opener. She climbed down and hoisted the bucket of coal onto the chair with her and pulled it level with the opening, then she tipped the coal in, dampening the inner furnace and feeding the hungry belly of the tortoise. She picked up the metal implement from its hook, closed the lid, and jumped from the chair to make her way back to the coalhouse for the next load. She knew she would need to make at least five or six more trips before the stove was full enough to be left to burn throughout the night.

When she approached the classroom with the second helping of coal, she heard a noise, like a chair scraping on a wooden floor. She stopped and held her breath. The silence was only broken by the owl hooting outside, so she pushed open the classroom door but stopped abruptly as soon as she had entered the room. A tall, dark figure was standing by the stove with his back to her. Emily dropped the bucket. Edwin Ball spun round and Emily's hands covered her nose and mouth in surprise and recognition.

'Hello, Emily Jane.' His face had a suspicious look. 'What are you doing here at this hour?'

'Oh, Mr Ball, I'm making the stove up for the night, sir.'

'I thought Mr Walker did that of an evening; that's what I pay him for.'

'Yes, Headmaster, sir,' Emily stammered, 'but I do it to pay for my keep.'

'Oh, I see.'

'I'm sorry I dropped the coal.' Emily began to pick the pieces from the floor and replace them whilst he watched. With a full again bucket, she walked forward and noticed the chair was no longer next to the stove. She glanced up at the headmaster, smiled, pulled the chair back over and climbed onto it ready to perform the opening ritual once more. Aware that Mr Ball was watching her, though in silence, the occasional shaking of his head caused her to wonder if she was fulfilling the stoking process correctly. She closed the lid, and jumped down to fetch the next load.

'Just a minute,' the headmaster called to her departing back. She stopped. He walked over to her and opened the door. 'Is there another bucket?' he asked.

'Yes, sir, but it's too big for me to carry so I use this one.'

'Then perhaps I could carry it.'

'Oh no, sir, it's my job, and it's a mucky one too.'

'So I see.' He smiled at her and she looked down at her completely black hands and wondered if her face was dirty too. 'Come along, I shall help you, and we'll be finished in no time.'

Mary picked up a brass key from the mantelpiece, and walked over to the Gustav Becker wall clock, glancing up at the eagle that sat proudly atop of it, scowling, as if it were admonishing her for forgetting to wind the timepiece earlier, rendering the pendulum still and its chimes silent. She pulled open the clock's glass door and inserted the key into one hole in the clockface, wound it until it would turn no more, then moved it to the other and did the same.

'What time is it?' she asked Alf, who took his pocket watch from his waistcoat pocket.

'It's a quarter to ten,' he told her. 'I'd better be going.'

'Just a moment,' Mary said, as she pushed the clock's hands into place, 'I'll wrap you some cake to take home for the boys.'

'Thank you, that'd be grand. Then I'll be off.'

'Come on, lads,' Mary called to her sons, as she went through to the scullery. 'Bedtime!'

'Whattoff's gone up already,' Charlie said, coming into the tiny kitchen, cheeks bulging.

'What are you eating?' Mary asked him.

'David's cake. He's too busy playing with his tiger and didn't want it.'

'Did you ask?'

'No. He was busy.'

'Charles Ernest Adcock. You do not take without asking. Now get to bed,' Mary scolded. 'David, come along. Time for bed – it's school tomorrow.'

David appeared in the kitchen clutching a wooden tiger. He looked up at Alf.

'Thank you for my tiger, sir,' he said. Alf bent and ruffled David's hair.

'Goodnight, lad,' Alf said.

'Goodnight, sir. Goodnight, Mam.'

The pounding of feet on the stairs soon stopped, doors slammed, and eventually the house was quiet. Mary closed the door that led from the kitchen to the staircase, and with her back to Alf, she turned the key in the lock. She walked over to the scrubbed kitchen table and lifted the parcel of wrapped cake.

'You can stay a while longer if you would like to,' Mary invited, placing the sweet dessert into his hands. 'I have a bottle of rum in the cupboard.'

'Maybe just a small one then.' Alf placed the cake back on the table and followed Mary back through to the living room. She walked over to an oak cabinet, her skirt swaying as she moved. Tendrils of her auburn hair had escaped the neat pleat and she pushed them back. She pulled open the cabinet's door, took out a bottle in one hand and a glass in the other, and then pressed the door to with her knee. When she turned round Alf was standing right in front of her. She raised her eyes to his and took a step forward so that she was even closer. He took the glass from her right hand and placed it on top of the cabinet, reaching across and behind her, nuzzling her neck as he did so. She breathed in and whispered his name. He rested his hand on her waist, rubbing her ribs with his thumb, and with his other hand he took the bottle and leaned across her left-hand side and placed it beside the glass. He kissed her beneath her ear and on her neck. She leaned back, and he kissed her throat, then his lips fell onto her eager mouth, which opened invitingly, giving him the permission he was seeking. Her arms snaked around his neck, over his solid shoulders, and he lifted her, gently laying her on the hearthrug. Heat from the dying embers warmed her skin. The release was urgent, greedy even, sweeping through their veins with a ferocity neither could remember having felt for many years, especially on a Sunday!

'You're back early,' Mrs Walker greeted Emily.

'Am I?' She feigned surprise. 'What time is it?'

'Twenty to ten. You don't normally get home until nearer ten. Are you sure you made the stove up proper?'

'Yes, quite sure,' Emily reassured her. 'I managed the bigger bucket tonight, and it didn't take as long. The moonlight was bright enough for me not to have to light the lamp either.' She didn't like telling fibs, but on this occasion thought it to be for the best.

'Wash your hands and face then up you go to bed – school tomorrow.'

Emily cleaned the coal dust away and climbed the stairs. She could hear Mr Walker's snores and hoped the headmaster wouldn't tell him about helping her with the stoking. Kneeling beside her bed, she prayed to St Luke, as she was sure that's what you were supposed to do on All Saints' Sunday, that her secret would remain safe in his keeping. Emily stood up and went to tuck Lizzie in. She was fast asleep. Emily kissed her on the forehead and then climbed into her own bed, in which Mrs Walker had placed a hot stone hot-water bottle.

Betsy closed the envelope containing the letter she had addressed to Mr and Mrs Hoyle of Bushby, and Emily's future as a girl in service was sealed. She banked up the fire and placed the guard in front of it, made sure all the candles were out, but for one, and lifted that to light her way as she climbed the stairs. She noticed that ice was already beginning to form on the inside of her bedroom window. Shivering, she blew out the candle and slipped into bed beside her husband. Outside, a tawny owl hooted and screeched as it swooped down on its prey.

Chapter 12

Tuesday, 19th September 1911

Private 10830

'Don't do that!'

David was just about to cut into a freshly-baked fruit cake when his mother's voice halted him.

'I thought it was for tea,' David grumbled.

'No, it's for the Wakes at the weekend.'

Mary took an old biscuit tin from the top of the Welsh dresser and pulled off its lid. Yellowing papers slid out onto the cracked oilcloth that covered the oak table and surrounded the cake. The number of rusty blemishes that decorated the tin had increased since the last time it was opened, creeping over what was once a mountain scene, leaving it hard to even recognise, and only a few letters from the *Huntley and Palmer's* name were still visible. She tutted, then scooped the documents together and began pushing them back into the grey metal box.

'You've missed one, Mother.' David bent to pick up a document that had fallen to the floor. He handed her his father's death certificate.

'Thanks, lad,' she said. 'I was just looking for that. I still can't believe I'm going to be getting married again after fifteen years of bringing you lot up on my own. I'll need the certificate for the vicar to prove I'm not a bigamist.' David smiled at his mother, who looked so happy after years of sorrow, which she had endured like a painful corn caused by second-hand shoes, after his father had died. He had felt angry when he found out that it was through drink that his mother had been left to raise the family, charring for others to feed and clothe them all, but since she had met Alf, his anger had left him, even if it had taken six years for them to finally 'tie the knot'. David picked up the *Daily Mirror* from the table and sat down.

'You'll need the light on if you're going to read, and don't get under my feet, I want to lay the table for tea,' his mother told him.

'It says here that some Indian chap's died in Bexhill. I wonder what he was doing in England,' David mused.

'Well, a lot of our soldiers went to India a long time before you were born – Hindustan I think it was – so there's no reason why he shouldn't come here.' His mother reached up and placed the old tin back on top of the dresser.

'This chap was a prince: Colonel His Highness Maharajah Sir Nripendra Narayan Bhup Bahadur of Cooch Behar,' David read. 'By heck, that's a mouthful. I'm glad I'm just plain David. Imagine putting that lot on a tombstone. He looks like a woman with his necklace, turban and fancy clothes.'

His mother laughed. 'Have a bit more respect,' she chided.

'It also says he were a fine shot and killed five hundred tigers. I hope they weren't our soldiers,' David joked. He put the paper down and looked up at his mother. 'Do you remember the tiger I had for my eleventh birthday?'

'Of course I do,' Mary answered. 'I'll never forget that night. You wouldn't let it out of your sight. Whatever happened to it?'

'It's upstairs in my drawer. When I learnt at school about our soldiers being nicknamed *Leicester Tigers*, I kept it safe.'

Alf looked into the mirror, which hung from the window mullion, and wiped soap lather from his face. He liked to have his evening wash at the kitchen sink before the lads came in for their tea. He felt a cool waft of early evening breeze and pulled the window to.

'What's that you've got?' Ernest came into the kitchen carrying a bucket of coal, which he put down next to the grate and pointed to a large brown envelope, bulging with papers.

'I was looking for your mother's death certificate,' Alf answered as he buttoned his shirt. 'I need it for the vicar otherwise I can't get married again.'

'What's the hurry? The wedding ain't till December.'

'I don't know, lad, summat to do with the banns being read.' Alf sat down and began to look through his documents. They both jumped when the back door flew open. A strong draught threatened to send the papers flying, and the chimney belched smoke into the room. Henry slammed the door behind him and shrugged off his jacket. He dropped his haversack onto the draining board and pulled out an empty bottle, removed its stopper and sniffed.

'Milk were off today,' he complained. 'I hope Alfred's going to bring some fresh home tonight after he's done milking.' He turned to Ernest. 'Where have you been all afternoon anyway? You'll cop it – foreman were lookin' for you.'

Alf looked up. 'You ain't been to work? Don't you get yourself the sack, lad – you need that job.'

'I'm sick of skiving leather,' Ernest answered. 'I want to do something more interesting. Besides, Whattoff clocked me in and out, so I'll still get paid.'

'So where were you?' Alf demanded.

'I went down to the recruitment office – I'm joining the army. Private 10830 George Ernest Wade reporting for duty!' Ernest stood to attention and saluted.

'What you done that for?' asked Henry. 'You must be barmy.'

'Haven't you seen the adverts? – "Join the army for travel and adventure"– when would I ever get to travel? I'll get regular meals, free uniform, no board to pay and a regular wage. It's everything I've always wanted.'

Alf pushed the papers back inside the envelope and looked at his son. 'Then take a look at the front page of that paper.' He pointed to a discarded copy of the *Daily Mirror*. Ernest picked it up and frowned as he read of a Lieutenant Cammell being killed when his plane crashed to the ground at the airfield in Hendon.

'But he was an airman – I'm joining the army. It says he's the sixth English victim of the new science of flight,' Ernest protested. 'Well, I'm not flying, new science or not.' The door opened and another plume of smoke billowed from the chimney to welcome Sydney home.

'What's for tea?' Sydney asked, but no one answered. He looked at Alf, then to his brothers, shrugged and sat down quietly. The tension in the room was treacle-like.

'Anyway,' Ernest said, as if he hadn't heard Sydney, 'it'll give you more room when you get married. Two families in one house will make it a tight squeeze, even though the one in Albert Street's bigger than this one.'

'We'll manage.' Alf stood up and laid his hand on Ernest's arm. 'You don't have to go, you're only seventeen. Whatever will Mary say? She looks on you lads as her own.'

'I'm sure she'll be fine. It's Jane who won't be best pleased.' Ernest hung his head and bit his bottom lip, then asked: 'When is she next home for a visit?'

'Sunday week,' Alf answered.

'Look, with Emily Jane in service it means you lads can have the other two bedrooms. You really don't have to go.' Alf spoke as if he was offering Ernest an escape route.

'It's too late,' Ernest told them. 'I've already signed up for six years with the Leicestershire Regiment. You never know, I might get to see somewhere abroad.'

'I doubt it,' Sydney replied.

David closed his eyes and breathed in the delicious aroma as his mother placed steaming plates of lamb stew and dumplings before her three boys.

'We shall need a bigger table,' she said and sat down. 'This one'll never get nine around it.' The kitchen was filled with the smell of the evening's dinner and the boys tucked in as if they hadn't eaten for days. Mary smiled. 'It's good to see you have such good appetites,' she told them. Whattoff paused and looked up from his meal.

'Ernest weren't at work this afternoon,' he said.

'He'll cop it if he gets caught – did somebody else clock him in then?' David asked.

'Yes, me,' Whattoff confessed.

'You'll cop it too!' David saw a shadow of concern flit across his mother's face.

'Where was he?' Mary's tone was one that had often put the fear of God into her sons. David bit his bottom lip and studied the carrots on his plate, swirling with parsnips in the rich gravy. 'Well?' Mary insisted.

'He went to the recruitment office,' Whattoff answered. 'He's joined up, Mam. He won't be at your wedding.' Mary looked at each of her sons in turn.

'Well, at least I'll have you three with me,' she said, 'and Ernest will be in a safe job, we should be thankful for that.'

'I wouldn't like to be in his shoes when Emily finds out,' David said. 'He won't be safe then.' They all chuckled and David continued: 'He'll be a *Leicester Tiger* – I wouldn't mind that me sen.'

Mary put her knife and fork down and wagged her finger at him: 'Don't you dare, my lad, or any of you.' She touched her purple, green and white necklace and narrowed her eyes, glancing round and dropping her voice to a stern whisper, 'Don't you dare.'

PART TWO

HEROISM IN THE ABSTRACT

Chapter 13

Friday, 7th August 1914

MacDonald

Emily pulled her shawl a little tighter and bent over close to a nettle patch. The sun promised a decent day, but the morning was cool and heavy dew on the grass soaked her stockings through sandal-clad feet and dampened the hem of her skirt. With gloved hands she reached over, and using kitchen scissors, she cut through a dozen of the square, hairy stalks. Handling them cautiously, she took the nettles indoors to the scullery and trimmed each to an even length. From a ball of string, Emily cut an arm's length and wound it around the vicious stems, creating a hanging loop before tying them securely. With her arm fully extended, she moved through the large kitchen and opened the pantry door. Reaching up, she hung the nettles from a ceiling hook.

'That should stop the little blighters,' she muttered, and swept a glance over the shelves to make sure there were none already in there. But there was – a fat bluebottle had landed on the marble thrawl next to the meat safe and was rubbing its front legs together as if anticipating a feast. She pulled off a glove and, with a flick of her wrist, dispatched the 'little blighter'.

The long-case clock in the hall chimed six as Emily turned on the tap and began to fill a tin bucket with cold water for keeping the milk cool. She smiled as the water flowed, grateful that she didn't have to take the pail to a well or pump any more. The smile faded when she remembered that she was going to ask her employer if she could leave a little earlier on Sunday, to see her family.

Each morning was tediously similar, but Emily was resigned to staying in service, at least until she married Franklin. His last letter had told her that when they were wed they would go to live with his uncle in Canada, where he would work in his family's business. She hadn't asked him what the business was, and although Franklin was very dear, the thought of leaving her own family, especially Ernest, caused knots to tighten and wrench at her insides until she felt sick. How naïve she had been to think that because Franklin was in the army she would have a closer connection to Ernest. With all this talk of the war, it was difficult to write to either of them knowing that any letters would be scrutinised by an anonymous overseer; she certainly didn't want a stranger reading her words of endearment.

Breakfast preparation underway, and pleased at having avoided being stung by the nettles, Emily cursed when a dollop of boiling porridge plopped onto the back of her hand as she stirred it.

'Wade!' Mr Hoyle's voiced boomed down the passageway. Emily licked the porridge away and grimaced at its saltiness and the smarting of the scald.

'Coming, sir,' she called, and blustered into the dining room. Mr Hoyle was sitting on his usual high-backed chair at the head of the table.

'Is *The Times* here yet, Wade?'

'Not yet, sir.'

'Well, bring it immediately when it's delivered.'

'Yes, sir.'

'And where's my tea?'

'Just coming, sir.' Emily nodded politely and slipped back to the kitchen. She was relieved to see that the kettle was sending a steady flow of steam from its spout. Her nose wrinkled as the smell of burning tickled her nostrils.

'Damn,' she cursed. She'd left the porridge on the stove unattended for too long. 'Of all the days when I needed everything to run smoothly.' There wasn't time to make another batch, so she carefully pulled it from the heat and spooned the top layer of unsullied oatmeal from the charred mess and dropped it into another saucepan. She poured boiling water onto tea leaves and placed the pot onto a tray she had already prepared with cups, milk and sugar, and took it through to Mr Hoyle. As she set the tea tray down, the letterbox clattered.

'Ah, at last. Well go and get it, girl.'

'Yes, sir.'

Emily scurried along the hall and scooped up the newspaper, which had been reduced from its pre-war size to a smaller publication, from the doormat. She was sure Mr Hoyle would have liked her to iron it, as the servants at the big houses did, but he was too impatient to wait, so she was spared that task. She handed it over and rushed back to the kitchen to rescue the porridge. Through a thick Virginia creeper that was already taking on the deep red of autumn and threatening to obscure the kitchen window completely, she could see the milk cart advancing up the lane. Something pressed against her shin and wrapped itself around her calf.

'Go away, Tabby.' Emily pushed the hungry animal aside with her foot and stirred the last of yesterday's milk into the porridge. As she hastily spooned the gloopy mass into two bowls, some fell onto the flagstone floor and was pounced upon by the cat, which was bloated with unborn kittens. A finger of guilt prodded at her conscience, causing another heaped spoonful of porridge to *accidently* drop down. A fleeting memory of kittens drowning at the hands of Aunt Eliza disturbed the moment, and then it was gone, chased away by Mr Hoyle's raised voice calling for his breakfast. Emily took the porridge through and saw that Mrs Hoyle had joined her husband at the table.

'Good morning, Emily.' She raised the cup of tea that Emily had poured to her smiling lips.

'Good morning, Mrs Hoyle,' Emily replied.

'That Lossie loon, MacDonald, has been voicing his radical ideas again.[3] What on earth is the bounder thinking of?' Mr Hoyle stabbed his finger at his newspaper. 'Of course we should support the war, stupid oaf! This kind of talk won't get our lads to join up.'

'He's thinking of the workers.' Mrs Hoyle tried to appease him.

'Tommyrot! What a ridiculous statement: that a war will settle nothing and put back the clock of civilisation a century.'

'If you say so, my love. Now, eat your porridge before it gets cold.'

A satisfied smile spread over Hoyle's face and he shook the paper like an excited child.

---

3. Ramsay MacDonald was from Lossiemouth in Scotland and when in his teens was part of a 'youth set' whose feat was that of swinging – squirrel like – round a circle of nineteen trees. It was a test of fitness for the "Lossie loons". When any of them had accomplished the feat he passed to a niche amongst heroes.

'Aha! At last! He's resigned his chairmanship, and a good thing too, I say.'

With a satisfied expression, Edwin Hoyle dropped *The Times* to the floor, lifted a spoonful of steaming porridge and guided it under his black, bushy moustache. Emily left the room in a hurry to fetch the morning's milk. As she neared the kitchen she heard Mr Hoyle's raised voice and her shoulders slumped.

'Pah, it's repellant! Wade!'

Esther Hoyle could then be heard trying to calm her husband:

'It is a little disagreeable this morning. Perhaps we should have something else instead.'

Emily pattered along the corridor, trying to push escaping tendrils of mousey-brown hair back under her mop-cap as she ran.

'Wade! Come here at once!'

Emily heard Mr Hoyle bang his fist onto the table.

'She'll be here in a minute.'

Esther Hoyle was sipping her tea when Emily reached the breakfast room. She put down her cup and dabbed at fine pink lips with a starched, linen napkin.

'Sorry, sir,' Emily panted as she entered.

'Where have you been, girl?'

'I was going to fetch milk from the cart, sir.'

'This porridge is revolting. Take it away and bring me some eggs.'

'Yes, sir.'

'And toast. Yes, toast.'

'Would you like eggs, Mrs Hoyle?'

'No, thank you, just some toast.'

Emily cleared the offending porridge away and rushed back to the kitchen. She prepared three eggs and wiped away beads of sweat, which had formed on her brow as she stood before the range holding a loaded toasting fork before the glowing coal. She could hear Mr Hoyle again; he was still ranting about Ramsay MacDonald and condemning the MP's stance that he didn't believe in war and thought it unnecessary. Emily smiled – she quite liked Mr MacDonald.

Having managed to catch up with the milk cart, Emily returned to the kitchen and placed the full churn into cold water just as the last grains of golden sand trickled through the egg timer. With toast buttered and the tray reset, Emily made her way back to her employers. After delivering the replacement breakfast, she drew herself upright and gave a little cough. Mrs Hoyle looked up and raised her eyebrows. Emily gripped her hands together behind her back to prevent them from shaking, pursed her lips and took a deep breath.

'Please, sir, ma'am, may I finish a little earlier on Sunday? I would like to go home straight after breakfast, if that's agreeable with you.'

'I don't see why not.' Mrs Hoyle smiled. Emily smiled back.

'No! You may not.' Emily noticed that Mrs Hoyle was staring at her husband with a quizzical expression. 'You ruined the porridge. You were late bringing the paper. You didn't fetch the milk early enough and you were late with the eggs. Your day off this month is cancelled.'

'But, sir, the paper was late being delivered and I had to run to get the milk.'

'Don't you backchat me, girl. Now get out of my sight. Leave cancelled.'

Emily began to shake with rage and disappointment. She wanted to give that man a piece of her mind, but she needed her position – for the moment. She drew in a deep breath and strode back to the kitchen. She could hear Mrs Hoyle trying, unsuccessfully, to reason with Mr Hoyle.

Sunday, 9th August 1914

David walked in time with the church bells as they called parishioners to Sunday morning worship. When he reached the village's allotments he pushed on a green gate, which creaked like an old crow on its rusty hinges. A clump of overgrown grass hindered its swing, but a swift kick dislodged the obstructing tuft and David walked through the now widened entrance, drawn by the smell of bacon frying as it drifted across the gardens. He spotted Alf, who was watering his beans with a stirrup pump, and headed towards him.

'Hello, lad. Have you come for your breakfast?'

David held up a brown paper bag. 'I've brought the bread.'

The last of the water was sucked up noisily and sprayed onto the dry ground.

'Shouldn't you be at church?'

'I'll go to chapel tonight, when Emily's home.'

'Come on then.' Alf picked up the pump and bucket. 'Let's go and get some snap.'

They walked together towards a glowing brazier where Joe Oswin was holding a shovel over burning coals. Rashers of thick bacon coated its metal front and the hot embers leapt as eight meaty strips spat their fat. David rubbed his hands together, in anticipation, and held out two pennies.

'It'll be three this week.' Joe's upturned palm remained outstretched, waiting for each of the men to drop three pennies, or a thruppenny-bit, into it.

'Bloody hell, that's dear,' Alf grumbled, digging deep in his pocket for another penny.

'That's the war for you.' Joe dropped the bacon-money into his own pocket and flipped the rashers over with his penknife, not offering to pay David for the bread.

Frank Swann, who was standing in the doorway of his shed, nodded to David and Alf in greeting, folded the newspaper he'd been reading, and dropped it to the floor. He then turned his attention to a kettle that was balancing precariously on a small stove. David noticed that the bench in Frank's shed was all very organised – four tin mugs, tea caddy, metal teapot and a small milk churn at the ready. With a dirty rag, Frank lifted the kettle and poured scalding water over tea leaves, and then snapped down the pot's lid. Leaving the tea to mash, he stepped outside and pulled a small silver box from his pocket and flipped it open with his thumb. Between his other thumb and forefinger he pinched a tiny amount of dried tobacco, held it to his right nostril and made a loud snorting noise. He repeated the snuffing to his other nostril, snapped the box closed and pushed it back inside his pocket. He gave a little shudder and went back into the shed to pour the tea.

David handed over the still-warm bread and Alf took an old knife with a bone handle from his pocket. With a blade that had been sharpened so often it was only half its original size, Alf sliced it and dealt it out. The four men each slapped two slices of well-cooked bacon onto their hunk, folded it over and tucked in.

'Good to see your lad 'ere, Alf.' Frank nodded towards David.

'I haven't seen your lad for nigh on three months,' Alf replied. 'What's 'e doing?'

'Three months,' Frank answered.

David almost choked on his bread but managed to hide

his amusement. He now knew why Bob Swann hadn't been seen in The Bell lately.

The church bells were ringing out their final call to worship, and a creeping dampness, caused by a spilt watering can, soaked through the seat of David's trousers as he sat on a grassy mound. He pushed the last of the bacon into his mouth and wiped away a greasy trickle that was running a path from the corner of his lips to his chin. He reached over and lifted Frank's discarded newspaper, thinking that it would make an excellent barrier to place between him and the wet grass. The front-page headline caught his attention, and instead of sitting on the paper, he scrutinised the words of *The Pioneer*. It was daubed with yellowish-brown snuff spots, which obscured some of the print, but the message was quite plain.

'What do you make of this?' David held the newspaper up.

'He's a good man.' Alf pointed to a photograph of Ramsay MacDonald. 'But he won't win votes if he doesn't change his attitude towards the war.'

'Wherever he speaks, there's trouble,' grumbled Frank.

'Well, he's speaking at the Corn Exchange in Leicester soon,' David replied, 'but it says here that he's told the mayor he refuses to attend the recruitment meeting in the city.'

'He was at the Trade Hall the other day.' Joe was cleaning his spade; the fat had given it a glossy sheen.

'Listen to this,' David read on. 'He said: "We are not really fighting for the independence of Belgium, but because we belong to the" – David frowned and stumbled over his words – ""triple en-tent." – what's that?'

'It's us, France and Russia,' Frank answered, and sneezed.

'Well, MacDonald says: "It's sad, because we love our own country best and hope we shall not be defeated or disgraced, we should have as counterpart to that, the desire that the great nation of Germany should be worsened, defeated and disgraced." And he finishes by saying: "how one almost hates the diplomacy that has brought us to this." What do you reckon to that?'

Alf blew out his cheeks and Joe scowled. David folded the newspaper and pushed it underneath him.

'The learned man speaks,' mused Frank. 'There'll be trouble, you mark my words.

Chapter 14

Sunday, 9th August 1914

Heroism in the Abstract

David stood up on the pedals as his bicycle juddered over potholes and ruts in the Barkby Road, and then, on even ground, he pumped as fast as he could. 'Come to church, come to church,' he heard Syston's distant church bells calling villagers to evensong. The sun hung low in the evening sky and he knew that in the hour it would take him to get to Bushby, it would slide further towards the horizon and a seven-thirty sunset. He pushed on through Barkby village where their church bells were silent, but he could hear singing as he sped past Saint Mary's. His legs ached as he pushed on up steep hills and through Scraptoft. It would be an easier journey home, at least. The streets of Thurnby were silent and his tyres crunched along dry roads. The Rose and Crown, had it been open, would have been a temptation difficult to resist; David's mouth watered at thoughts of a pint of ale. He licked his dry lips and pressed on, keeping Emily firmly in his thoughts. No one else had seemed perturbed at her absence, and the usual Sunday tea became a discussion about how the war had forced prices to rise and how the Government was now requisitioning corporation horses. David chuckled when he remembered Alf's remark that Mother would be tying herself to the chairs in St Peter's just as the London suffragettes had in St Paul's Cathedral. He hoped she hadn't been involved in the burning of Blaby station last month. Even though she had denied being there, David wasn't so sure.

The Bushby lanes were quiet, and on the evening air David caught a whiff of cigarette smoke. The road curved round to the left and his front wheel slipped as he tried to avoid a collision with a soldier who was strolling down the lane, swagger stick tucked under his arm.

'Look out, you clumsy idiot!'

'Sorry, sir.' David recognised the officer's authority from the crown on his epaulette. He didn't know whether he should stop or carry on. He stopped. Through narrowed eyes, the major looked down to David's dusty boots and then up to his face. David smoothed his upturned collar. The major drew a deep drag on his cigarette and threw it to the ground.

'Why aren't you in uniform, boy?'

David's tongue felt like a hammer beam. He swallowed and stared at the officer.

'Well, answer me, boy.'

'Erm, well, I, er... I haven't joined up, sir.'

'Why the blazes not? Get yourself down to the recruiting office first thing.'

'But, I'm a clicker, sir... you know, in the boot and shoe.'

'How old are you?'

'Nineteen, sir.'

'Then you're old enough.'

Trying to think of an acceptable reply, David kicked at a stone in the road. Just as he opened his mouth to speak, the major jerked his chin upwards and bawled at him: 'Get down to the recruiting office, boy. We don't want any shirkers round here. You hear me?'

'Yes, sir.' David jumped back onto his bike and pedalled away as hard as he could. His back wheel slipped as he rounded the next corner onto the lane that ran behind the house where the Hoyles lived. Freewheeling to the back gate, David dismounted and rested his bicycle against a low privet hedge, which ran the length of the back garden. He pushed open the high black wrought-iron gate, its hinges still dripping with recently administered oil, and made his way through the orchard, ducking to avoid low-hanging branches laden with apples, which were almost ripe, and pears, which were not. A lazy wasp had buried its head in a misshapen fruit that had been left hanging on the Syston White plum tree. David dodged it and, leaving the orchard, made his way alongside a well-stocked vegetable plot. A bed of flamboyant dahlias formed a border between the lettuces and a parched lawn. David walked on up to the house, the dry grass muffling his footsteps. He wiped his sweaty palms down his trousers before tapping on the back door. Something pushed him from behind. A fat, tabby cat wrapped itself around his legs and sat down expectantly between him and the doorstep, ready to slide inside once his knock was answered. No one came. He rapped again, stepped away, and waited. A wave of disappointment rose up and he peered through a small diamond-shaped window but saw no movement. Then a voice cut through the evening's stillness, startling him.

'What are you doing here?' Emily asked. David spun round and laughed a little louder than he had intended. He stepped forward and took her cool hands in his. He thought how beautiful she looked, her hair escaping its clips and her dress, albeit quite drab, clinging to her in all the right places. Her eyes appeared red and belied the smile she was wearing.

'I came to see if you are all right. You were supposed to come home today. I was worried. Where were you?'

'I was sitting in the summer house,' she teased, then replied more fittingly, 'I'm quite well, thank you, but my leave was cancelled.' Before he could ask why, she pulled him towards the house. 'Come and have some lemonade, you look as though you might burst,' she said.

Shadows were lengthening across the lawn and the wooden bench by the back door held its warmth. David leaned back against its slats, closed his eyes and stretched out his legs so that his heels rested on a low wall. He thought that life was good and time alone with Emily fuelled his contentment.

'Wake up, sleepy head.' Emily placed a tray beside his feet. On it were two glasses and a large jug containing a cloudy liquid. 'Sorry it isn't ale.' He took the glass she was offering; it was cold and he held it against his forehead before taking a generous gulp. His throat tightened at the sharpness of lemon and then relaxed as the sugar smoothed the thirst-quenching liquid.

'Why didn't you come home, Em?'

'I told you, I had my leave cancelled.'

'But that's twice in the last three months. Why?'

Emily recounted the incidents that had caused Mr Hoyle's displeasure, her voice wobbly with indignation and sadness.

'The bastard! He can't treat you like this.'

'Sshh, yes he can. I am, after all, a domestic servant.'

'But it ain't right. How would he like it if —' Emily leaned across and pressed her index finger against his lips. He felt his heart thump at her touch and playfully caught her finger, curling a fist around it, and held on.

'Let go.'

'No.' He kissed the top of her protruding finger. She giggled and pulled her hand free.

'Oooh, our David, you always cheer me up.' She reached over and straightened his collar. He caught her hand again.

'Emily!' Mrs Hoyle was in the kitchen. Emily pulled her hand free for a second time and stood up. 'I thought I heard a man's voice.' Esther Hoyle stepped outside. David jumped to his feet, and on seeing him she raised her eyebrows.

'My brother came to see if I had taken ill as I hadn't gone home today,' Emily answered the quizzical brows.

'Oh, your brother. I see.'

'Stepbrother.' David held out his hand. Mrs Hoyle didn't take it.

'And how is Franklin, Emily?'

'Quite well, thank you.' David saw a redness rising from her neck and the flush covered her cheeks.

'Would you bring some warm milk through to the front parlour for Mr Hoyle and me, please?'

'Yes, ma'am.' Emily followed Esther Hoyle inside, leaving David alone with his resentment. He sat down and poured himself another drink. He hated Edwin Hoyle and he hated Franklin. If only Emily would turn her affections his way instead.

A bird was singing in the evening twilight when Emily returned and sat down a little closer to David than she had earlier.

'Listen! Do you hear the nightingale?' he asked.

'It isn't a nightingale.'

'Yes, it is.' David sat up and turned towards Emily.

'No, it's a robin.'

'It's a nightingale – listen to it sing.'

'It's a robin!'

'Mmm.' David wasn't sure he liked being contradicted by a girl, – well, a woman. Neither spoke for a few minutes, then David, realising he must leave very soon, broke the silence. 'Em, do you think I should join up?'

'Oh, I don't know. Mother wouldn't like it. Why do you ask?'

'I bumped into an officer on the way here, almost knocked him over, and he told me I was a shirker, spoke to me as though he hated me. Do you think that's how officers talk to their men?'

'I don't know. Perhaps it's because you haven't taken the King's shilling. He may have spoken differently had you been in uniform.'

'So, you do think I should enlist?'

'Only if you really want to. Do you?'

'I'm not sure. I'm not a shirker, but Mr Garner says I don't have to as I'm a worker in the boot and shoe.'

Emily held his gaze, pursed her lips and asked: 'Do you hate the Germans?'

'Not really.'

'It said in the *Leicester Mercury* that more than fifty Germans were marched to the Corn Exchange this week. What will happen to them?'

'I don't know.'

'Do you like the French?'

'Not really.'

'And the Belgians?'

'I don't know any.'

'Then I can't think of a reason for you to enlist, other than a desire to be some sort of hero. Now, it's time you were leaving. I have to be up at five in the morning.' David opened his mouth to reply, but again she placed her finger to his lips, more gently than the last time. He closed his eyes and wished it had been her mouth. He kissed it, took it between his thumb and forefinger and pressed it against her lips.

A flash of lightning lit the orchard and a clap of thunder, which followed seconds behind, rattled the slates. David knew he was in for a soaking before he reached home.

Chapter 15

Monday, 26th October 1914

Fog

The fog hadn't lifted all morning and spirals of blue smoke that rose up to join it added to the smoggy shroud around the factory yard. A production line of men, puffing on their lunchtime tobacco, leaned against the outside wall as if to absorb any warmth it had to offer. The air was chilly and already hoar frosts had begun to cover the ground and coat hedges every morning. Steadily, one after another and as if by clockwork, the workforce threw cigarette ends to the ground, emptied pipe bowls against brickwork, and pressed down with the toes of their boots to extinguish remnants of glowing ash. The factory's hooter clamoured out its message, although it became muffled in the thick, smoggy air that clung to the streets like a benediction. The workforce pushed themselves from the wall and headed towards the large double doors that had varying shades of dull umber paint flaking from them.

'Hey, Dave!' David turned to see his brother striding towards him. 'Wait up.' David paused momentarily whilst Whattoff caught up with him.

'What's up?'

'Lend us five bob till payday?'

'No. I ain't got five bob. What do you want it for anyroad?'

'Rent's due tomorra. Go on, just till Saturday. You get paid more than me; you must have a few bob to spare.'

David sighed and pushed his hand into his trouser pocket. Before he pulled it out again he frowned at his brother. 'Rent ain't five bob.'

'I'm a couple of weeks behind.' Whattoff looked past David, seemingly to avoid eye contact.

'You've only been there a month, how can you be?'

'Six weeks,' Whattoff contradicted. David shook his head. 'Well' – Whattoff scratched behind his left ear as if looking for an answer under his cap – 'I've had to get stuff.'

'What stuff?'

'Bloody hell, Dave, you sound like Mam. Are you gonna lend me it or not?'

David countered the question with a disconnected one of his own: 'You comin' down The Bell tonight?'

Whattoff shrugged. 'You buyin?' he asked.

The shriek of an impatient whistle being blown by Mr Garner halted the conversation and David quickly pulled two shillings from his pocket and pressed them into his brother's hand.

'Here. That's all I've got.'

Whattoff slapped him on the shoulder and grinned. 'And that's the last time an' all,' David warned him, but he was speaking to his brother's back as they both joined the workforce, who, like ants returning to their nest, filtered back inside the factory. Whattoff raised his hand above his shoulder in dismissal and turned left towards the lasting track. Before David turned right for the clicking room he stopped and watched his brother lift the coins to his lips and kiss them with a gesture of gratification before plunging them into his own trouser pocket and tapping them triumphantly as he stepped out to join the tack lasters.

David lifted a dark-brown skin from a trestle behind him and turned back to the thick wooden block where he placed it and smoothed it over. The smell of freshly tanned leather was always more intense when it was first placed on the bench and he breathed in salty chrome mixed with rich, peaty bark before its redolence dispersed into the general atmosphere of the leather-filled room. Satisfied that the skin was even and positioned close to the block's top edge, he placed a vamp pattern on its right-hand side and lifted his knife. He had sharpened its blade on the strop that hung from his bench before leaving off for his dinner break and the knife sliced through the full-grain material as he guided it around the brass pattern. With a final click, the circuit was completed. The room was a cacophony of clicks as the men cut around patterns and placed the vamps, quarters, tongues, toecaps and heel pieces in bundles of twelve on wooden trolleys standing next to each bench. The clickers only stopped to sign cards, which they fastened to each three-dozen bundle with a pre-cut piece of string. These cards were a representation of the piecework totals used for filling their pay packets every Saturday.

David lifted another skin from the trestle and, as he turned back to his bench, he looked up at a poster hanging on the whitewashed wall. It was different from the one he had been looking at the day before. Although the message was identical, the number had changed. The smart soldier was the same one, standing erect with a rifle held proudly in front of him, haversack on his straight back. *A Soldier of the King* was emblazoned to his left – a cleverly chosen headline to draw the young men in.

'A soldier of the King,' thought David. That sounded important. He'd always wanted to be a bit important. Then the poster became more personal: *To the Men of Leicestershire* it called out. He couldn't read the smaller print, but below that he read: *4th Battalion Leicestershire Regiment*, some more small print and then in large letters: *800 RECRUITS, COME AT ONCE*. He was sure it had said one thousand yesterday. There was a block of even smaller printing and then at the bottom of the poster: *DON'T WAIT – APPLY AT THE DRILL HALLS*. David had been smoothing the skin over and over whilst he stared at the poster.

'Come on, Adcock, no dawdling.' The foreman was pacing behind him along the row of clickers.

'Sorry, Mr Sharp.' David wiped the blade of his knife on his apron, which had started the week white and unblemished but was now bearing the streaks of skived-off leather from each wiping. At least it no longer bore the bloodstains from knife-nicks, which had represented the lion's share of the markings when he first started work at Garner's six years earlier. With a quick glance at the notice, he went back to his task and muttered under his breath, 'God save the King,' the final words at the foot of the recruitment poster.

All afternoon he carefully arranged patterns over different skins, so that at the end of the day there was little waste in the wooden box under his bench. Every so often he glanced up at the poster. Eight hundred wanted – it had definitely been a thousand all last week. David asked himself if he really wanted to spend the rest of his life in the factory. This was his opportunity to get out, see the world, and serve the King. Ernest seemed to be doing all right; he'd been to Ireland and was now in France, or maybe Belgium, David couldn't quite remember. His last letter home had told them how he had been playing rugby, hockey and football for the battalion. Yes, thought David, that's what I'd like to do one day.

Whattoff was watching the hands turn on the white face of the large clock at the far end of the lasting room. The final hour had gone agonisingly slowly and it felt like midnight, even though it was only ten minutes to six. The gas lamps in the factory had been lit early, at around half past two, and the afternoon had dragged on. Every so often he touched the coins in his pocket to remind him that he would be all right that evening. He loaded the final three-dozen uppers he had lasted onto a wooden trolley and signed his sheet. Having already removed his dirty apron for when the hooter sounded knocking-off time, he grabbed his jacket from its hook and ran across to the time clock, where he was the first to push his card into its top just as the hour clunked over. He reached up and dropped the card into a metal rack on the wall next to the machine and ran back through the factory, weaving between the tide of workers coming towards him, rushing to clock out. Pulling his cap on as he went, he bolted through the double doors and out of the factory, plunging into thick fog that wrapped around him like a comfort blanket. He hurried down the yard and out of the gate, leaving Garner's behind for another day, and quickened his pace along High Street where gas lamps were straining to throw any light onto the pavements below. As he neared the chemist's shop he slowed down and walked, almost nonchalantly, towards its entrance. He reached for the handle, but the door flew open before he could grasp it and the bell above played its tuneless chimes. Mrs Hubbard bustled out of the shop, clutching a bottle of Brilliant Green.

'Good evening, Mr Whattoff,' she beamed at him, 'and how's that lovely wife of yours?'

'She's grand, Mrs Hubbard.' He tried to be civil but really just wanted to push past her and into the shop. Fortunately, he didn't need to, as Reverend Avery had appeared behind her.

'Excuse me, Mrs Hubbard.' The vicar tried not to cough as his lungs filled with smoggy air, which was seeping into the shop through the open doorway.

'Sorry, Vicar,' she apologised, and moved on into the street, soon to be swallowed up by the swirling mist. Before the vicar could speak to him, Whattoff had slipped inside. He swept his eyes around the shop to see if there were any other customers, and, satisfied that he was alone apart from the chemist, he pushed his hand into his pocket and pulled out the warm coins. The chemist nodded and reached under the counter, giving a quick glance towards the door as he did so. He held out his upturned left palm towards Whattoff, who dropped the coins into it and snatched a package the size of a shaving brush from the chemist's right hand. Both men nodded, not a word was spoken, and Whattoff headed out into the night.

'Is that you, Alf?' David heard his mother call from the kitchen.

'No. It's me, Mam,' David replied as he hung his jacket and cap on a hook in the hallway. 'Brr, it's a filthy night,' he told his mother, and rubbed his hands together.

'What's that?' he asked, pointing to a piece of paper that lay on the oilcloth-covered table.

'There's going to be a meeting in the village hall.' His mother scowled and wiped her wet hands on her apron. 'That Mrs Walker-Holmes has organised it. She's invited some high-ranking officer to come and talk about *why your country needs you.*' She almost spat the words. David picked up the paper. He recognised the soldier standing proudly with his rifle.

'He looks a bit like our Ernest.' David grinned, but his mother frowned in reply and lifted a saucepan of freshly peeled potatoes onto the stove. 'I suppose we'd all better go then,' he said, and placed the paper on the sideboard, next to a photograph of Ernest, who smiled back at them from under his regimental cap. 'I'll ask around when I'm in The Bell tonight to see who else is going. The poster in the factory says they need eight hundred men to enlist.'

'That's a lot,' his mother said, as she clattered a pile of plates onto the table.

'Well, there's four in this house, plus Whattoff and Alfred.'

'Alfred's needed on the farm, and Whattoff won't sign up, he's only just got married.'

'Has Whattoff been to see you lately?' David asked.

'Yes, last Sunday.'

'Was he all right?' David tried not to show too much concern for his brother; it would only worry his mother.

'As far as I know. Why?'

'Oh, I just wondered if he had taken on too much with that house.'

'You worry too much, lad,' Mary told him.

'Perhaps,' David said, and he headed into the small scullery to wash off the day's grime.

The house was in darkness and Whattoff breathed a sigh of relief. It was cold and he really needed to light the fire, which Kathy had set before heading off to work that morning. Instead he lit the gas mantle, which soon grew into a healthy glow and afforded him enough light to see by. He lifted a full jug from the draining board and poured some cold water into a metal mug that had been upturned in the granite sink. He pulled the packet from his inside pocket and unwrapped it with clumsy fingers. His heart pounded as he ripped at the paper, and then the familiar brown bottle, no bigger than his thumb, was exposed. He pulled out the stopper and carefully dripped six drops into the water, swished it round, then shook in another three for good measure. He pressed the stopper back in, pushed the bottle deep into his jacket pocket, and took a deep breath. It didn't matter now if Kathy appeared; he would just be having a drink of water. Before putting the tin mug to his lips, he opened the sideboard cupboard where their cups and plates were kept and looked inside for the sugar bowl. A round white net that was edged with coloured beads covered it. Pushing the net aside he quickly scooped two teaspoons of sugar into the water and straightened up. He was swirling it round when the back door opened and he pushed the cupboard door to with his knee, a little harder than he had intended, but Kathy didn't appear to notice.

'Hello, love.' Whattoff raised the mug and gulped down its contents. The water was still bitter despite the added sugar, and he struggled not to grimace as it washed over his tongue.

'It's a horrible night,' Kathy replied. 'Oh, you haven't lit the fire. Have you only just got in?'

'Yes, just this minute,' he lied. She smiled and walked over to the brown-tiled fireplace and struck a match. Yellow flames were soon leaping up the chimney.

He watched his wife slip her coat off and lift a parcel from her bag.

'Mrs Fortescue gave us a ham hock,' she told him.

'I ain't hungry,' he said, roughly. His appetite quashed, he began to feel the effects of the opium beginning to unfurl. 'Leave that.'

Kathy looked surprised and tipped her head to one side as if to question his last remark, a gesture that always excited him. He gripped her arm and pulled her towards him. She gasped but didn't resist him. In the orange lamplight, and warmed by the red glow of the now roaring fire, he pushed her onto the small sofa and pressed his hungry mouth onto hers. Kathy didn't struggle but remained passive, taking him in her arms, a signal to him that this was what she wanted. Frantically, he pulled at her clothes and took her with a drug-induced passion. Her cries spurred him on, and he didn't care if he left bruises on her thighs and buttocks. Eventually he gasped in fulfilment and lay still, holding her secure until the flames died down.

The Bell was quiet. David took a seat by the fireplace and placed his glass of nutty dark-brown ale onto the round table in front of him. Paraffin lamps and a few candles supplemented gas mantles; such was the blackness of the night. He pulled a packet of Woodbines from his top pocket and searched for his matches. John Wing tossed a box of Swan Vestas to him from behind the bar and David struck one and lit a cigarette. He drew in deeply and blew out a cloud of blue smoke, which rose to the ceiling and swirled around the beams until it vanished into the cracks. He noticed a pile of buff-coloured leaflets on a nearby table;

they were showing the proud soldier holding his rifle and information about the meeting next month.

''Ow do, Dave,' a tall, handsome young man with dark hair and even darker eyes called to him. George Oswin took his drink from the bar, rather awkwardly, and crossed the room, ale splashing over the sides of the glass he carried. He changed hands and shook his wet one, causing the fire to sputter and hiss when spots of ale landed in the grate. 'You can play on Saturday afternoon, can't you?'

'Yes, of course I can.' David's second love was football, and the Saturday matches were when he could lose himself in in the mud and glory of the game.

'That's grand.' George looked relieved. 'Bernard's gone and signed up, so you'll have to play centre. We're against Loughborough, so it'll be a tough game.'

'Nah, we'll give 'em a battering,' David promised. George grinned, still only a boy at eighteen, but man enough to be given the captain's shirt for Syston Town. John Oswin, George's elder brother, joined them and tipped dominoes from a battered box onto the table. A few more men trickled into the bar – mainly railway and factory workers. Every time the door opened David looked up from the game to see if it was Whattoff coming in. But he never showed.

At ten to nine, and four pence richer than he had been at the start of the evening due to some good hands of dominoes, David finished his second pint and stood up.

'You off?' George Partridge had joined them in the domino school, his protruding ears glowing red in the firelight.

'Yes, that's me done.' David put his cap on and turned to his teammates. 'Don't be late in the morning,' he joked, and stepped out into the murky night. Instead of turning towards Albert Street and home, he headed in the opposite direction towards Turn Street. It was unusual for his brother to miss the opportunity of a free drink. Smog clung to the streets, creeping into every doorway, down drains and along the gutters. Although he passed a few people and bid them a good evening, he had no idea who they were; identities were hidden and voices muffled by the grey shroud.

Number forty-two appeared to be in darkness. David tried the back door and it gave no resistance, so he pushed it wider and went inside.

'It's only me,' he called, sounding more jovial than he felt. The door to the tiny living room opened and a shard of welcoming light fell across the flagstone floor. Kathy slipped in and pulled the door to behind her.

'What are you doing here at this time of night?' she asked in a nasal, snuffly voice.

'He didn't turn up at The Bell so I thought I'd just drop by to see as nowt's up.'

'Oh, he must have forgotten.' Kathy wiped her nose on a white rag handkerchief; its movement was all David could see in the dark kitchen.

'I'll light the lamp. Pass me the matches.'

'No! Leave it.'

'But you can't see. Give me the matches.'

'Whattoff's asleep. You'll wake him. Now, it was very kind of you to call, but I think it best if you go now.'

'What's to do, Kathy?'

'I don't know what you mean, I'm sure.' Her voice faltered, just a little, but the darkness had sharpened David's instinct, and it didn't go unnoticed.

'Where is he?'

'I told you, he's asleep.'

David moved across the kitchen and opened the door into the living room. He heard Kathy groan behind him. 'Please don't wake him.'

David turned to Kathy, who had slipped in like a shadow.

'What's that?' David's voice was just above a whisper

– he was pointing to a red mark on her arm. She pulled a thick grey sleeve down over the fingermarks.

'Oh, it's nothing – I caught it on the stove this morning.'

'Then why have you been crying?'

Kathy didn't answer. She crumpled onto a hard-backed chair and shook her head.

'He ain't hit you, has he?'

Kathy shook her head. 'No, he'd never do that. He's not been himself lately though. I'm so worried about him, David, but I don't know what to do.'

'Make some tea, eh?'

Kathy got up and moved back into the tiny kitchen, leaving the door open to afford her the light she needed to see by. David walked over to his sleeping brother and kicked his foot, which dangled from the sofa.

'What?'

'Wake up!'

'Uh?' Whattoff seemed to be struggling to open his eyes and sit up. 'What are you doin' 'ere?'

'You were supposed to come to The Bell tonight. I thought there might be summat up.'

'Ha, yes, of course. Let's go now.' Whattoff had woken up remarkably quickly and was grinning. He hoisted himself from the sofa.

'No.' David squared up to him. 'Sit down!'

'Come on! Let's go!'

'I said no. Besides, it's getting on for ten, John'll be closing up afore we get there,' David reasoned.

Whattoff shrugged. He put his arm around David's shoulder. 'My good man.' He wasn't slurring, but his voice was different, high-pitched and almost euphoric. 'I'm going to be a foreman – you didn't know that, did you?'

'No, I didn't. How come?'

'Well, with all these silly buggers signing up, I'm going to fill their boots, then we'll see who earns the most.' He patted David's chest and laughed almost demoniacally.

Kathy came in and placed a tray holding three cups of steaming tea onto the table.

'Just make sure you pay the rent on time.' David pushed a cup of tea into his brother's hand.

'You've no need to worry about that,' Kathy said. 'My wage covers it with a little more besides. That's why I don't want to stop working just yet.'

David turned to his brother: 'You told me you're behind with the rent.'

Whattoff didn't answer, but gave another shrug. He was beginning to irritate David. Kathy's eyes widened, and she looked from David to Whattoff but said nothing.

'Well, we ain't now.' Whattoff laughed again and David lunged towards him. He grasped his brother's shirt and pushed his face close in. Tea slopped onto David's hand but he didn't flinch as the hot liquid left its angry mark. Kathy gasped. The atmosphere was poisonous.

'What did you want the money for?' David demanded. 'Have you been gamblin'? Do you owe someone?'

'I told you. I had to buy stuff.'

'You told me you were behind with the rent. What stuff?'

'Aw, leave me alone.' Whattoff knocked David's hand away and sat down.

'No, I want to know what's going on.' David had noticed that the black centres of his brother's eyes were like pinheads, even in the dimly lit room, and there was a strange smell on his breath. He looked at Kathy. A tear began to slide over her high cheekbone, and in contrast the pupils of her eyes were relaxed and large, in an effort to see in the poor light.

'I want my money back,' David growled.

'Well, I ain't got it.'

'Where is it then? What have you spent it on? Tell me!' David was shouting.

'I don't have to tell you owt.' Whattoff leaned back into the sofa. 'Goodnight, mind how you go.' It was as if he hadn't heard his brother's demands. David shook his head and clenched, then unclenched his fists. He felt a hand on his arm and looked into Kathy's rheumy brown eyes. He nodded his unspoken agreement and turned towards the door. With his hand on the brass knob, he looked back over his shoulder and opened his mouth to speak. Whattoff and Kathy were sitting together contentedly on the sofa and David slipped away into the dense night, unconvinced.

Chapter 16

Saturday, 31st October 1914

Match

When the whistle blew for half-time, Syston Town was losing one–nil to Loughborough. Two lads from the junior team had been recruited by George to make up his squad and the players grouped together behind their respective goals, having changed ends ready for the second half. The ground around them was flecked with cigarette ends. David tipped the last of his lukewarm tea down his throat and put his tin mug back onto a tray that Henry was trying to hold steady as he shivered in the north-easterly wind. His puckered eye gave the impression that he was squinting, or winking, at anyone to his left and suggested he was older than his eighteen years.

David tried to reach over with his right arm to give his back a rub. He had been barged twice and the second time a shoulder-bone had slammed into his muscle, which was beginning to tighten in acknowledgement. He looked around the edges of the pitch and saw Whattoff leaning on one of the fence posts; he'd have a word with him later.

Further along, and nearer to the gate, a woman was handing out pieces of paper – it was Mrs Walker-Holmes, no doubt whipping up enthusiasm for the recruitment meeting. And then he saw his mother. Her green coat stood out among the dark, drab greys and browns of the other spectators and she was striding along the perimeter of the pitch. Every so often she paused, speaking to whoever was holding one of Mrs Walker-Holmes's papers. On reaching the corner flag her pace quickened and she made her way along the field towards the Syston lads. David looked at Henry, who also appeared to be watching her.

'Are you going to the meeting?' Henry had directed his question to David, but most of the team who heard him nodded.

'Yes,' David answered, still keeping his eye on his mother. 'Are you?'

'Yes, and I'm gonna join up as soon as I can.'

'You'd best not let Mother hear you say that.'

'I'll tell her after I've done it, just like our Ernest did.'

David grinned at his stepbrother, who only had half his sight and no hope of fulfilling his recruitment wish.

Mary stopped in front of the goalpost. David followed her gaze as it swept over the mud-spattered men.

'Now look here...' Her voice had reached a fortissimo and it carried across the team, playing to every ear. 'If you go to that meeting, think very carefully about what you are doing. There's plenty of jobs that need doing at home. Men are getting killed out there – you might not come back, never see your family again, or they you. Come on, lads, it just isn't worth it. Think of your mam worrying about if she'll ever see you again.'

David looked at Henry, who had turned scarlet. Even his ears had taken on the look of a danger signal.

'My mam wants me to go,' one of the three Bills in the team stated.

'And mine,' another voice called out.

'Then may God be with you,' Mary responded.

A whistle blew for the second half to begin and David pulled his socks up high. He smiled at his mother, whose cheeks were pink from wind-chill and exhilaration. She raised her eyebrows quizzically. David nodded.

'Well you might change your mind when you get home,' she told him. 'Emily's there and the poor lass is heartbroken.'

David stopped to speak, but George was calling his team to take Loughborough by storm, and they made their charge. All thoughts of meetings, and even Emily, for the next three quarters of an hour were pushed from his conscious mind; the match was his only concern. Although in his subconscious his beloved Emily remained, unrequited though it was, and the question as to why she was home a day early, and distressed.

Emily was sitting at the scrubbed kitchen table, which was strewn with papers and cards. Rather clumsily, Alf set down a cup of hot, sweet tea in front of his daughter and sat down opposite. She could see that he was struggling to find words of comfort, and when none came, he reached across and took her hands in his. She raised her head. Swollen, red-rimmed eyes, lashes dewy with tears, must have conveyed the starkness of her sorrow. She tried to smile, but her mouth merely twitched and then gave up hope. They sat in silence until the clock chimed.

'Drink your tea, love, afore it gets cold.' Alf broke the stillness and Emily raised the china cup, with violets painted around its rim, to her lips and took a sip.

'Where is everyone?' She thought her voice sounded distant, as though she was in another room.

'At the football match.' Emily knew that Alf was on safer ground, speaking of the match rather than the stark reality of what lay between them.

'What about Mother?' Emily yearned for another woman's comfort.

'Aye, even Mother.'

Emily was surprised by the fact that her stepmother had gone to a football match and her face must have born witness to that. Alf gave a low chuckle. 'She's trying to persuade as many as she can not to go to some meeting in the village hall.'

'What meeting?'

'Oh, just summat that Mrs Walker-Holmes has organised.'

'It's about the war, isn't it?'

'Aye, lass, it is.' She knew Alf couldn't lie to her – there'd be no point.

The final whistle blew. With the wind behind them, Syston had beaten Loughborough by three goals to one. Everyone was patting George Oswin on the back – he in turn shook hands with the goal scorers: David and the two Bills.

'See you in The Bell,' George called to his team. David didn't reply. He snatched his jacket from the post it was hanging from and rushed home, the studs of his boots clattering on the cobbled streets as he ran. Whattoff had disappeared too, but he could wait until another day.

When David reached the back door, dusk was spreading through the streets. He pulled off his muddy boots, left them on the step his mother had scrubbed clean that morning, took a deep breath and pushed open the back door. Emily and Alf were sitting either side of the kitchen table and both turned their heads towards him. He felt awkward when he saw Emily's puffy face. He wanted to hug her and kiss her swollen eyes and lips, but instead he slipped through to the scullery muttering something about getting cleaned up.

'Did you win?' Alf called.

'We thrashed 'em, three–one,' David replied, relieved to have found his voice. He heard the back door open. His mother was home.

When David finally made his way back to the kitchen, Henry and Sydney were also back and Emily was talking to Sydney about his chickens.

'Go and light a fire in the front room,' Mary told David, who was trying to flatten his hair down without much success, 'and take Emily with you.' Emily picked up some papers from the table and followed David. They normally only used that room at Easter, Christmas and on Sundays; it smelled of lavender polish and soot. The fire had already been set and David took a box of matches from the mantelpiece. He lit a paraffin lamp that stood on a small table beside the sofa, then set light to some paper and kindling in the grate. He noticed the now familiar, proud soldier with his rifle and backpack beneath the coal and sticks. The paper curled as the fire caught, and flames swallowed up the soldier. He turned to Emily, who was sitting on the sofa.

'What's happened, Em?' He found it easier to talk when it was just the two of them. She handed a letter to him. He took it and leaned in towards the lamp. When he had finished reading the news from Franklin's father, his emotions were in turmoil. He had been jealous of Franklin, resentful that Emily had found love with the Canadian serving with the British Army rather than him, but he hadn't wanted this.

'They'd crossed a river at a place called Aisne and everything seemed to be going all right, but the Germans had made some trenches and they used machine guns. Oh God, David, hundreds were killed. Apparently it had been foggy when they went across the river and the Germans couldn't see them, but when the sun came up they had a clear view and they just shot them all down, including Franklin.'

David nodded; he had read it all in Franklin's father's letter. He moved away from the lamp and sat down beside her. The wind had become stronger and it was roaring in the chimney like a bear. The flames leapt upwards throwing a flickering radiance around the room.

'What are they?' He pointed to some embroidered postcards that she was holding. She offered them and he took them. Turning each one over he read the messages, not really sure that he wanted to, but curiosity overcame reluctance.

'That was for my birthday,' Emily told him as he read the words: 'With fondest love, Franklin.'

The next card was from a Mr and Mrs Green wishing her a happy birthday followed by: 'May you celebrate your next in Canada with dear Franklin.'

'Canada!' David spoke more loudly than he had intended and Emily started.

'Yes, we were going to Canada after we were married.'

'Sorry.' David felt churlish and picked up the next, which was an Easter card, again sent, with fondest love, from Franklin.

'That one only arrived last week.' Emily pointed to the last card; a tear had escaped and was sliding down her cheek. The neat, swirling writing said: 'From your sweetheart across the sea.' And on the side where the address should have been was the now familiar greeting: 'To Emily, with fondest love from Franklin,' followed by x x x.

David felt as though something had taken his insides and wrung them out. He felt sick; sick that Emily had loved another and sick that he couldn't feel sad for her loss.

'He'd been dead for all this time when I thought he was still alive, until... Oh, David, what am I going to do?' she wailed.

'Ssh,' he blew through his teeth and placed the cards onto the table. He wanted to throw them on the fire, but Emily would never have forgiven him. She began to shake as sobs swept through her body, and he placed his arm around her shoulders and pulled her close. His back twinged as the football injury tightened under his shoulder blade. He really wanted Emily to rub it for him, gently, but thought it improper to intrude on her distress for what he ashamedly knew would be his own self-gratification. Despite his pain, he held her and she turned her face into his chest. Her hand reached out to his free arm and held on. He could feel tears soaking into his shirt and onto his skin. His embrace tightened and he could smell soap on her hair. He planted a light kiss on her forehead.

'It will be all right,' he tried to comfort her. 'I'll look after you.' He felt her body relax into his. He wanted to take her and make love to her there and then, her vulnerability an instrument of arousal in him. He cradled her until the sobbing grew less. Conscience-stricken, he eased his hold and she pulled away. Her face was level with his and she smiled. Then she reached out. His heart thumped and he swallowed. Her hand fell on his collar and she pressed it down.

'Will you ever learn to put your collar straight?' she scolded. He laughed and hugged her.

Chapter 17

Monday, 9th November 1914

Gathering

David could still feel beads of sweat trickling down his neck as he punched his new time card into the clock. Six twenty-eight. He had made it with two minutes to spare and was thankful that he was fit and could run faster than most, especially on a Monday morning when the foreman was waiting by the door to reprimand latecomers. He made his way through to the clicking room and nodded good-mornings to his fellow workers as they filtered in. Taking out a clean, white handkerchief that Emily had given to him last Christmas, he wiped the back of his neck. The weather had turned mild since the wind changed from east to south-west and few were wearing overcoats to work. He turned and walked through the racks of leather where George Partridge was lifting a roll of hide onto his shoulder. As they walked together onto the factory floor David noticed a new poster displayed at the back of the room. The picture wasn't that of a soldier with a rifle and fixed bayonet, but of two men: an officer and a civilian. The officer was pointing to a framed list, underneath which was written, in bold lettering: *Is YOUR Name on a Roll of Honour?*

'Are you going to the meeting tonight?' George asked, peering over the brown skins that were balanced on his left shoulder.

'I am that,' David replied, pushing the handkerchief back into his pocket.

'Me an' all.' George dropped the heavy load onto the first trestle and pointed to the poster. 'We've got nowt to lose according to that; Garner's gonna keep our jobs open till we get back.' Then he was gone, back to the store to collect more leather.

David unrolled his clean apron. Mam always made sure the week began with clean clothes, even if it did sometimes cause him to be late leaving. He picked up his knife and gave it a few swishes up and down the strop before lifting his first hide of the day. He placed patterns on skins and went through the routine of cutting and bundling his work. The repetitive monotony prompted his mind to wander, and it settled on the weekend with Emily, which tended to remain at the forefront of his mind, even though it had been a week ago. He had escorted her back to Bushby on the Sunday afternoon, which had been his twentieth birthday, and she had kissed him on his cheek when he left her at the Hoyle's residence. He remembered how his stomach had clenched when he felt her lips on his face and hoped he had shaved closely enough so that she wouldn't feel stubble. If he did join up, he would ask her for a photograph to take with him whilst he was over there. He must have been smiling, as young Albert Rowbotham, on the bench in front of him, called over: 'What are you smirking at, Mr Adcock?' David shook off his daydream and looked at the lad who was heaving a skin of poorer quality leather onto his bench.

'Nowt for you to be concerned with,' David fenced back. Fancy, the lads called him Mr Adcock and he had been a teenager himself only last week, but now he was twenty it was time to make something of his life, and he wouldn't do that by standing in a factory every day for the next forty years.

'Summat secret, is it?' Albert turned and flashed a toothy grin.

'Look out!' David yelled, but it was too late. Albert hadn't been concentrating and his knife had slipped, grotesquely. David ran forward and grabbed Albert's hand. The blade had sliced between his thumb and forefinger and an ugly gash stretched to the palm of his hand. Albert had put the leather grain-side down onto the bench and blood was pooling into the flesh. David pulled the boy's wrist away from the bench. Blood trickled down Albert's fingers and onto his shoes. David drew his handkerchief from his pocket and wound it around the wound, but it was soon soaked.

'Take your apron off!' David instructed, but Albert just stared at him. 'Come on, take it off!' Someone was tugging at the apron and rough hands pulled it over Albert's head and handed it to David. He used it to bind the laceration, and as he did, a rose of blood bloomed into it.

'What's going on?' Mr Sharp had appeared, his face dark and angry.

'Young Albert's cut 'is sen,' Harry Hamson said.

'You should get to the doctor's,' David told Albert, whose colour had drained from his face; he appeared to be on the verge of collapse.

'Mind you clock out afore you go,' Mr Sharp snapped. 'And the cost of that side o' leather will come out of your wages, boy.'

'Yes, Mr Sharp,' Albert groaned, and made his way, unsteadily, out of the room.

'Back to work you lot, show's over.' Mr Sharp had puffed out his chest and was strutting like a cockerel along the benches until he was satisfied that everyone was working efficiently.

At noon, the hooter sounded for lunchtime and the clicks stopped, tapping and hammering ceased and the steam powering the presses hissed a weary sigh, which immobilised them for the time being. Workers spilled into the passageway where the time clock was and a symphony of cluncks and thumps resounded from the orchestra of a workforce freed.

David shrugged on his jacket and walked over to the new poster to find out what George meant by Garner keeping their jobs for them. He read:

> *'If your name goes down on your firm's Roll of Honour, it also goes on that mighty Scroll which records the names of all who have rallied around the Flag. There is room for your name on the Roll of Honour.'*

'What do you reckon then?' George was standing beside him. 'Sounds all right, don't it?'

'It tells us what we have to do here.' David pointed to the next paragraph and read it out loud:

> *'Ask your employer to keep your position open for you. Tell him that you are going to help the Empire. Every patriotic employer is assisting his men to enlist, and he'll do the right thing by you. Tell him now – Your King and Country want you – today.'*

'At least if we don't like it we can come back.' George was nodding his approval.

'Don't you have to sign up for a set time? Our Ernest joined for six years, until nineteen seventeen.'

'Well, we'll soon find out.'

When the hooter sounded at the end of the day, the workers left in an increasingly rushed manner; they only had an hour and a half before the meeting was to begin and the men were hungry. David pushed his way through, as he had something more pressing to deal with before attending the meeting, even if it meant missing his tea. He squeezed past and slipped his card into the clock, pulled it out and dropped it into the rack. Whattoff's card was two below his, so it was easy for David to see that his brother hadn't already clocked off. After leaving through the peeling brown doors, David stepped into the shadows and waited. He really wanted to pull out a cigarette and light up, but he remained still until his brother emerged and made his way towards the factory gates. Whattoff was halfway down the yard before David slipped out and followed, keeping a good distance between them but always keeping him in his sight. From the route they followed, David guessed they were heading towards High Street. The gas lamps had been lit and he was careful to remain in the gathering darkness, only stepping out briefly to run the gauntlet of a stream of light. Whattoff didn't look behind; his head was down and he was walking determinedly. When he did stop, he faced a shop's entrance, and from where David was standing, about five shops away, he knew it was the chemist's. Whattoff looked up and down the empty street and then entered the shop. David moved quickly, stopping at the edge of the apothecary's frontage. Through the window display he could see Whattoff; there was no one else inside apart from the chemist himself. An exchange took place, coins dropped into the chemist's hand and a package was given over, then Whattoff strode towards the door. David slipped into the unlit doorway behind him, listening for metal heel segs on cobbles getting closer. When a figure emerged, level with the entry, David stepped out, and grabbing his brother by the lapels, he propelled him inside the dark doorway.

'What the fuck?' Whattoff was outraged and raised his fist.

'Shut up!' David hissed. 'Give me the package.'

'Piss off and get yer own.'

'I mean it. What's in the packet you just collected?'

'Nowt for you. Now bugger off and leave me alone.'

David pushed Whattoff back against the wall. 'Give me the package.' He pushed his forearm against Whattoff's throat and searched his brother's pockets until he found the small, wrapped bottle. He pulled it out, shook the wrapping to the floor and held it in front of his brother's face.

'Explain this!'

'I need it, please, Dave, I need it.' Whattoff had become more congenial, almost contrite.

'You stupid sod. You don't need it. You'll kill yourself if you take this stuff.'

'No I won't, it's safe, and I need it. I've got a bad back and it eases the pain.'

'Take an aspirin. You don't need this.' David threw the bottle to the ground where it smashed, laudanum seeping out into the cold cobbles.

'No!' It was a strangled scream that descended into a sob, and Whattoff slid down the wall. He was on his hands and knees picking at the pieces of brown glass, seemingly oblivious to any pain as the shards cut his fingers. After a while, Whattoff conceded defeat; he appeared broken.

'Get up. I'll walk home with you,' David said and helped his brother to his feet. They walked to Turn Street in silence. On the way, David bought a *Leicester Mercury* from the tobacconist's and they arrived home before Kathy. David lit the gas mantles, then the fire, and finally the paraffin stove to boil a kettle. Whattoff sat on the sofa, head in hands. David had found some aspirin in the kitchen cupboard and offered one to his brother, who knocked it to the floor.

'You don't know what you've done.'

'I think I do.' David sat on the sofa and passed his brother the newspaper. On the front page was a photograph of a man who had been hanged in Leicester Prison for murder. Whattoff pushed the paper aside. 'Read it,' David ordered, and stabbed his finger at the story. Whattoff shrugged, lifted the paper and began to read. He fell silent and his face paled to a grey realisation. David knew he had won this particular battle and leaned back into the sofa.

When David arrived home, with just enough time to wash and change, his mother was sitting at the kitchen table reading the *Leicester Mercury*. Alf was in his armchair beside the fire with the *Daily Mirror*.

'Have you seen this?' David's mother looked over her dark round spectacles and pointed to the front-page story.

'Yes, it's a rum do,' David replied.

'Poor little mite. And that was the stuff I was giving your father before he died.'

David laid his hand on his mother's shoulder as if by way of comfort.

'What's that then?' Alf removed his half-moon spectacles and turned towards them.

'There's been a hanging at Leicester Prison,' Mary told him. 'It was that chap who killed his baby son in Western Park after he'd taken laudanum.'

Sydney came into the kitchen from putting his chickens to roost and tried to see the newspaper over his mother's shoulder.

'How did he kill him?' Sydney seemed to be enjoying the grisly tale.

'He slit his throat with a razor,' their mother said, and visibly shuddered. 'It just shows what damage that stuff can do. It should be banned.'

'Well, I'd best get a move on, the meeting starts in half an hour.' David looked at his mother, who didn't respond but carried on reading the newspaper. The door to the stairs opened and Henry appeared in his best suit, looking as though he had scrubbed himself with a stiff brush, his hair all smoothed down.

'I'm ready. Come on our Dave, get a move on, we don't want to be late.' David saw his mother look up and raise her eyebrows quizzically towards Alf, who shrugged and went back to reading his own paper.

The village hall was almost full when David and Henry arrived. There was a low muttering, which burbled throughout and hung from the rafters around the gas lamps like an invocation. They found two chairs at the end of a row halfway down the room and behind the Oswin brothers. David did a quick calculation in his head; he could count eleven rows of chairs, six on either side of the aisle, which meant a hundred and thirty-two people could be seated. The chairs on the stage were of the same kind, and there were just four.

Mrs Walker-Holmes stepped up onto the platform followed by an army officer who David recognised – he had a swagger stick tucked under his arm and a crown on his epaulettes. The gentleman on the right of the officer, they later found out, was Campbell Baxter, a dentist from Leicester who had agreed to help with recruitment by ensuring soldiers' teeth were in good order. The fourth was another army officer with less swank and fewer pips on his uniform than his senior officer. On each side of the platform was a large poster showing the soldier with his rifle and bayonet and, Henry pointed out, rather odd footwear. A hush descended, as just before a snowstorm, and the room was expectant. Mrs Walker-Holmes rose from her seat and stepped forward. There was a polite ripple of applause to which she almost bashfully raised her hand and inclined her head. A few people were still arriving and she waited for them to settle, and then a wave of muttering swept the room like a fever and David turned to see who was causing the almost suppressed sensation. He first saw his mother, and then, standing next to her, he noticed a smartly dressed, very handsome man. Ramsay MacDonald was leaning down to speak to his mother, who was a good head and shoulders shorter. She was laughing, and MacDonald's distinguished moustache lifted as he returned her smile. David shook his head as he watched his mother lay her hand on MacDonald's arm. Good God, she was flirting with him! His face twitched into a smile and he turned back to the platform.

Mrs Walker-Holmes pointed to the soldier, who everyone knew, a familiar face in every household.

'A soldier of the King' – her voice was shrill – 'Field Marshal Sir John French says that it is an honour to belong to such an army.' She swept her gaze over the room, which was mostly made up of young men. 'Every fit man from nineteen to thirty-eight is eligible for this great honour. Friends can join in a body and serve together in the same regiment.' David felt Henry nudge him. The piercing voice continued: 'Rapid promotion! There is rapid promotion for intelligence and zeal. Hundreds who enlisted as private soldiers have already become officers because of their merits and courage, and thousands have reached non-commissioned rank. After the war, every man who has served will command his country's gratitude. He will be looked up to and respected because he answered his country's call. The regiments at the front are covering themselves with glory.' There was applause; it began with a few hands being slapped together and rose to a crescendo, like a rousing orchestration. Mrs Walker-Holmes was laughing, her cheeks pink with exhilaration.

Amidst the cheering a slightly stooped man with round spectacles and thinning grey hair took a seat at the piano to the left of the stage. David recognised him as the church organist. A pretty auburn-haired young woman, with grace and determination, climbed the few steps and joined him. David leaned forward and spoke into George Oswin's ear:

'Ain't that your Gertie?'

George turned and grinned. 'Ahh, it is that.'

Accompanied by the skillfully played piano, Gertie began to sing. The new song of patriotism that was filling towns and villages had a calming effect, and those who had been standing sat down again and listened. The village hall had perfect acoustics and the purity of Gertie's voice trespassed on the men's souls.

'... turn the dark cloud inside out, till the boys come home.'

Gertie finished her song, smiled and curtsied. The room remained still, then men rose to their feet, clapping and cheering. Mrs Walker-Holmes saw her opportunity and took to the stage once more. She ushered Gertie away and wafted her flattened hands up and down until everyone settled. She paused for a moment and then declared:

'I see that Mr MacDonald is present this evening.' Mrs Walker-Holmes stared at him. A cheer rose up and everyone turned towards the radical MP, who raised his hand in acknowledgement. 'Perhaps you might like to say a few words?' she invited. MacDonald nodded his assent and moved down the hall towards the platform. As he passed, every mothers' son rose from their seat, clapping and cheering. He climbed the steps, and once again the room fell silent.

'My opinion regarding the war is well known, but we are in it. Victory, therefore, must be ours. We cannot go back now.' He spoke of apportioning praise and blame and he appealed to everyone's love of country. 'You young men must settle the issue of victory. I want the serious men of the trade unions, the brotherhood, to face their duty – England has need of you.'

He left the stage to a standing ovation and Mrs Walker-Holmes resumed her position at the fore. She whipped them up into a state of frenzy once more when she shouted, 'Enlist today! Enter your name on the nation's roll of honour and do your part. God save the King!' The words she had spoken were well known. They had been read often enough as they appeared on recruitment posters and leaflets, but still the applause increased, chairs clattered and fell backwards and Mrs Walker-Holmes left the stage. No one saw Ramsay MacDonald leave the building.

The atmosphere in The Bell was euphoric. John Wing had needed help to satisfy demand and the room was blue with cigarette and pipe smoke. David was standing in the corner with others from the football team. They had all been drinking since the meeting ended; first John Wing's finest ale, and now whisky, brandy or rum.

'Old Garner won't have many hands left,' George Partridge joked, 'only them as is over thirty-eight or under nineteen.'

'I ain't nineteen.' Henry was put out.

'You will be soon enough,' David told him, relieved that his brother wouldn't be able to enlist just yet; he would only experience further disappointment when he took his medical. And Mam would be pleased.

'Well' – George Oswin swayed a little as he spoke – 'I ain't nineteen neither, but I'm goin'. How are they to know how old I am anyway?'

John Wing called time.

'Don't be late in the morning,' David called to his pals as he left The Bell. He swayed and staggered home, wishing he hadn't missed his tea but determined to tell Mr Garner to hold his job whilst he went and did his bit.

Chapter 18

Tuesday, 10th November 1914

Enlist

The moon was still hanging low in the early morning sky, doing its best to light up the day. David pushed back the bedclothes and rose, his bed giving a friendly creak as he left it. He padded across the bedroom to a chest of drawers and pulled one open, as quietly as he could. He wasn't a fussy fellow but he did like to wear matching socks. Eventually, after much fumbling, he had two dark socks; the grey ones just wouldn't do, not for today. He crept past his brother's bed, where Charlie was snoring softly, making the most of the extra half an hour of being warm in welcome unconsciousness before the bells on the alarm clock clattered.

David's head was heavy. The persistent, dull ache behind his eyes thumped with every step as he went downstairs, reminding him that perhaps he shouldn't have drunk so much ale last night, let alone whisky, to round off the evening.

The kitchen was warm, a glow still evident in the range. He closed the door to the stairs and dropped his jacket over the back of a chair. There was some coal in the scuttle and, as quietly as he could, he fed the smouldering embers. After lighting the gas mantle, he put a pan of water on to boil and sat down at the table, pressing cold fingertips to closed eyes. Drawing his hands down his cheeks he rested them under his chin. The night's stubble prickled, and he tilted his head back and stared at the ceiling.

After a few minutes, he stood up and poured water from the pan into an enamel mug and took it into the scullery, where he lit a lamp and peered into a mirror that was hanging lopsidedly from the window-frame. The face that looked back at him seemed to be Whattoff's; the same dreamy eyes, same full lips, just like their father's according to Mam. A leaden feeling hit David's stomach when he remembered his brother's secret. He picked up his shaving brush and began to work up a lather. Whattoff would have to wait until another day; he had more important things to prepare for today.

'Just look at you!'

'Mornin', Mam.' David went back into the kitchen and sat down.

'Why are you dressed like that? It isn't Sunday.'

'You know why.' David smoothed his hair down with one hand and tugged at his collar with the other.

'You don't have to go.' His mother placed a cup of tea in front of him. 'You have a good job, and they'll be making army boots soon, so you'll be needed here.'

'Yes, I do. I'm needed at the front.'

'Let the others go. Wait a bit longer. It won't last long, you'll see. It'll be a waste of time you getting all trained, and –'

'Mam!' David interrupted. Then his voice dropped to a softer tone. 'I'm going.'

The day had changed colour, and by the time David cycled into Town Hall Square the sun had painted the town in brighter shades than the greys of earlier. He propped his bike up against a red-brick wall and pulled off his cycle clips.

'Bugger!' He was wearing one black sock and one brown.

He looked up at the notices that bedecked the Town Hall, the main one saying: *Recruiting Office*, and beneath it a banner ran the length of the building: *5,000 Leicesters now at the front ask 2,000 more Leicester men to join them.* The queue of men snaked up the Town Hall's steps, each in his Sunday-best suit. David looked around for a familiar face. It was the ears he noticed; George Partridge was further up the line, freshly scrubbed. They shuffled forward and David gradually neared the front. Every so often a Boy Scout ran past heading towards the barracks clutching a bundle of papers.

Inside the Town Hall, a soldier, who looked about nineteen, was sitting at a makeshift desk constructed from a six-foot board balancing across two chair backs. The soldier didn't have his jacket on – the only man in the room dressed that way. Once the soldier had written down David's name and address he waved him into the next room to be weighed and measured. David stood in line and waited. When it was his turn, he took off his cap, jacket and shoes. The soldier who was scrutinising operations narrowed his eyes.

'Are you colour-blind?' he bawled, 'because if you are, you're no bloody good to us.'

'No, sir.'

'Then why are you wearing odd socks?'

David's heart sank. 'It was dark this morning, sir,' he answered by way of explanation.

'Of course it was bloody dark,' the officer snapped, 'it's bleedin' November.'

'Sorry, sir.' David didn't know what else to say, but the soldier was already inspecting the next volunteer.

When instructed, David stepped up to a measuring pole in the corner of the room and felt the wooden rule press onto his head. A series of measurements were shouted out to another soldier sitting at a desk in his shirtsleeves:

'Height: five feet four and three-quarters. Weight: ten stone. Chest: thirty-four inches. Expansion: thirty-six inches. Physical development: good.'

David breathed a sigh of relief and put his shoes and jacket back on. He was sent to another desk where he was ordered: 'Sign here,' by the recruiting officer. When David had sealed his fate with a spidery signature he was handed his pay-book and told to report to the barracks the next morning.

'What about my uniform?' he asked a soldier who had two stripes on his sleeve and was standing by the exit.

'There ain't none,' was his reply, 'so don't come in your Sunday best, but make sure you're smart. And don't be late – 0700 hours, sharp!'

'Yes, sir.'

'Yes, Corporal!'

'Yes, Corporal.'

David walked down the steps and felt more confused than when he had entered the building. There was slap on his back and he turned to see George Oswin holding up his papers. David raised his eyebrows.

'You got in then?'

'I did, fit as a fuckin' flea and rarin' to go,' George said.

'But you ain't old enough,' David whispered, looking around to make sure no one could hear.

'Told 'em I were nineteen and they didn't ask no questions.' He grinned then almost shouted: 'We're off to France, Dave, to sort out the bloody Boche.'

The church clock struck three. High Street was quiet and the only sound, apart from the clock, was that of an elderly horse pulling a creaking cart full of mangel beets along the cobbles. David propped his bike against some railings and walked towards the chemist's shop. He looked around and, when he saw no one, pushed open the door. The bell jangled, and Mrs Walker-Holmes, who was handing over some coins, turned towards him and raised her head, as if questioning his being there. He decided not to give her the satisfaction of an answer but merely lifted his cap in begrudged greeting. He moved over to a rack of postcards and began to flick through them. Eventually Mrs Walker-Holmes left the shop, the bell clanging its farewell. David pulled a card from the rack then walked over to the door and flicked the 'Open' sign to 'Closed'. He turned back into the shop and moved towards the counter, but he didn't stop when he was opposite the chemist; he walked around the end of the bench and behind it into the shopkeeper's sacred space.

'What are you doing?' John Lewin was spluttering and his face had turned the colour of an over-ripe tomato. David stared into the chemist's widened eyes and breathed in, but said nothing.

'Get out. You've no right to be behind here!' Lewin shouted.

'And you've no right to be selling my brother opium tincture.' David kept his voice low, yet menacing.

'I don't know what you're talking about. Now get out.'

David took hold of John Lewin's white overall lapels and pulled, unsteadying him. 'If you so much as sell my brother one drop of that stuff, I'll see to it that you don't sell anything, to anyone, ever again.' Beads of sweat had formed on the older man's top lip and forehead. David tightened his grip, squeezing the material into the chemist's throat. 'Do you hear me?'

David shook his quarry, like a dog shakes a rat, and flung him onto the floor. John Lewin nodded, his head bobbing up and down, eyes even wider with fear.

'Not one drop,' David snarled.

He moved back to the other side of the counter and placed a halfpenny onto it. 'For the postcard,' he said, and pocketed the card.

David flipped the sign back to 'Open' and left John Lewin on the floor.

The house was chilly and the late afternoon's silence oppressive. David didn't feel right being at home during the day. He felt uncomfortable, guilty, even though Mr Garner had been fine with him when he'd told him he had enlisted and had assured them all that their jobs were safe. He'd even said he would like to be going himself and maybe he would if they raised the age limit. He'd wished them well and told them he was proud of them.

The house creaked as if to tell him he shouldn't be there.

David pulled open the top drawer of a chest, which stood under the window in his and Charlie's bedroom, and took out a grey woollen jersey. He pulled it on, and when his head emerged he saw, tucked into the corner of the drawer, a small wooden tiger. He lifted it and held it in his palm. Memories from the day when Alf had given it to him for his birthday kindled a smile. He shook his head.

'Well,' he said to the toy, 'I never thought I'd be a Tiger, a Leicester Tiger, a proud, fighting Leicester Tiger.' His grip tightened as he spoke. He looked out onto a village of smoking chimney stacks and well-tended allotments. A barrage of unanswerable questions burst into his head and he spoke them out loud:

'What if I'm not good enough?'

'What if it gets really bad?'

'What if I get injured?'

He paused for a moment and looked around, taking in the plain furniture and bare floor.

'What if I don't come back?'

His voice had dropped to a whisper and his hands shook as he put the tiger back. His fingers caught on a card and he took it and smiled. It was the birthday card Emily had sent to him. He turned it over and frowned. The words, which should have made him happy, frustrated him: *To my dear brother on your birthday. Love Emily.* He wanted her to love him, but not as a brother – as a lover. She was only his stepsister, for goodness' sake, not his real sister. He felt the card begin to buckle under his grip. Letting go, he dropped it down beside the tiger and rammed the drawer shut.

'I'll write to her,' he said aloud. 'I'll tell her I've joined up, just like her beloved Ernest. Just like her bloody precious Franklin.'

'Is that you, David?' His mother was calling from the foot of the stairs.

'Yes, Mam.'

He shivered. The bedroom had grown colder as the sun set, and he went downstairs and into the kitchen, where he found his mother stoking the fire. Without turning, she greeted him.

'You've done it then?'

'Yes, Mam, I've done it.'

She bombarded him with questions about when, how, what and where – which he couldn't answer, apart from the one about his uniform. His Mam only stopped asking when the kettle began to sing.

The letterbox rattled and November's parish magazine slid in and dropped onto the mat. David walked over and picked it up. Even the vicar had adopted the war orphan and the front page read: *To parents and friends of our soldiers and sailors*. He put the magazine down. His mother poured them both a cup of tea and, sitting at the kitchen table with him, she picked up the magazine and flicked through it. David sipped his tea in silence as she read about church services, the harvest festival and a collection for waifs and strays.

'Apparently we have Belgian refugees now,' she grumbled, 'and the members of the Girls' Friendly Society are busy knitting scarves and cholera belts for the troops.'

'What's a cholera belt?' David asked. No one had mentioned cholera at the recruitment office.

'They keep you warm and dry and stop you getting cholera,' she answered without looking up. 'They had them in the Boer War, too. Anyroad, there's no need to worry about that.' Her eyes flashed. 'There's a letter from a chaplain; here, listen to this: "*The front is unspeakable. I have known men die of shots. I have known men go mad. I have known men come into the hospital with shattered nerves. Do tell the Territorials*" – that's you,' Mary pointed a bony finger at David – '"*that they must know God before they come out if they want to adequately face what lies before them. There are no atheists at the front and men are not ashamed to say that though they have not prayed before, they are praying now.*" You'd better get praying, lad.' She stuck her chin out towards David and narrowed her eyes. David shrugged.

The back door opened and Alf came into the kitchen.

'What you doin' home?' he asked. 'You got the sack?' Mary sighed and stood up. She poured her husband a cup of tea and lifted yesterday's stew onto the hotplate. David told Alf of the day's events and his stepfather nodded and took out his pipe. David picked up the magazine and turned the pages in pursuit of happier stories.

'I see our Whattoff's wedding has a mention.' He began to laugh. His mother, lips still pursed, raised her eyebrows. 'They've spelt his name wrong – it says Whattott.' He would pay Whattoff a visit later. He scanned the list of names serving in His Majesty's naval and military forces, and then he spotted the extracts from soldiers' letters. He stood up and walked over to his mother who was scrubbing potatoes as though they were about to escape.

'Listen to this, Mam.' His voice was gentle, reassuring. Alf looked up. 'This is from one of our boys at the front:

> *"I am getting on very nicely and having a fine time. It is like being out on a holiday. It seemed a bit strange to me for a day or two, but I am getting over that. I am getting on well with my drill thanks to the Lads' Brigade. We are getting on fine now, talking French, as we have had books issued to us to enable us to ask for things we require."'*

See, it ain't all bad.' David looked up at his mother and smiled, but he was shocked to see a tear roll down her cheek and plop onto the potato in her hand. He'd never seen his mother cry; he felt his throat tighten as it tried to push back the sickly guilt that rose up from his stomach.

The back door crashed open and Sydney entered. Mary brushed her cheek and returned to scrubbing the spuds. David put the magazine face down on the mantelpiece. The back cover bore the words of a Serjeant[4] Graves, who was in the Fifth Northern General Hospital in Leicester, and David could almost hear him shouting at them: 'Tell your young men who are able-bodied and of military age to enlist at

---

4. Serjeant is the traditional spelling with Sergeant becoming popular after 1918.

once and to train, so that they can take their turn in the trenches and give their brothers at the front a rest.'

Sydney looked around the silent kitchen.

'What's for tea, Mam?' he asked.

Chapter 19

Wednesday, 11th November 1914

Barracks

'Watch out!'

David recovered his footing and glanced round to see who was calling out to him.

'You nearly went a cropper there, mate.'

'Slipped on the ice.'

David looked towards the young man who was just leaving the urinal where ice had formed on the surrounding cobbles. He was taller than David and looked as though he would do well to eat a decent meal; his clothes hung loosely off his slender frame. He pushed his flattened hand down his trousers and then offered it to David.

'Ray Kirkby,' the young man said, slicking back his dark hair with his free hand.

'David Adcock.'

The two men shook hands, hitched their haversacks higher onto their backs, and together walked along The Newarke, their breath forming visible clouds of watery vapour that floated in the air around them. They joined a steady stream of men who were making their way past the drill hall to stand before a pair of huge double-gates that led into the Victorian barrack block. Coming from Oxford Street, others joined them under the arch of The Magazine building at the end of the road, which housed the regimental headquarters.

'Hey, Dave!'

A large hand fell on David's shoulder. He was surprised that it was still sore from that Loughborough lad's barge at the match last month. Harry Hamson punched the flat of his left hand with his fisted right.

'This is it then, Dave. We're gonna be soldiers. Fightin' men. Heroes.' He punctuated each phrase with another slap of his fist.

David looked about him at the hundreds of men who had taken the King's shilling and were now anticipating doing their bit, getting decent meals, and proudly wearing the uniform. Although, to appease his mother, David hadn't signed up to go abroad – even though he was old enough – he believed he would get that opportunity if the war carried on much longer.

'Yes, this is it.' He playfully thumped Harry's arm.

When the bells of St Mary de Castro tolled seven o'clock, the huge gates swung open. So loud was the cheering that David couldn't hear a word of what Ray Kirkby was saying, and they were swept through the entrance into Magazine Square with the hundreds of men that surged forward. Filtered and directed into lines by uniformed soldiers, they stood and they waited.

A stocky white dog sat beside a wall and observed the raw recruits who had been lined up in rows of ten throughout The Magazine parade ground. As it turned its head, David noticed that the fur around one eye was a patch of jet black, giving it the appearance of a pirate. Each section had a corporal telling its men to 'stand up straight' and 'shut the fuck up'. Serjeants grouped sections into platoons. David's line stepped forward and joined another three, then each platoon joined three others, where a captain came over and inspected them. The four companies of young men formed a battalion and David soon realised that these soldiers would be his army family. The adjutant moved slowly among them, scratching his head with his pencil and making notes every so often. After a morning of standing, which made David's feet ache, the adjutant finally saluted and strode back to HQ. The dog continued to observe them and shuffled along the wall, following the sun as it moved across the wintry morning sky.

After a mid-day meal of bread and dripping with a mug of sweet tea, David marched with his section to the quartermaster's stores, his haversack weighing heavy on his back. After a few steps, his arms swung and hit the person behind, and as he stepped forward with his left foot, the man in front stepped out with his right and their feet collided, throwing them off-balance. They eventually reached a building with very few windows and where other new recruits were queuing in front of an arched doorway.

'Right, you shoddy lot, you're like a bleedin' load of cripples. Get in line and wait your turn.'

David and Ray looked at each other.

'Eyes front!' the corporal bawled.

No one spoke.

'Well? I said "eyes front" – answer me!'

'Yes, sir,' the men mumbled their response.

'Yes, Corporal! Now, let me hear you.'

'Yes, Corporal,' they shouted.

David didn't dare stamp his feet in an attempt to keep them warm, so he stood still and waited, although he wasn't sure what they were all waiting for. The line of men gradually shuffled forward as the weak afternoon sun began to set and the air became frosty.

Eventually, David's section entered the dimly lit building and from the stores the men drew bed-boards, palliasses and grey blankets. They staggered back to their barrack room. David noticed that he wasn't the only one struggling to carry the unwieldy items – a board was dropped, the next man tripped and lost his blanket, the farce continued – David thought it was like a circus scene and they were the clowns.

Four sections occupied the room that David, Ray Kirkby, Harry Hamson and George Oswin were in. A stiff-backed serjeant was waiting for them. The forty men were each given a numbered bed place and they clumsily positioned their boards and bedding. The serjeant strolled up and down.

'Squad, attention!' the serjeant commanded, and there was much shuffling and some stamping of feet. The platoon was in disarray. Some stood at the foot of their bed, some at the head, others just anywhere.

'My name is Serjeant Mills. We'll soon have you boys in shape. Now, let's get these beds in order, and then back on parade.' He moved among the men, giving instructions: 'Move that to the left. Shift it over. Not there! Straighten it up, for God's sake!' He waved his hands back and forth until the beds were lined up like flattened dominoes. Satisfied, Serjeant Mills moved back and stood in the middle of the room.

'Stand by your beds!' The corporals had joined in and quickly moved the men in their section to the correct position. Serjeant Mills spoke again: 'When I say atten-shun, you will bring your left foot to your right with your heels together and in line. Keep your knees straight and turn your feet out at an angle of forty-five degrees. Let your arms hang down, wrists straight, palms turned towards your thighs and thumbs behind the seam in your trousers. Neck erect, not poking forward, eyes front.' The serjeant watched as the men pulled themselves to attention, the bristles of his moustache twitching as his mouth tried hard not to smile. 'Shoulders down and back. No slouching!' His blue eyes swept the room. 'Have you got that?'

'Yes, sir.'

'Yes, Sarge!'

'Yes, Sarge.'

'Good. Stand – at ease.'

David glanced to his left at George Oswin, who stared back. No one moved. The serjeant shook his head. 'Carry your left foot twelve inches to the left, hands behind your back, place one hand in the palm of the other, and hold.' His voice became louder. 'Slovenly attitudes are not permitted.'

David concentrated whilst Serjeant Mills gave directions for their daily routine and, as if he were delivering a gift, told them that their officer was Second Lieutenant Harvey, who would be present at squad drill in the morning. Not wanting to miss a command, David kept his mind focused on the instructions for the evening: after parade, get a meal in the canteen and be back by nine thirty for roll call. Lights out at ten. Serjeant Mills concluded:

'When I say dismiss, you will turn to your right, pause briefly, then move off quietly. Squad, Dis-miss!'

Supper was a noisy occasion. Cigarette smoke hung and swirled beneath the beams and around the lights; every man's words were wrapped in spent tobacco. David wiped his mouth. His stomach was stuffed with a stew of nameless meat, mashed potatoes and over-boiled cabbage, followed by an apple dumpling. He was sipping his tea when George Partridge pushed his chair back and almost fell over.

'Watch out, you clumsy bugger,' a voice that David recognised, but couldn't place snarled.

'Sorry, mate,' George apologised to the man who remained with his back to them.

The Syston lads had gathered together, and it reminded David of when he had been camping with the Boy Scouts and he began to look forward to the adventure that lay ahead.

'What a load of instructions.' Ray took a gulp of his tea.

'And that were only the start of it,' George said, chuckling.

'They don't speak very nice, do they?' Ray's face was serious.

'You'll be swearin' like them afore long.' David was amused by Ray's reserve. He felt something push against his leg; the white dog with the black eye looked up at him, its tongue lolling over the side of its mouth. David offered it a piece of apple dumpling, which he hadn't been able to eat, and the dog took it, swallowed it down in one gulp, then moved on to the next table.

'That's a butcher's dog if ever I saw one,' Harry said.

To complete the holiday-camp feeling, an older man in uniform climbed onto a raised platform at the far end of the canteen where a piano was positioned. Above it hung a six-foot banner that declared *God Save the King* in huge letters.[5]

For the rest of the evening, the old soldier bashed out familiar tunes, and even Ray joined in as the songs became more raucous.

It was chilly when they stepped outside to cross the parade ground. In their room, Serjeant Mills called the roll. At ten o'clock a bugle played 'Taps' and lights were extinguished. The men slid under their grey blankets, which blended into the dull grey walls and the steel-grey night.

---

5. See photograph 2, page 319

'It's bloody stark in 'ere,' George Oswin said in a stage whisper.

'A bit like prison,' Ray said from under his blanket in the bed next to David; just the top of his head protruded.

'It's nowt like prison.' The same rough yet familiar voice that David had heard in the canteen sounded from somewhere on the other side of Ray. Then he remembered.

'Is that you, Swanny?'

'Well who the fuck else did you think it was?' Bob Swann growled.

'When did you get out?'

'Last month. Ended up 'avin' to do a bit more time for fightin'.'

'How the hell did you get to enlist then, you being a convict an' all?'

Bob gave a hollow laugh. 'Gen 'em me brother's name, didn't I?'

'But he ain't old enough.'

'They don't know that. Told 'em I were Bill and I'm twenty. Don't want to be a Tommy really though.'

'Why did you join up then?'

'Coz I done another job and they're lookin' for me.'

'When? Ain't you 'ad enough of gaol?'

'Yeah, but when everyone started fightin' after that politician 'ad been speaking, I just sort of joined in.' David knew about the trouble in Leicester after Ramsay MacDonald's speech. 'Hooligans' the papers had called them. David had been there but had dragged Whattoff away before his brother had joined in too.

'What happened then?' David was whispering, as he didn't want to wake Ray, who was snoring softly.

'Well, I hit some bloke who pushed me, and the poor bugger went an' died. I didn't mean to hit 'im that 'ard. It were probably that piece of iron I were carryin' that did it. Went down like a stone 'e did.'

Bob went quiet for a moment, then in a muffled voice said: 'So, I'll swing if they catch me. I'll be safe here, and when we go abroad, they'll never find me.' Bob hoicked and then spat. David was glad he wasn't in the bed next to him.

'Shut up and get down to it,' Serjeant Mills shouted from his cubicle. The room fell silent.

David's blanket felt rough and he scratched at his neck. It was so cold he was still wearing his shirt and trousers. He tossed and turned on the hard board, barely cushioned by the straw palliasse. He thought of Emily. He'd only been at the barracks a day and was already looking forward to his first leave when he could stand before her in his uniform, if they were ever given one, and maybe she would love him as much as she did her brother Ernest, and Franklin, God rest his soul.

Chapter 20

Thursday, 12th November 1914

Rope

At the sound of the reveille, David shifted into consciousness. The bugle's notes rang around the parade ground and bounced off the walls. He lay for a moment, listening to the grunts of the men around him as they left sleep behind and reluctantly left their beds. Convinced he had only been asleep for about an hour, and that the bugler had got it all wrong, he screwed his eyes shut and wished he could do the same with his ears.

'Jump to it!' Serjeant Mills shouted. David rolled from his own palliasse onto the cold floor.

'Come on, come on!' Serjeant Mills marched back up the room. 'Stand by your beds.'

David scrambled to his feet and looked around. Even though the men were a raggedy, unshaven lot with loose shirts and braces hanging in low loops, ostensibly they presented a reasonably tight unit. David relaxed when he noticed that Serjeant Mills didn't suppress a smile as he called the roll.

With a piece of dry bread, David wiped the last of the bacon fat from his tin plate and threw it to the white dog that waddled between tables, scrounging for every morsel it could. Breakfast was a much quieter affair than the night before's supper, until orders were shouted. David gulped down the last of his strong, lukewarm tea and made his way outside along with the others, who were slapping the tops of their arms to keep warm. The dog followed them out onto the parade ground, where David lined up with the rest of his platoon.

''Ten-shun!' Corporal Green shouted, his breath streaming before him like a smokestack on a steam engine. The simultaneous clicking of forty pairs of heels acknowledged the command and the men stood to attention. The white dog walked across the drill square and sat facing, and in front of, the platoon.

'Officer approaching.' The men turned towards Second Lieutenant Harvey, who was crossing the quadrangle.

'Eyes front!' Corporal Green called out. Looking forward, all eyes fell on the dog, who stood up and wagged its tail.

Second Lieutenant Harvey leaned down and patted the animal.

'Sit, Patch.' The dog obeyed, never taking its eyes off the junior officer.

'Stand the men at ease, Corporal,' Second Lieutenant Harvey ordered.

'Platoon, stand... at ease!'

David moved his left foot over and gripped one hand in the other behind his back, just as Serjeant Mills had shown them.

Second Lieutenant Harvey inspected his men. David thought he looked about his own age, with a strong chest and kind face. The dog followed him as if it was tied to his leg. Robert Harvey returned to face his men and told them who their officers were, what training they would have, that the rest of the battalion was in Luton and that they would join them when the order was given. Until then they would be trained into fit fighting men.

Corporal Green brought them to attention again. Second Lieutenant Harvey saluted and left them in the hands of Serjeant Mills for some physical training. David watched the dog look up at its master and then amble across the yard towards the warm barrack room, away from any physical training.

Serjeant Mills soon had them bending and stretching, doing press-ups and running on the spot until sweat trickled down their spines and soaked their shirts. After a morning's exercise, the afternoon was spent queuing, once again, outside the quartermaster's stores with the rest of the company. By sundown two hundred and forty men had been given khaki trousers and puttees, plus tunics and caps with brass Leicester Tiger badges on. They were also given shirts, vests, socks and pants, and much of the sizes were guessed, but boots were measured. They were told to 'bleedin' well look after 'em', as the uniforms had 'taken a month of Sundays to get here.'

Back in their barrack room they began to dress like soldiers.

'How the fuck do you put these on?' Bob Swann was spouting expletives as he tried to get his puttees right.

'Buggered if I know.' David was trying to roll his own around his leg, but it was proving a mystery to him too. He noticed that George Oswin had managed to wrap his quite well, but Ray Kirkby's were up to his thighs. George walked over to help, and as he moved, his roll began to gape until it flopped around his ankles.

'Bugger!' George sat on the floor and tried again.

Although it would probably take them another week to master the puttees, when Serjeant Mills strode in to call the roll, they were all dressed in khaki, and looking more like professional soldiers than the raw recruits of the day before.

Each day brought with it a new discipline. They would spend the entire time learning words of command, how to salute, left-turn, right-turn, about-turn. When the day came for them to learn marching, Serjeant Mills brought out his pace stick, which reminded David of the compasses he had used when measuring leather patterns; the clicking room was already becoming a distant memory. Serjeant Mills told them the distance for each pace in marching time and used the stick to demonstrate, flicking it deftly for each man as they took turns to keep their strides the correct length. When it was David's turn, he tried to keep to the correct pace but was always out of step when he arrived at the end of the parade ground.

'Do it again, and get it right this time!' Serjeant Mills called at each failed attempt. Finally, after covering the ground twenty times, he did get it right. The corporal led the cheering and David proudly marched back into line. Corporal Green burst out laughing when Serjeant Mills readjusted the pace stick to what it should have been throughout David's incorrect pacing. The men were helpless, George Oswin was doubled over and Ray wiped his eyes; even Swanny was laughing. The serjeant grinned, raised one eyebrow, and snapped the stick closed. David knew his face must be red, both from marching and embarrassment.

By sundown they were all able to correctly relate the length of each step to the distance they moved their feet, even David. Corporal Green brought the platoon to attention, and after roll call they were told to 'Fall out!' The bells of St Mary de Castro told them it was dinnertime, and they staggered towards the canteen, most of them swearing and cursing about their day's exercise, especially those who, like David, had been subjected to a serjeant's practical joke.

'You're not fuckin' fit,' Corporal Green told them when they passed him at the entrance to the mess hall. 'But believe you me, you will be by the time we've finished with you!'

'Pass a ciggie.' Harry Hamson held his hand out to David. The packet had only five left in it, and after putting one between his own lips, David threw another to Harry and held out the packet to Ray.

'No, ta, I don't smoke.'

For a moment, David studied Ray's pale face, then closed the pack and pushed it back into his pocket before lighting up.

Supper had been similar to that of the night before, but with a different stodgy pudding. There was no pianist this time and 'The Tigers' sat in groups, smoking and drinking strong, sweet tea.

'What was prison like?' Ray asked Bob Swann.

'What do you want to know that for?'

'Well, you said this isn't like prison. Is it worse?'

Bob's hollow laugh sprayed them with the tea he had just swigged. He placed his tin mug on the table and then, as soulless as a hawk claiming its kill, he seized Ray's collar and pulled the young man's pallid face towards his own. Harry pushed his chair back and David stood up too. The rest of the men in the canteen paid little attention to the scuffle and carried on drinking their tea.

Ray's eyes were wide and bulging as he choked in Bob's grip.

'Leave him be.' David leaned forward, his face close to Bob's ear.

'Or what?'

'Or you'll be in bother again and you might end up being found out.' Knowing he had struck a chord, David backed off and sat down. Bob loosened his grip, allowing Ray to pull away.

They sat in silence for a while, and then Ray, after straightening his collar, spoke: 'Before I joined up, I worked at the Turk's Head.'

'The pub opposite the prison?' George Partridge asked.

'Yes, that's the one. Well, the landlord used to tell tales of when they'd rent out their attic rooms so folks could see the public hangings.'

'When were that?' George Oswin was open-mouthed.

'Oh, ages ago, they ain't hung anybody outside the gates for about fifty years.'

David looked at Bob, but his expression was empty.

'They didn't hang the women there though, and some of the others made money renting out their attic to see them dangle.' Ray was animated.

'Where did they hang the women then?' George encouraged Ray to tell them more.

'The governor, I think his name were Musson, wanted the women hanging on their own scaffold, so they were taken to Infirmary Square. The landlord of the Turk's Head had an arrangement with the hangman and used to buy the rope from him, and then he'd cut it up and sell it to folks as souvenirs. There are still some bits at the pub now. Made my skin crawl they did when I seen 'em.'

'Well?' David asked Bob.

'Well, what?'

'What is it like inside "The Big House"?'

Bob leaned back in his chair and held out his hand. David reluctantly gave him another cigarette.

'It were fuckin' awful. I were locked in this tiny cell an' all I 'ad were a metal bed and a filthy blanket. When I were in there, I 'ad an iron manacle round my ankle and they only took it off for an hour a day so I could walk round the yard with the other Scotch caps.[6] I had a tin bucket to piss and shit in, and that were only emptied when it were full, and even then I had to wait till it were my hour outside.'

'What were you in for?' Harry Hamson asked.

'Poachin''

'Poachin'? You were treated like that for poachin'?' David shook his head.

'Everybody's treated the same, but some for longer.'

'And some until they go quietly to the scaffold,' Ray added.

Bob took a long drag on his cigarette and blew the smoke into Ray's face.

'If you think they go quietly, you can think again.' Bob rolled the cigarette between his lips as he spoke, his voice a growl. Ray sat back.

'Just afore I were released, some bloke were hung for killin' his baby in Western Park after he'd been taking laudanum. His screams made my blood run cold. From the minute the key went into the lock of his cell door, he started to beg and plead with 'em. I covered my ears, but I couldn't block out his caterwaulin'. I could still 'ere 'im bawlin' when 'e were out in the yard. And do you know what the worst thing was?' The cigarette hung from his bottom lip. The Syston men sitting near to Bob shook their heads. No one spoke.

'The worst thing was the quietness after they let the trapdoor down and his neck snapped.' They sat in silence

---

6. Scotch cap was a nickname given to prisoners, which began in Victorian times when they had to wear a leather hood called a Scotch cap to conceal their identity and ensure they could not communicate with each other when they were not in their cells.

until Bob took a last drag on his cigarette and threw it to the floor.

'Well, Swanny,' David said to Bob, 'you'll never have to hear anything like that again now that you're here with us.' The others nodded their agreement. George Oswin patted Bob on his shoulder and Ray held out his hand to David.

'Can I have that cigarette now please?'

Chapter 21

Friday, 20th November 1914

Training

'Another day in the park for us, boys.' Ray was always joking about their routine, which was becoming increasingly boring. They marched along Braunstone Gate and folks cheered and waved as they passed. Soldiers of the Royal Horse Artillery also trotted by on their mounts, heading towards the Filbert Street recreation ground to carry out their training.

The soldiers of the 2/4th Leicesters were smartly turned out, although David still found the tightness of his puttees uncomfortable. When marching, he no longer kicked the man in front or misjudged the pace; their section was a much more disciplined unit.

In Western Park, Drummer Archie Phillips beat out time and they marched up and down, their boots making dark tracks in the frosted grass. Second Lieutenant Harvey marched with them and his white dog waddled beside him. David thought that it was looking fatter than ever as it struggled to keep pace with its master.

By mid-morning, although the soldiers' breath still formed visible clouds, they had all warmed up and David was pleased that his legs no longer ached after drill. His shirt felt tight across his chest though. He would need to see if he could get a bigger size when there was a uniform delivery.

The dog had stopped marching.

Second Lieutenant Harvey nodded to Serjeant Mills. The serjeant shouted across the park:

'Squad... halt. About... turn. By the left... quick march!'

Their speed increased with the beat of Archie's drum and Serjeant Mills hurried them along.

'At the double, left-right, left-right, left right, lef' right, lef' right.' They reached the far edge of the park, turned and made their way back along the dark tracks. Each time they reached, and climbed, the slope at the top end of Western Park, Serjeant Mills turned them around and sent them back again. Drummer Phillips was struggling to keep up. After some time, they were brought to a halt on the crest of the rise.

'Stand... easy.' Corporal Green instructed. The park was silent except for a loud whining. David could just see Robert Harvey kneeling under a tree, and beside him, lying on a bed of half-decomposed leaves, was the dog.

Corporal Green ordered his section to fall out and they slid back down the incline. The whole platoon sat down in groups, each man perching on his backpack. Serjeant Mills and Corporal Green remained standing, positioned between the platoon and their officer.

The dog howled. The men were becoming restless. It was almost lunchtime.

'It's only a fuckin' dog.' Bob Swann spat.

'But it's the liuetenant's dog,' Ray said.

'I don't know why he don't shoot the bloody thing an' put it out of its misery.'

'Because it ain't bad,' Ray told them.

'What's it makin' a fuckin' noise like that for then?' Bob kicked at the ground.

'Coz it's droppin' its pups.' Ray was grinning.

'Bloody 'ell, you've got good eyesight.' David screwed up his eyes, trying to see the same as Ray, who was laughing.

'What's so fuckin' funny?' Bob stood up.

'Sit down,' David told him.

'Well,' Ray said, chuckling, 'we all thought the lieutenant's dog was a fat lad, but it's a bitch full o' pups.'

'No wonder it was always hungry.' David started laughing too.

Bob Swann looked away.

'Shoot the fucker, I say.'

'An' I say shut the fuck up.' David was on his feet, and so was Bob. The men around them fell silent.

'Right you lot, fall in,' Corporal Green shouted as he strode towards them.

Bob stuck his chin out towards David and narrowed his eyes.

'Piss off,' David hissed, and heaved his backpack onto his shoulders, all set to march back to barracks.

Corporal Green's section joined the others in the platoon and they stood ready in four straight lines. Corporal Green gave his command:

'By the left... quick march!'

The dog, too, was on its feet and managed to keep up, close by her master's heels.

Back at the parade ground, Serjeant Mills dismissed the men and they ran towards the canteen, hungry after the morning's marching. David stood for a moment and watched the dog go into a barrack room, followed by Second

Lieutenant Harvey, whose tunic was bulging and stained with blood from the morning's event.

'Not like that!' Serjeant Mills walked among the platoon. The men had been issued with rifles and were being instructed on how to hold them properly.

'Now then, Private.' Serjeant Mills stood beside David. 'Start with your balance controlled.' He pointed to David's boots. 'Feet well apart.'

David moved his left foot out.

'Grip your rifle; firm, like as you'd cuddle a girl.'

The rifle was almost as heavy as any girl too, David thought, and he felt the sinews of his arm muscles tighten as he tried to hold his Lee Enfield steady. He hadn't expected it to weigh as much as it did. The men in the platoon stood in four lines, their rifles dipping as the soldiers grew weary. The serjeant lifted his own rifle with just his right arm and held it straight. He pulled the trigger; a bullet flew across the parade ground and into a pile of sandbags. He grinned and turned back to the platoon.

'Hold them straight,' Serjeant Mills yelled. He was smiling as he watched the men struggling to hold up their heavy weapons using both arms.

The following days were spent learning the names of the different parts of their rifles and how to clean and care for them. They learnt how to 'Present... arms' and 'Slope... arms'. David thought that most of the time it was as if the drill serjeant was speaking in code.

'Now then you 'orrible lot,' Corporal Green addressed his section, 'Fix... bayonets!'

The men were holding shiny blades in one hand and their rifles, with their butts resting on the ground, in the other.

Along with the rest, David tried to put the two together, but, as with all things in the army, there was a correct way to do this, and they were not doing it.

'For Christ's sake,' Corporal Green bawled, 'take the handle of the bayonet in your left hand and push the muzzle of the rifle forward, sharp like. Eyes... right!' The men looked confused. The corporal marched along the section as the men tried to fix their bayonets whilst at the same time, turning their heads to the right. On reaching David, who was at the end of the line, Corporal Green pushed his face forward and shouted: 'Eyes... left!' David turned his head to the left, and so did all the others in the line.

'Not you lot, just him – the end man.'

Blank faces followed the corporal as he moved in front of them. 'Look lively. Draw it upwards, elbows down. Press it home to the catch. And stand up straight!'

'You!' Corporal Green pointed his bayonet at David. 'When I say "fix" you take three paces forward and you don't step back until all bayonets are fixed. Have you got that?'

'Yes, Corporal.' But David didn't really have any idea.

'Unfix... bayonets.' The men just stared at their weapons. Corporal Green carried on with his instruction:

'Mother o' God, you're like a load o' blind badgers. Keep your heels together, put the rifle between your knees... careful like... I don't want to be taking anyone to the infirmary before you've even left the country.' The men placed their rifles between their knees. 'Now, grasp the handle with your right hand and put your left thumb on the bolt spring.' He watched as they fumbled for the spring. 'Now, draw the rifle into your body with your knees, like you would a pretty girl, and press the spring. Raise the bayonet about an inch. Eyes... left.'

By the end of the day, only four out of the ten men in the section didn't have cuts on their hands. They had learnt to fix and unfix their bayonets as well as put them into scabbards whilst facing this way and then that, taking time from David at one end of the row, and George Oswin, the other end man.

That night, the muscles in David's shoulders and arms ached as if he had been in a brawl. Despite the cold, sleep came easily, his Lee Enfield within three paces of his bed.

'Mother o' God, it isn't a sack o' straw, 'tis the bloody Hun!' Corporal Green, watched by Second Lieutenant Harvey, was directing David's section in using their bayonets to dispatch *the bloody Hun*. All morning, they had been running towards sacks of straw with yellow circles painted onto the hessian – run forward, thrust the bayonet, twist it, pull it out, move on.

David ran towards a straw-filled sack that was hanging from a wooden frame; he aimed at the yellow circle and pushed his rifle forward, felt the blade cut into the straw, and pulled it out.

'Twist it, man, for God's sake, twist it. If you don't twist when it's inside Jerry, it won't bloody do for 'im and come out clean.'

David doubted it would *come out clean* if it had been in Jerry's guts. He ran back to the end of the line and waited his turn for the next assault on the sacks. Bob Swann was standing in front of him, face flushed, and David noticed that Swanny's hands were shaking. He followed Bob's gaze to the six fat sacks of straw hanging from their gibbets.

'All right, Swanny?' David asked.

Bob turned and his body relaxed.

'Yes.' He almost smiled. 'Let me at the fuckin' Hun.'

When it was Ray's turn, he ran forward and lunged, almost missing the sack when Corporal Green pulled it aside.

'Kill him or he'll fuckin' kill you,' the corporal bawled.

Second Lieutenant Harvey had left the training ground.[7]

Tuesday, 1st December 1914

A day closer to Christmas and rifle training moved to the firing range. About fifty yards ahead, there was a line of shapes cut from boards. Each resembled a German soldier, complete with the outline of a spiked helmet, and they were pitted with old bullet holes.

Corporal Green marched up and down his section calling out instructions.

'Fire! Not like that! To the left. For God's sake, right a bit.'

David was lying belly down on the frosted ground with his Lee Enfield resting on a straw bale. His rifle was heavy, his arms ached and his shirtsleeves were tight around his solid biceps.

'Mother o' God, aim straight, 'tis the bloody Hun!'

'He's said it again!' Ray muttered through gritted teeth; he was lying next to David and appeared irritated by Corporal Green's favourite description of any target they were to aim at. The shape Ray had been firing at had been precisely hit with every pull of the trigger. The holes, in what represented the Hun's chest and knees, didn't grow, and they simply allowed Ray's bullet to pass through on its accurate flight path.

7. A corporal would never swear in the presence of an officer.

David closed one eye and took aim. He squeezed the trigger and the rifle kicked into his shoulder.

'Get them brought closer,' Second Lieutenant Harvey told his serjeant, 'except for that one.' He pointed to Ray's target. 'Push that one back.'

David was grateful for a few minutes respite whilst the targets were repositioned and he could rub his sore shoulder. Ray, however, didn't seem troubled by the recoil from his rifle, his slender frame now appearing more muscular.

Targets were repositioned and they resumed.

After days of practice, observers were brought in and targets gradually pushed back to five hundred yards. Fire discipline was learnt, and observed, and very soon every man in the section could load his rifle, commence firing and cease firing, on command. They could also fire twelve well-aimed shots in one minute.

Ray's target, however, was always placed further away than the others and was peppered with fewer bullet holes, each round repeatedly finding exactly the same objective.

'Kirkby!' Corporal Green shouted as Ray fired his last bullet through the hole in the centre of his target's head.

Robert Harvey was standing beside Corporal Green, close to Ray's feet. He was holding field binoculars and wore a satisfied smile.

'Yes, Corporal.' Ray jumped up.

'This way.' Second Lieutenant Harvey turned and strode away.

'Well go on man, get a move on,' Corporal Green bawled.

'Yes, Corporal.' Ray saluted and ran after Harvey. David watched him go and then returned to firing at the distant targets.

Chapter 22

Thursday, 24th December 1914

Leave

David pushed his head down into a bitter north wind, grateful for the overcoat he had finally been issued. His haversack was heavy, but he had become used to carrying such a weight and it was no hardship any more. The silver crescent moon, surrounded by a million bright stars, smiled down on him as he trudged along the dark streets. He pushed against the gate and it creaked open in welcome. His steps quickened. When he reached the front door he paused, taking in the familiarity of the old house. Reaching for the doorknob, he heard footsteps approaching and turned to look back down the path. A young man wearing a high-domed hat with a wide brim hurried towards him. David grinned and put his arm across his stepbrother's shoulder.

'Dave! It's good to see you. How long are you home for? Does Mother know?'

'Hey, steady on.' David laughed at Sid's exuberance. 'Where have you been in your Scout's uniform at this time of night?'

'Collecting playing cards.'

'What do you want playing cards for?'

'We're helping the police to collect them for the wounded.' Sid's teeth began to chatter.

'Come on, let's go inside and get you warmed up.' David pushed the door open and warm air wrapped around them.

'Look who's here,' Sid called out as he shrugged off his coat and hung up his hat. Their mother appeared from the kitchen, sleeves rolled up to her elbows, flour on her cheeks.

'David!' She looked tired. 'Oh, it's good to see you, and on Christmas Eve an' all. How long are you home for?'

David put his haversack down carefully onto the flagstone floor and hugged his mother.

'Take your coat off, or aren't you stopping?' she teased.

'Oh, I'm stoppin' all right – I've got six days' leave.'

'You'll be here for Christmas then. That's grand. Come and sit yourself down by the fire and I'll make some tea.'

David hung his overcoat on a peg and put his cap on top. He smiled, feeling proud of the badge that showed a fearless brass tiger with its paw raised, as if it was offering it in greeting. With great care, he lifted the haversack and followed his mother into the kitchen.

The normally dimly lit room was bright, the gas mantle helped by two paraffin lamps. David watched his mother as she poured boiling water onto fresh leaves, pushed a tray of mince pies into the oven and then turned her attention to an ox tongue, which she had already cooked and pressed. The back door swung open and Henry appeared, accompanied by the smell of burning. He was holding two of Sydney's plucked chickens by their feet, pinfeathers all singed away. Dropping the birds onto the table, he stepped towards David and slapped his back.

'Dave! I didn't know you were coming home.'

'Neither did I until yesterday.'

'You look... well, bigger.' David flexed his muscles and grinned at Henry, who was studying him with his good eye.

'Do you want me to gut them for you, Mam?' David nodded towards the birds. Their heads were hanging over the edge of the table, feathers still attached above their plucked necks.

'What's that noise?' Sydney was looking around.

'What kind of noise?' Mary asked him.

'Like a baby crying.'

'Don't be daft,' she said, as she finished slicing the tongue and handed the knife to David. 'There ain't no babies here.'

'Ah,' said David, 'that'll be...' Before he could finish, the back door opened and Emily came in clutching a paper bag.

'What did you manage to get, love?' Mary asked, but Emily didn't answer. She put the bag down and rushed over to David.

'David! You're back. Oh it's going to be a good Christmas.' Emily's cheeks were flushed. 'We'll have the whole family here.' Then her voice flattened and she looked over towards the fireplace and the photograph that stood on the mantelpiece. 'Except for Ernest.'

David felt a rising wave of jealousy.

'And Charles,' Mary added. Peering into the paper bag she said: 'Oh good, Emily, you've brought oranges and chestnuts.'

'There it is again!' Sydney insisted, looking round. David began to laugh.

'What's so funny?' Sydney looked puzzled.

David put the knife down and walked over to his haversack.

'It's moving!' Emily shrieked.

David knelt beside his bag and undid the straps, then he reached inside, and when he pulled his hand out he was holding a tiny black-and-white animal that was wriggling and whimpering.

'It's a kitten!' Henry looked dumbfounded.

'Put your glasses on.' Emily pushed Henry aside. 'It's a puppy!' She clapped her hands together. 'He's adorable, and so tiny.'

'He's only a few weeks old,' David told them. He took Emily's hands and gently put the writhing pup into them. 'And he's all yours,' he said to her. 'Happy Christmas, Emily.'

David knew he'd played his ace; Emily was radiant, and he was sure that if Mam hadn't been there she would have kissed him. Then a dark thought struck him. 'You'll have to leave it here though, you won't be able to take it to Bushby.'

Emily smiled, then threw her head back and laughed. The laughter was infectious; his mother joined in, and then Henry and Sydney. David was mystified, but couldn't help himself as he began to laugh with them. Emily caught her breath and put her hand on David's arm.

'Why do you think I'm here and not fulfilling my duties as a domestic servant?' She wobbled her head, mockingly.

'Have you been sacked?'

'No. I've left their employ.'

'But?' David was puzzled.

'I'm working for the Post Office instead. This war ain't so bad after all. Lots of men have gone and joined up, so there's good work for women now, and with all the post to and from the front line, I'll be kept busy, and I'll be doing my bit.'

'Well, at least I won't have to bike all the way to Bushby in this weather.' David was smiling.

'You'd 'ave a job, lad.' Alf had come in and was pulling his threadbare overcoat from his muscular shoulders.

'Good evening, Father.' David shook Alf's hand. 'Why would I have a job?'

Alf pulled a pipe from his pocket and reached for his tobacco. 'You ain't got a bike no more. It's gone to the military,' he said.

David's mouth fell open. 'How am I supposed to get about?'

'It's all right,' his mother reassured him, lifting a tray of pies from the oven, 'we've one bike between us. We'll manage. Now, get them birds gutted and that pup can have their lights for its supper.'

David lifted the knife and took a sharpening stone from the table-drawer; he honed the blade to a razor-edged sharpness and swiftly chopped the two heads from limp necks and then separated clawed feet from singed legs. He teased Emily by pulling on the white tendons that were protruding from the severed feet, causing the toes to twitch in a macabre dance. He took one of the hens and slit its body from the end of its breastbone to the parson's nose and then pushed his hand into the still-warm carcass. He slid his fingers under the membrane, separating it from the breastbone and with a swift pull drew the entrails from the first bird, and then did the same with the second. His mother took the hearts, gizzards, necks and livers to make gravy and David chopped up the lungs and dropped them onto an old dish for the puppy.

Looking forward to a cheerful family Christmas, everyone except David and Emily eventually went to bed. Emily sat on the hearthrug with the puppy curled up in her lap, fast asleep.

'What are you going to call him?' David asked. He was sitting opposite her on one of the hard kitchen chairs.

'I don't know.' Emily looked thoughtful. 'Where did you get him?'

'The lieutenant's dog had four pups and I asked if I could have one.'

'Is he nice?'

'Who?'

'Your lieutenant, of course.'

David looked down at the sleeping pup. 'Yes he is. He's a gentleman.'

'What's his name?'

'Second Lieutenant Robert Harvey, but we call him Lieutenant Rob when he can't hear us.'

'Then I shall call him Robbie.'

David chuckled and Emily laughed with him, then, very gently, so that she didn't wake Robbie, she put her puppy onto a scarf that she had placed in a wicker shopping basket and put it within the warmth of the range.

The kitchen was quiet. The table had been set for breakfast with a large pork pie in the centre and a dish of brown sauce beside it.

'Let's go and sing carols at the church service.' Emily took David's hands and pulled to get him to stand up.

'But we normally go to chapel on Christmas morning,' David protested.

'But if we go tonight, we don't have to go in the morning and can stay here whilst the others go.'

'Just you and me?'

'Well of course just you and me.'

David held Emily's hands tightly and looked into her eyes; she looked so happy.

'Emily, I want to ask you something.'

But she was on her way out of the kitchen and reaching for her coat.

'Come on, we'll be late; the bells are ringing already,' she called to him.

David was taken aback by the amount of hand shaking and nodding of heads by the congregation. They were treating him like a hero, even though he hadn't ventured any further than Leicester. Every man wearing a uniform was greeted in a similar way, and in the candlelight their cap badges glistened. Hard pews welcomed khaki-clad soldiers.

Reverend Avery finished his sermon and reminded the congregation of the next day's services and, in particular, the '8.00 p.m. intercessions for our soldiers and sailors'.

Heads were bowed in prayer and David knelt beside Emily. The reverend spoke, and the congregation responded in low voices that rumbled through the pews. At the next response, David leaned towards Emily, his lips almost touching her ear; he could smell the fresh scent of soap in her hair.

'Will you marry me?' he whispered.

Emily's kneeling body jolted slightly, but she didn't look up. She remained with her head bowed low, eyes firmly closed until prayers were over. When they stood to sing the last carol, she turned towards him and gave a slight smile before returning to her hymn book.

'Merry Christmas!' Villagers were calling to one another as they left St Peter and St Paul's and handshakes of encouragement were once again bestowed on those in uniform. The north wind swept through the streets, chilling everyone who was still out, and Emily slipped her arm through David's as they made their way back.

The house was silent; it felt snug compared to the outdoor chill. Henry and Sydney were sound asleep upstairs, as were his parents. David lifted a blanket that had been left on the back of a kitchen chair. He assumed it was for him and took it into the front room; Emily would have taken his and Charlie's old bedroom. He returned to the warmth of the kitchen where the puppy was sleeping soundly in its basket under the gas mantle that was affording a low light to the room. The smell of baking still hung in the air and the grate in the range glowed orange, keeping it warm and ready for Christmas Day.

Emily checked on the puppy and turned to face David, who was standing between her and the door to the staircase. Neither had spoken on the way home from church, and they stood in awkward silence; the only sound was from the popping and hissing of the gaslight.

David stepped forward and took Emily's hands. She didn't pull away but stepped in closer, her eyes looking up into his. He released one small, soft hand and gently cupped her chin in his rough one. They drew together and he tilted her head back slightly. She closed her eyes. He pulled her towards him and felt her other hand slide around his back. He kissed her, gently at first, scarcely brushing his lips against hers, then she began to kiss him back. Their arms laced around each other and he felt her breasts soft against his well-muscled chest. His hands slid down to her hips and he pulled her closer still. He kissed her neck, the flesh above her collar and the dip at the base of her throat. The puppy whimpered. Emily pulled away and walked over to check the basket, then turned out the gas lamp. She took David's hand and he followed her upstairs, both treading quietly in the still of the night.

Christmas dinner had been a triumph for Mary; the whole family had enjoyed eating Sydney's hens as well as an enormous plum pudding; one or two had even found a silver sixpence in their portion. Whattoff and Kathy left for the afternoon carol service, leaving the rest of the family to enjoy their day off together. A holly branch in the corner of the front room was decorated with wooden figures carved by Alf – a new one added each year. This Christmas he had carved a toy soldier and named it Ernest. Candles flickered, throwing long shadows around their front room. Roasting chestnuts popped their skins open and everyone took a turn at picking one up without getting burned. Henry and Sydney were playing cards, Alf was dozing, Mary was admiring her new brooch, a dainty piece set in stones of the purple, green and white of the suffragettes, and Emily played with the puppy as it chased chestnut shells. David was reading the parish magazine; on the inside page he saw his name in a list of those serving in His Majesty's Forces. He then turned to 'Extracts from our own Soldiers' Letters'. He chuckled when he read one from Driver F Mann: *We are on duty one day in four and the other days we go drilling or route marching* – David could identify with what was said – *We have plenty to eat and are very comfortable in our billets. I am just getting into the way of getting up early, but it does take some doing. We do not stop up late at night.* 'Well,' David thought, 'that sounds all right'. He read a few more, then his attention was drawn to one by Fred Butler from the No. 8 General Hospital, Rouen: *I have been wounded in the right hand by shrapnel. We had it hot last week. Pals killed all around me, but, thank God, I escaped. It was terrible. We mowed the Germans down as fast as they came up.* David shivered.

'Throw another log on the fire if you're cold,' his mother told him. As he stood up and lifted some wood he heard the back door slam. David made to see who it was, but before he reached the front-room door it flew open and in rushed a khaki-clad soldier sporting a Tiger badge on his cap.

'Ernest!' Emily cried out and jumped to her feet. She rushed over to her brother and flung her arms around his neck.

'Eee, lad, it's good to see you. Come and sit down.' His mother patted the chair that David had just risen from. Ernest took off his overcoat and cap and settled himself. Emily sat close by, at his feet. David knew that the rest of Christmas would now revolve around Ernest. He fought to curb his rising jealousy, especially when he watched Emily doting on her brother's every word.

'Leicester Fosse are playing Derby County on Monday,' David said to Ernest. 'You coming?'

'I'd like to, but I have to be at the station for nine o'clock on Sunday morning to take the train to Luton, and then back to France.'

'I didn't know you were in France, I thought you were in Ireland. Why didn't you say in your letters?' Emily asked.

'You know I can't tell you where I am when I write, and if I did it would just be crossed out.'

'Why are you home then?' David asked. He was sitting on a hard chair that he'd fetched from the kitchen.

'We've got to take back sandbags, shovels and trench pumps. It ain't half wet, and so bloomin' cold. Trenches are flooded and some chaps got frostbite. When they pulled their socks off some of their toes came away an' all.'

'Oh,' Emily's hand flew to her throat, 'are they all right?'

'They've been sent home to recover.'

'Where is your battalion then?' David quizzed Ernest further.

'We've just taken over the front-line trenches in Bois-Grenier, near Armentières.'

'Seen any Mademoiselles then?'

'Oh yes, plenty.' Ernest laughed and ruffled Emily's hair. Then he fell silent and stared into the fire. David sensed that Ernest was reflecting on whatever was happening in France.

'I'll come to the game,' Sydney said. David nodded and smiled, satisfied that Ernest wouldn't be around for very long.

'That's the second match in a row that we've lost six–nil,' David grumbled as he and Sydney left the ground. 'We haven't won owt since the beginning of November.'

'That's because all our best players have joined up,' Sydney offered by way of explanation.

'So have Derby's. I mean, losing seven–two against Leeds. I could play better than they do.' David was probably right. He was looking forward to playing for his regiment in France or Belgium.

Football always made David hungry, whether he was playing or watching, and he was looking forward to one of his mother's hearty meals. There was a fire blazing in the front room and David stood before it, warming his hands. Robbie waddled in, his feet slipping on the floorboards, and began biting and tugging at David's turn-ups. David scooped the puppy up and held it in front of him.

'What are you doing? Put him down,' Emily scolded.

'He was biting my leg,' David joked. He put the pup down on the hearthrug and pushed the door to. He pulled Emily towards him and kissed her, running his hands up and down her back. She pushed her full breasts against his well-muscled chest and his kisses became more urgent.

'Emily!' Mam called from the kitchen.

'Yes, Mother.'

'Will you butter some bread please?'

Emily made to move towards the door, but David caught her hand.

'You haven't given me an answer yet, Em, and I have to go back tomorrow.'

Emily giggled and pulled her hand free.

'I'll tell you in the morning,' she teased, 'and then you'll know whether or not you'll have to ask Father's permission.'

Chapter 23

Saturday, 9th January 1915

Pageant

David was standing easy with his battalion in a thronged Victoria Park. The 4th Leicesters were assembled alongside those training with Kitchener's New Army from the Glen Parva Barracks. There was hardly a spare inch of ground. Police officers, Boy Scouts, contingents from the Church Lads' Brigades, about a thousand lads from the Leicester Junior Training Corps and two thousand members of the Leicester Citizens' Training League spread themselves across every available space.

'Ay-up,' Harry Hamson whispered, 'I think we're off.' David watched Second Lieutenant Harvey and Corporal Green move towards them.

'Atten... shun!' The stamping of boots onto hard ground thundered across the park. 'By the left, Quick... march.'

David and his men proudly led the procession, and the gathering moved off at 1.45 p.m. precisely. A lorry was waiting on the Welford Road, and as the soldiers approached, it began to move off. David saw that it was carrying two captured German machine guns and was escorted by eight wounded men from the 2nd Battalion, marching with fixed bayonets, and led by a serjeant. David had read about the night-attack a month earlier by the 2nd Battalion on the German trenches when the guns had been seized. He considered himself honoured to be accompanying the brave men who had been part of that action. Old men, young men, women and children lined the streets, cheering as they passed, and David felt the warm glow of almost being heroic ripple through his veins.

The lorry stopped outside the rugby football ground and massed bands played as the parade dispersed inside. Corporal Green instructed his men to fall out. David and the others mingled with the ever-growing crowd who were preparing to listen to speeches before the promised rugby match against a team of Canadians commenced.

The Lord Lieutenant spoke first. It was difficult to hear his words over the roar of the gathering. David managed to catch: 'Until Germany is utterly crushed, and the menace of its armed forces destroyed, England will go on fighting.' Well-wishers patted David on the back throughout, almost knocking him over in their enthusiasm. '... rely on Leicester men of both borough and county to take their full share of this grave responsibility,' the Lord Lieutenant continued. Bob Swann stayed close to David. He had his cap pulled down over his eyes, his overcoat collar turned up and a woollen scarf wrapped around his face; only his red nose was visible.

'Police behind us,' David muttered. He saw Bob's body stiffen and then he bent down as if tying his bootlace. Bob looked up at David, who was laughing at the dread he had induced. Bob stood up.

'Bastard!' he hissed, and then his eyes twinkled. David knew he was grinning under his scarf.

They watched as the mayor took to the platform, his chain of office glinting in the weak afternoon sunlight. He puffed out his chest and swept his gaze over the masses. When he spoke, his voice was forceful, but it cracked occasionally on emphasising the righteousness of the cause. He concluded with the sentiment that everyone should be 'looking forward to the future with hope and confidence.' Polite applause rippled around the ground, then the mayor called out: 'Are we downhearted?'

David's voice joined over twenty thousand others who shouted back:

'No!'

'We are not,' the mayor continued. 'We need to be patient, steadfast, and confident, fully assured that we shall emerge from the conflict not only triumphant but with a truer exemplification of those qualities by which alone a nation can be great.'

The mayor left the platform to loud cheers and David rubbed his hands together as everyone made ready for the match. The enthusiastic applause for Tom Crumbie and his team was also extended to the Canadian side as they ran out onto the pitch.

By half-time Leicester was in command of the game. Tom Crumbie spoke to the supporting crowd, encouraging those who hadn't enlisted to do so. He announced that there would be no more matches on the ground until the war was over – it was to be used for military training. The crowd quieted down as they awaited the second half, and David felt a hand press his forearm.

'Emily!' He took her hands in his and squeezed them. 'What are you doing here?'

'The same as everyone else I should think.' She laughed and then said: 'I've something for you.'

'And what might that be?' David slipped his arm around her waist and whispered into her ear, smelling her familiar soap as his nose brushed against her hair.

'This.' She pulled a paper rectangle from her pocket and pressed it into his hand. He turned it over and grinned at the photograph of Emily smiling back at him. He squeezed her more tightly.

'Thank you,' he said, wishing that he could kiss her.

'That's so as you won't forget what I look like.'

Her words were lost in the roars of the crowd as the game resumed, and Leicester stormed on, scoring a try within the first minute. David noticed Emily give a puzzled look towards Swanny, who was still standing close by, but neither of them said anything. A hush fell over the ground as the Canadians' fullback prepared to convert a try.

'I'm going back now,' Emily whispered. David nodded, his eyes never leaving the kicker. Another roar from the crowd filled the ground as the ball soared between the goalposts. David turned, but Emily was gone.

'Thank God that's over.' Swanny sat down opposite David in the canteen.

'It were a grand day, though.' David was tucking in to his dinner – meat with onions and gravy, cabbage and mashed potatoes. The smell of boiled cabbage hung in the air.

'Might 'ave been for you. I had to keep that bloody scarf round me face all the time. I were glad to get back 'ere.'

'Grand result!' George Oswin joined in.

'Yeah, we were too good for them Johnny Canucks. Forty-two points to six, eh?' Harry Hamson sprayed potato as he spoke.

'Were that your sister I saw at the match?' George Partridge asked David.

'She ain't me sister.' David finished his meal and lit a cigarette.

'But it were your Emily, weren't it?' George insisted.

'Yes, she were there. Did your girl show up then?'

'Annie couldn't come. Besides, she don't like rugby, or crowds.'

'What do you mean, your girl?' Harry had finished his meal and wiped his mouth with the back of his hand. 'Emily ain't your girl, she's your sister.'

'No she ain't!' David slammed his fist down onto the table.

Swanny looked from David to George Partridge. 'Shut up,' he growled, 'and get on with the game.' He threw a battered deck of cards onto the table. David nodded his acknowledgement.

The games had gone mostly in Swanny's favour, but the last one hadn't been won, and at a farthing a game, the pot was a wealthy one.

'I'm out.' Harry Hamson threw his cards onto the upturned deck.

'Nine, ten, Jack, to the board,' George Oswin offered. George Partridge threw in.

'What you got then?' Swanny rolled his cigarette between his lips and waited for David to turn over his first hand.

'Prial of threes,' David said as he turned over the cards.

Swanny shook his head and turned his over.

'Jack, queen, king, basher, and spades at that. What's your backhand?'

David grinned and very slowly turned over an ace of spades, then a two of spades and a two of hearts.

'Bugger! You jammy sod.' Swanny turned over his backhand to reveal the two of diamonds and two of clubs, but with a ten of hearts.

David scooped up the pot and tipped his winnings into his pocket.

'You won't be able to spend that in France – if we ever go,' George Oswin said, and tipped the dregs of his tea down his throat.

'Do you think Ray's there already?' Harry Hamson asked.

'Dunno.' David lit another cigarette. 'He might be, but I think we'd have known if any more Leicesters had gone.'

'It's getting a bit hotter now, ain't it?' George Oswin said. 'The Germans are getting closer. There was that air raid near Dover just afore Christmas, and now they've sunk one of our ships in the channel.'

'Which one?' David asked. He knew Charlie had signed up to join the navy but didn't know where he was.

'*Formidable*, I think it said.' George was a reliable reporter of any news and no one doubted him.

'Did we lose many?' David asked.

'They said about six-hundred and about a hundred and fifty survivors.'

'Bloody Jerrys. Let's get at 'em,' Swanny growled, a look of utter hatred in his eyes.

No one had seen Serjeant Mills come into the canteen and walk across to where Swanny was sitting.

'Private Swann!'

Swanny jumped to his feet.

'Yes, Serjeant.'

'Come with me.'

'Yes, Serjeant.' Swanny threw a puzzled look towards David, who shrugged.

The two men marched across the canteen towards the exit, and it was then that David saw two military police officers waiting by the door.

Chapter 24

Saturday, 16th January 2015

Colours

Emily put the last of the letters onto a pile ready for delivery. She shivered and pulled her cardigan closer around her.

'Oh Ernest, why don't you write?' she shouted to the pile of envelopes, which contained quite a number for the Reverend Avery from overseas. There was even one from Malta. It was difficult to read the addresses in the weak glow of the lamp.

She tipped more coal onto the fire that was beginning to come alive and throw warmth into the post office. A blackened kettle, which was balancing on a trivet over the flames, would soon begin to sing, and she would make tea for herself and Gertie, whenever she turned up.

Emily stepped out into the street to see if the milk cart was near and was almost blown over by a forceful westerly wind. The pounding of feet joined the sound of heavy rain, which had been lashing down since midnight, and Gertie Oswin ran into the post office. Emily followed her inside. The church clock was striking eight as Gertie pulled off her hat and shook it over Robbie, who was lying on the rug in front of the fire, which hissed as fat droplets fell into the grate.

'I ain't goin' out again in that,' Gertie said. 'The delivery will have to wait.'

'But it's your turn,' Emily told her, 'and don't shake your wet things all over the place.'

Gertie patted Robbie and sat down on a low stool beside the fire. Presently, the clopping of hooves outside told them that the milk cart had arrived. Emily looked at Gertie, who didn't move.

'I'll go then,' Emily said, and grabbed her coat. When she returned Gertie was holding her head in her hands.

'Is anything the matter?' Emily asked, and hung up her wet overcoat.

Gertie shook her head.

'I can see there is, what is it?'

'Oh, Em, I've done summat stupid and now I don't know what to do.'

Emily made tea and pushed the hot cup into Gertie's hands.

'Come on, it can't be that bad. You can tell me, can't you?'

'You'll never forgive me.'

Emily sat down on a hard chair. She glanced up at the clock: twenty past eight. Customers usually started to arrive around half past, but the bad weather might keep then away a little longer. The dark clouds outside sent murky shadows into the room, and even though the sun had risen, Emily kept the lamp lit in an attempt to dispel the gloom.

'Come on, afore folks start coming in. Tell me, Gertie.'

'I can't.'

'It's a man, isn't it?' Emily asked.

Gertie nodded.

'What have you done then? Given him a white feather? Given him a kiss?'

'Worse than that.' Gertie looked ashamed.

'You haven't!' Emily said, but felt no conviction to cast judgement considering her time spent with David.

Gertie nodded.

'Well, it's not the end of the world. Who was it?'

'I can't say.'

'Will you see him again?'

'He's gone.'

'Gone? Where?'

'France.'

'Oh, I see. It's a soldier, ain't it?'

Gertie nodded again.

'Don't be upset, Gertie, he'll be back.'

'You don't understand.' Tears had begun to roll down Gertie's cheeks.

'Yes, I do. He's told you he loves you and he'll miss you and wanted to remember you so you went with him. You should have waited until you were wed, but there's no harm done really. I won't tell, and whoever you do marry, if it isn't him, need never know.'

Gertie stood up and threw back her head. 'I think I'm having his child!' she cried.

Emily almost dropped her teacup. 'Oh my God, you stupid girl. Who was it?'

Gertie shook her head.

'Tell me.'

Gertie straightened her shoulders and pursed her lips. She looked Emily in the eye and blurted out the answer: 'Ernest!'

Emily stood up and reached for the counter to steady herself.

'No. It can't have been. He wouldn't.'

'Well he did. We did. And I haven't heard anything from him since.'

The bell above the door chimed and the day's first customer entered.

Gertie left with the deliveries sooner than she had originally intended, although the rain had eased a little, but Emily found it difficult to concentrate. Her thoughts slid back to Christmas Eve and David making love to her whilst the family slept. She closed her eyes and prayed that she too hadn't caught. She loved David and was wearing his ring, but please God, don't let me be so, she thought. The door opened and Emily's heart sank when Mrs Walker-Holmes came in.

'Is there anything for me?' the older woman demanded.

'I'll just check.' Emily knew there wasn't but went through all the items for collection once more. Mrs Walker-Holmes was surveying the cramped office, her eyes peering into every corner as she waited.

'Sorry, nothing today, although the post has already left, so there may be a letter waiting for you when you get home.' Emily made an effort to be polite.

'I can't see any recruitment posters in here.'

Emily didn't answer.

'They're all off now so more young men will be needed. Is that brother of yours going?'

'Ernest is already serving at the front,' Emily said in response.

'Not him, the other one you went to church with at Christmas.'

'Oh, you mean David. He's not my brother, he's my fiancé,' Emily said, and smiled at her stepmother's adversary.

Mrs Walker-Holmes's mouth fell open, and for an extraordinary moment, she was speechless. Then she found her voice:

'Don't be ridiculous. He's your brother... it's immoral... it's illegal.'

'He's my stepbrother!' Emily countered. 'We are not related. We love each other and we are getting married.'

Mrs Walker-Holmes's eyes were blazing. 'Well, now he's being sent to the front, you may not get that chance, and that might be a good thing.'

'How dare you speak like that!' Emily was incensed. 'And what do you mean now that he's being sent to the front?'

'Didn't you know? The train is leaving this afternoon to take our boys to France, and not before time.' Mrs Walker-Holmes looked smug.

'Wh-what time?' Emily felt a wave of alarm rising.

'As I said, the train leaves this afternoon. I shan't be going – my son is at Officers' Training about to get his commission, and I've work to do here.'

'How do you know all this? I haven't heard anything.'

'I thought everyone knew.' Mrs Walker-Holmes was smirking. 'Now, get some posters up in here, and that' – she pointed to Robbie – 'should be given to the regiment so it can be put to work.'

'Goodbye, Mrs Walker-Holmes,' was Emily's reply.

Emily felt hope slide out of her as she saw the omnibus pulling away. She stamped her foot and cold water splashed up her leg.

'Damn you, Gertie!' Emily's voice caught in her throat and she pushed the back of her gloved hand over her mouth. Because of that strumpet she had missed the bus into Leicester. If Gertie had been back from the deliveries five minutes earlier Emily would have made it to the bus stop in time. By means of apology Gertie had agreed to take Robbie home, which was of little consolation now. Emily squared her shoulders and began to stride out down the

Leicester Road. It would be ages before another omnibus came by, but at least she would be well on the way. She walked as briskly as she could, and although the rain had eased, the roads held deep puddles and her feet slipped and slid, hindering her progress.

David marched with his company out of Magazine Square and they formed a line. Corporal Green stood them at ease and they waited. One by one the other companies marched through the gates and took up their positions in quarter column. The men were all dressed in Field Service Marching Order and each carried one hundred rounds of ammunition, which didn't hinder them as it would have done two months earlier when they were fresh from the factories.

'Thank Christ we're going at last,' Bob Swann said to David as he leaned on his rifle.

'No more close calls for you then,' David replied. 'I thought you were for it when they came to get you last week.'

'So did I. I thought me brother'd turned up at home, but he ain't, so the sooner I get to France the safer I'll be. They wanted to question me as to the whereabouts of my brother.'

'Bill? Why, what's he done?'

'Nowt, you duffer. I'm supposed to be Bill, ain't I? They're lookin' for Bob.'

'You're a bloody liar, Swanny, and you should face up to your crime, but you'll soon be facing Jerry, so I suppose that'll have to do.'

Suddenly there was a sharp word of command:

'Fix... bayonets!' The men deftly secured their blades.

'Present... arms!' Arms were brought to the 'present'.

The Colours were raised and the Colour Party began to march past. David watched the silk of the King's Colours held high on the left of the party, and the Regimental Colours on the right, departing down Newarke Street towards St Martin's Church where they would be laid up whilst the battalion was away on active service. The Tiger in the centre of the Regimental Colours appeared to be waving a greeting as it passed, or was it farewell?

David looked about him and he could tell that every soldier was experiencing the same thrill as he was. He felt his stomach clench and his chest expand as if his whole body was being inflated with the pride of allegiance. There was something sacred and thrilling about those rich pieces of silk that caused a lump to rise in his throat, and his chin to lift slightly as he watched the Colour Party disappear from view. It was as if the Colours embodied their souls.

When the Colour Party returned, David and the battalion moved off. The streets were full and as they passed the Leicestershire Club, he saw Mr Garner standing on the steps with a group of employers, who were wishing their lads 'Godspeed'. David had never really understood what that meant, but he smiled up at them, accepting their good wishes. At the end of Belvoir Street, and all along Granby Street, the crowd was dense and folks cheered: mothers calling goodbye to their sons, sweethearts to their lovers, and friends to their pals. Children were held for their fathers to give a parting kiss, and strangers called out encouragement. David saw George Partridge's Annie run out to him and plant a kiss on his cheek, but there was no sign of Emily.

When they arrived at Midland Station it was bustling with activity; a military band played and the mood was festive. Second Lieutenant Harvey led his men onto the platform and David saw a shabby woman rush up to the officer and place her dirty hand on his arm.

'I'll be here waiting for ya when ya get back, ma duck,' she said in a gravelly voice, and she grinned, showing a few blackened teeth. Rob Harvey smiled congenially and waved his men, who were laughing helplessly, towards the waiting train. Doors were swung open and the men clambered aboard, throwing their equipment onto overhead racks, unbuttoning their collars and jostling for a widow seat. David hesitated and looked along the length of the platform. The last few goodbyes were being trapped under the station roof, sucking the oxygen from the smoky air. And the band played on.

'What's up, Dave?' George Oswin dropped down onto the seat next to David, who shook his head but said nothing. Doors slammed and the train wheezed and grunted as khaki-clad men continued to squeeze in and pile the racks high with their packs. An air of excited anticipation filled the carriages, and when the battalion was entrained and the final door banged to, the guard waved his green flag and a whistle signalled their departure. Soldiers leaned out of door-windows and others pressed their faces against the carriages' sooty glass, bidding farewell to their flag-waving loved ones who lined the platform. A resounding cheer rattled the ironwork as the click-clack of turning wheels increased and they steamed out of the station into the Leicestershire countryside. Cows looked up as the train sped past, as if offering their valediction to the departing soldiers. David sat in silence. An overwhelming sadness enveloped him and he didn't trust himself to speak. He took a cigarette from George and said a silent prayer, wondering what would be the end of it all.

Emily hurried along the damp roads, praying that another omnibus would soon arrive. She knew it was futile to try to walk the distance to the Midland Station, but the buses did run more frequently on Saturdays and she clung to the hope that another would be along at any minute. A horse and cart passed her, heading in the opposite direction, but nothing was going towards town.

'Please, God, don't let me be too late,' she prayed, knowing in her heart that she might not get there in time.

Emily trudged on, making as much haste as she could down the muddy lanes. Presently, she heard a regular thudding of hooves on the softened earth. As they drew nearer she turned; it was the horse and cart that had passed her earlier.

'Whoa,' the driver called to his mud-splattered horse that slid to a halt beside Emily. 'Where are you going, lass? It ain't fit to be out walkin' tha knows.'

'Oh, Mr Gamble.' Emily recognised the driver now. He was the joiner who was also the village undertaker. 'I'm trying to get to Midland Station before the soldiers leave for France this afternoon. I missed the bus and I don't know when the next one will come, if there is a next one.'

'Jump up then.' Tom Gamble held out his hand and pulled Emily up onto the cart's damp, narrow seat. 'I can take you as far as Shady Lane.'

'That would be most helpful, thank you.' Tom shared his blanket with Emily, throwing it over her knees, and slapped the reins on his horse's back. They clattered down winding country lanes and Emily told Tom all about David and Mrs Walker-Holmes's comments.

'Well it won't be easy. Some folks'll try and make trouble for you,' Tom told her, 'but it's nobody's business but your own.' He slapped the reins again as an encouragement for the horse to go faster.

At last an omnibus arrived at Shady Lane and trundled along into the town. Emily alighted when it stopped close by the station and quickened her pace again. She could hear a band playing, its music muted by the damp weather, and made haste, exhilarated that she would be able to see David before he left. She pushed her way onto the platform against a crowd of people who were moving back towards the London Road. Then her excitement curdled to sour disappointment, as, to her utmost horror, she watched the train chug its way round the bend and out of sight. Hot tears flowed down her cheeks and her heart sank in sadness and despair. The man she loved had slipped away and she hadn't been there; she had let him down. The band stopped playing and its members marched from the platform. Emily stood alone, staring down the track, and as the daylight faded she slipped into a listless torpor, weighed down with absolute wretchedness.

Emily was exhausted. She pushed open the back door and hung up her damp coat.

'Come and sit by the fire,' Mary told her. 'You look starved through.' Emily sat and held her hands out towards the grate. Robbie was in his favoured position on the hearthrug and Emily patted his head; she accepted a cup of tea from her stepmother.

I see Gertie brought him home,' Emily said. 'At least she managed to get that right.' Mary gave her a quizzical look then took an envelope from the sideboard.

'There's a letter for you. It's from the barracks.'

Emily ripped open the military-issue envelope and pored over David's words.

'When did this come?'

'Gertie brought it this morning.'

'But she can't have. I sorted the post myself this morning.'

'Well, she did. I thought it was strange that it came here when you were at the post office.'

'Damn Gertie!'

'Well, it wasn't really her fault if you didn't see it,' Mary offered in Gertie's defence.

'You don't know what she's done,' Emily wailed, still regarding Ernest as blameless. Mary looked even more puzzled but didn't press Emily. Instead, she asked to see David's letter. Emily handed it to her and for the second time that day cried as Mary read her son's words telling them that he would be leaving for Luton that afternoon and then to France shortly afterwards.

'Why didn't she bring the letter to me sooner?' Emily said, still blaming Gertie.

'She wouldn't have known what was in the letter,' Mary tried to reason.

'Well, if she'd been quicker with the post I could have caught the bus and I wouldn't have missed him. He'll think I don't care. He'll think I don't love him.'

'Then you must write to him and tell him why you weren't there to see him off. And get yourself a backbone, girl – it's no use crying when things go wrong. There's going to be some hard times ahead of us and you're not to be so thin-skinned.'

Chapter 25

Friday, 19th February 1915

Inspection

When they arrived at Luton, the battalion was billeted in different places around the town. Some were in private homes, some in schools, and David, with his section, was in a chapel. Training was even more rigorous than it had been at the barracks and once again the men needed larger uniforms.

Shortly after arriving in Luton, David received a letter. Post from home was always a frantic and happy event and something the soldiers welcomed with cheerful anticipation.

'You seem in better spirits today,' Swanny said.

David waved the envelope. 'Letter from home.'

'Well it seems to have put you in a better mood than you have been of late.'

'It's from Emily; she didn't miss seeing us off on purpose. She didn't get my letter and got to the station too late. She was heartbroken.'

Swanny slapped David on his back. 'Come on, we're doin' range firing today.'

They marched the short distance to the firing range, each man having a hundred rounds of ammunition. When they strode onto the field, David saw a young man running towards them, his grin wider than a piano keyboard. There was much back-slapping and shaking of hands.

'Ray!' David greeted him. 'Good to see you.'

'You an' all, mate. Won't be long now – the whole division is here, and loads of stuff has been sent from the ordnance.'

'About bloody time,' Swanny said. 'What the hell's that?' He was pointing to Ray's rifle. Ray laughed.

'Ain't you never seen a telescopic sight afore?'

'How come you get one o' them and we just get ordinary sights?' Swanny looked resentful. Ray leaned in towards them and patted the side of his nose with his forefinger.

'Sniping,' he whispered.

David raised his eyebrows. 'I'll stick wi' you then,' he told Ray, and they moved towards the straw bales. All that morning they lay on the soggy ground firing at distant targets until their arms ached.

Emily thanked the milkman, who was now bringing post into the village as well. Inside the post office she had already made up the fire and filled the kettle so that she could concentrate on sorting out the first delivery of the day. The bag was heavy and she tipped it out onto the counter. It wasn't her turn to take the letters around the village, but Gertie, as usual, was late. Emily's stomach clenched and her heart fluttered when she saw a letter for her, the address written in David's neat, swirling handwriting. She pressed it against where she thought her heart should be and then slid it into her apron pocket before continuing to sort the morning post into piles, one for each street. There was a letter for Gertie, too. Emily recognised the writing and felt vexed that Ernest should write to Gertie and not her. Perhaps Gertie had written telling him of her condition. She propped the letter up above the key shelf next to the cellar door and carried on dividing up the delivery. Her stomach cramped, but instead of feeling bothered by it, she felt relief. It was, at least, reassurance that she wasn't in a similar situation to Gertie.

Emily was drinking her second cup of tea when Gertie finally arrived, and she was about to give her a telling off when she noticed how pale her friend looked.

'Are you all right?'

'Been throwing up ever since I got out of bed,' Gertie told her. Emily pursed her lips and offered her a cup of tea. Gertie swayed and Emily pulled a chair over.

'Sit down,' Emily said. 'I'll do the deliveries today, you're in no fit state.' Gertie nodded. Emily put on her hat and coat and then slung the postbag across her shoulders. 'There's a letter for you,' Emily called on her way out. Gertie looked up. 'It's on the key shelf,' Emily told her, omitting to say who it was from, and closed the door behind her.

The biggest bundle of letters was for Reverend Avery, and Emily took those to the vicarage first. After she had delivered to Church Street, her bag was lighter and she stopped and took her own letter from her pinafore pocket. She had been going to wait until later to open it, but she wanted to read David's words and imagine his voice as if he were speaking them to her.

> *Dear Emily,*
>
> *Thank you for your letter. I hope you are well. We are in fine spirits here. We first went to Luton, but only stayed there three days before we were drafted to Bishop's Stortford to complete our training. After being there a few weeks, I was again sent to Luton,*

where I am now, for a week of range firing before returning to Bishop's Stortford to receive our orders that we are going abroad on active service. The lads are looking forward to it, but I would rather be with you, my dearest. We have been told that on Friday we shall be inspected before leaving by somebody very important. What do you think to that then? I hope you like the photo. It was took outside the hut I used to be in. It was only took for fun. Write soon, my love. Fondest love, from David. x x x

'Oh my word,' thought Emily. 'What a lot of to-ing and fro-ing.' She pulled the photograph from the envelope and laughed out loud. Fifteen Leicester lads, nine standing and six seated, including David, looked relaxed. David had his arms and legs crossed and his cap pulled down over his eyes. The soldier in the middle of the row had turned his head just as the photograph was taken and his face was a blur. The two George's stood together: George Oswin, handsome and smiling, George Partridge, ears protruding and with a cigarette in his hand.[8]

'You look happy.' A small woman wearing a thick but threadbare coat had stopped by and was smiling at Emily.

'Oh, hello, Mrs Pollard. Yes, I've had a letter from David.'

Emma Pollard nodded, and then laid a gloved hand on Emily's arm.

'You know they're cankin' about you, don't you?'[9]

Emily squared her shoulders and tilted her chin upwards. 'What do you mean?' she asked.

'Well, you and David being engaged. Folk are sayin' it ain't right.'

---

8. See photograph 3, page 320.

9. Canking is a Leicester term for gossip that originated from Tudor times when women went to a washhouse on Cank Street to catch up with the stories and scandal of Leicester.

'And what about you? What do you say?' Emily challenged her. Mrs Pollard smiled. She still lived in the small cottage on Paddock Row between the one where Mary had brought up her young family before marrying Emily's father and the one where George Partridge's family lived. She had always made a fuss of David and had often looked after him whilst Mary had gone to work cleaning other people's houses.

'I say it ain't nobody's business but yours,' Emma Pollard told her. 'Anyroad, he ain't your proper brother like your Ernest, is he? So I can't see nowt wrong.'

'Thank you, Mrs Pollard. I think I know where the catty comments are coming from.' Both women nodded in unspoken agreement. Emily showed the photograph to Mrs Pollard, who also laughed at the Leicester lads whilst pointing to David, then George Partridge and Harry Hamson.

'I have a letter for you, too.' Emily pulled a now familiar censored-and-stamped envelope from her bag and handed it to Mrs Pollard, who dropped her own shopping bag onto the ground and, hands trembling, ripped open the letter.

'It's from Percy!' Mrs Pollard's plump cheeks glowed as her smile pushed them upwards. 'He's in the Guards, you know.' Slightly ashamedly, she held out the letter to Emily. 'Will you read it for me?'

'Of course.' Emily was delighted to help her new-found ally and took the letter. 'He wrote this on the twenty-sixth of December,' Emily said, quickly looking over Percy's words, and then she read them aloud to his mother:

'I am still alive and kicking. We were in the trenches Christmas Eve and Christmas Day. It was very cold. The Germans kept sending us a few greetings. We saw an Indian soldier do a brave deed. He went right out in the front of our trenches to get one of our wounded in. He carried him about twenty yards

and then he got wounded. Then another Indian went out and brought them both safely in. It was worth a V.C. It did not seem much like Christmas. We did not have any Christmas carols but instead the sound of the German guns. We had some Christmas pudding on Christmas night. It went down all right! Percy.'

Mrs Pollard thanked Emily, who then pressed on with her other deliveries, which didn't take very long and she was soon on her way back again. When she reached the post office the kettle was boiling, although the fire had died down and was in need of making up. Gertie was nowhere to be seen.

'Where is she now?' Emily said aloud. The cellar door was open and a cold draught penetrated the room. 'She must have gone to fetch more coal,' Emily thought, but there was no noise from the cellar. Ernest's letter remained unopened on the shelf.

'Hurry up, Gertie, the fire's almost out,' Emily called, and she pushed the door to a little.

Tom Gamble came in and asked for some sealing wax and string.

'On your own today?'

'No, Gertie's down the cellar getting some coal.'

'She weren't 'ere when I called ten minutes ago,' he said. Emily frowned and went over to the cellar door. She pulled it open and called Gertie again. Then she saw her – Gertie lay at the foot of the cellar steps, her leg at an impossible angle, and she was as still as the coal that lay beneath her.

David had been busy fixing soles, hammering tacks into heels and replacing burst stitching. He had accumulated a bountiful supply of cigarettes in exchange for cobbling. After roll call, the order came for the men to get tidied up as they were going to be inspected by someone of great importance. Everyone's bayonets were highly polished, their uniforms were clean with no buttons missing and their boots, now in good order, shone to match the bayonets.

The men washed quickly and readied themselves. At the command they fell into line and began to march from their huts in Bishop's Stortford to Great Hallingbury Park. David was used to gauging distance by time and he thought they had marched for about five miles when the road led them into a large park where other battalions of the North Midland Division were already assembled. He could see that the Sherwood Foresters and South Staffords were there. The Leicesters fell into columns and waited. Nothing seemed to be happening and David shifted his weight from one foot to the other to prevent pins and needles from running up and down his legs. It was about two hours before a contingent of staff cars arrived and the officers got out and mounted their horses, which were waiting for them.

'Bloody hell,' David heard Swanny mutter under his breath, and as he stared ahead he recognised the King on one of the horses and the royal standard-bearer on a smaller horse that followed. King George rode towards the assembled ranks, nodding to the officers, and then he reined in his horse to inspect the men. They marched past him, eight abreast. The senior officers saluted and the men in the ranks turned their heads towards their sovereign. A band played a rousing tune, guns and bayonets glistened, officers looked forceful and the transport rumbled along. At the rear the mules in their new harnesses grinned as they went by. The men had been told that when the inspection was complete they were to place their caps on the points of their bayonets and wave and cheer.

The King steadied his horse and saluted and hundreds of soldiers waved and shouted: 'Hip, hip hooray!' The King's horse was startled and reared; His Majesty only just managed to stay in the saddle to accept the resounding greeting.

Their journey back to the barracks took just under two hours, with everyone pushing their heads down against the biting wind. Back at base, the hungry men piled into the mess hut, where they were given green soup – which they assumed, though on no obvious evidence, was either pea or cabbage – followed by bully beef with turnips. There was also suet pudding and hot, sweet tea.

David took his mug of tea outside and lit a cigarette. He could see the communications office from where he was standing and there seemed to be quite a lot of activity going on inside. He finished his drink and pinched out his cigarette. As he turned to go back inside, he heard a commotion. He rushed in and saw Swanny standing over Ray, who was sprawled on the floor with blood pouring from his mouth.

Chapter 26

Friday, 26th February 1915

Mobilisation

David was wide awake and reveille hadn't even sounded. If he went to wash and shave before the rest of them woke up, he wouldn't have to jostle for a space. He made his way to get water from a pump in the small yard next to the latrines, where thick mud had frozen, making it slippery underfoot. Picking up a tin bucket, he began to work the handle up and down until fresh water flowed. He carried the pail back into the washroom and shaved as swiftly as he could. The razor stung his cheeks and the cold water was painful to his face and fingers. He smiled as he looked into the mirror on the washroom wall. His face was distorted by a crack that ran across it and his eyes appeared lopsided.

'What you got to laugh about?' Ray gave David a friendly thump on the shoulder and then poured some of the cold water into a basin. He still sported a black eye, although the split on his lip had almost healed.

'This mirror makes my face look funny,' David replied.

'It's not the mirror, you stupid sod,' Ray joked, and David thumped him back.

Ablutions over, the two men picked up their shaving kits and hurried across the cold yard back into their hut. Reveille had sounded and the other soldiers were stirring.

'Swanny still not back then?' Ray called as they were packing up their blankets.

'Nah, should be back soon though,' replied George Partridge. He then put more coal onto the tortoise stove in an attempt to warm the large barrack room. One blanket remained neatly folded at the end of its palliasse – Swanny's blanket. Bob Swann had been given field punishment number one for hitting Ray and putting him out of action on the firing range.

Less than a minute later, Serjeant Mills entered the room and the men all jumped to attention. It was almost as if he had been listening to the conversation; he instructed the two Georges to go and release Private Swann. He said no more than that and left again. David and Ray went and stood by the door to watch as Swanny was released. He had been tied spread-eagled on a wagon wheel for two hours, and it was so bitterly cold it would be a while before his circulation got going again. His two rescuers helped him back into the warm, and as he sat down on his palliasse, rubbing his numb limbs, David hunkered down next to him.

'You stupid sod, what did you go and hit him like that for?'

Bob Swann gave a swift sideways glance, his dark eyes meeting David's blue ones, and he then went back to rubbing his wrists.

'Well?' David pressed him. Bob stopped rubbing and looked David square on.

'He said he saw me at the riots when MacDonald was speaking in Leicester.'

David was silent for a moment. He bit down on his bottom lip, as if to aid concentration.

'But why hit him?'

'I said I weren't there, but he kept saying I was.'

'Why didn't you just walk away?'

Swanny sighed. 'I said if he didn't shut the fuck up, then I'd shut him up.'

David raised his eyebrows.

'Well, he said he definitely saw me, so I shut his mouth for him.'

'And his eye an' all by the look of him. You know he's not been allowed on the firing range, don't you?'

Swanny shrugged.

'Ray,' David called, 'come here.'

Ray looked dubious, and then strode over. David and Bob stood up.

'Shake!' David growled.

Bob Swann offered his hand and Ray took it.

David patted them both on the shoulder and they all moved off to line up with the others for a final medical check prior to their leaving for France.

Pay-books were made up and issued. All the men had been given new boots.

Serjeant Mills returned.

'Tomorrow,' the serjeant announced, 'is your lucky day. The War Office has commanded that we mobilise our troops – you are off to France.' Cheering rippled through the entire barracks and David thought it would probably be heard in the communications office and beyond. The exuberance died down when Serjeant Mills put a pile of War Office postcards onto a table and nodded towards them, saying simply, 'Send a few words home, lads.' Then his voice became stern as he commanded: 'Make sure you get a good night's sleep, as you all leave for Southampton docks at 0800 hours.' There was a scramble to get a postcard, or two, and when they were written the soldiers ran down the road to the nearest pillar box. Only the first arrivals were able to put their cards into the box, as it was soon overflowing. Gradually the pile of postcards grew, and when the postman came to make his collection the following morning he would have seen only the top half of the red pillar emerging from a stack of cards covered in a layer of white frost.

At last, everything was ready, and on Saturday, 27th February 1915, the battalion paraded, ready to leave Bishop's Stortford.

David stood with the rest of the men of the North Midland Division. They all carried their rifles and bayonets, one hundred rounds of ammunition and a haversack containing spare shirt, socks, vest, pants and anything else they could cram in. David had managed to fit in his shoe knife and pincers, and his tack hammer was wrapped in his spare vest. The cobbling he had been doing of late had proved lucrative, and he didn't want to miss out on any extra earnings. It was a damp, cold morning and David stamped his feet to warm them up as they waited near the railway station for everything to be loaded.

Everyone seemed happy to be leaving; pleased that their training was complete and was now going to be put to the test.

David felt a wave of pride and enthusiasm sweep through his veins, and he looked at Ray, who was grinning lopsidedly, his lip still appearing to give him some discomfort.

'What an honour for us, lads,' Ray said as they squeezed into a carriage.

'If you say so,' Swanny grumbled.

'You want to get out of here, don't you?' David asked.

'Too bloody right I do.'

Ray stepped up onto the seat, and speaking in a high-pitched tone, he pretended to imitate the voice of a high-ranking officer but sounded more like Mr Punch.

'Then it is an honour,' he declared, pointing upwards with his trigger finger, 'to be part of the first Territorial division to go to France and fight the Hun alongside the regulars. Remember this, chaps, it isn't only our standing that's at stake' – he paused and changed his accent to a more local dialect – 'it's the whole bleedin' Territorial Army's.'

Everyone in the carriage was laughing at Ray's mimickery, even Swanny.

'There's going to be some tough fightin' over there,' Harry Hamson said.

'Yeah,' George Partridge agreed, 'but just think how great it will be when we've beaten the bloody Boche and we come back to Leicester as heroes tellin' all them that haven't joined up what we think of them.'

The others in the carriage shouted out their agreement and, as the train rumbled out of the station, David watched another slide past in the opposite direction, bringing a contingent of blue-coated wounded back to Blighty.

Emily had left the deliveries for Brookside until last, and it was early afternoon by the time she had delivered all the postcards from serving soldiers to the villagers. She had put the ones to her and to Mary into her apron pocket for safe keeping and was grateful that theirs were dry and legible; some were damp and the writing distorted as if they had been left out in the open all night.

'Only me,' Emily called as she pushed open the door into the Oswin's house. The smell of boiled potatoes and damp clothes flowed over her as she entered, and Mrs Oswin called to her from the kitchen. Gertie's two youngest brothers were playing with some smooth stones under the table and the morning's washing was dangling from an airer that almost touched the ceiling. Emily had often wondered how on earth Mrs Oswin had managed to raise eleven healthy children, who were always polite and well turned out, in this house, which she thought must also have elastic walls. Emily handed over a postcard and a letter to Mrs Oswin, one from George and the other from John, his elder brother who was serving as a regular, just like Ernest.

'Will you take a cup of tea?' Mrs Oswin offered.

'Thank you, yes. May I see Gertie please, Mrs Oswin?'

'Ah, tek her one up an' all will ya? She's feelin' a lot better now – she'll be glad to see you.'

Emily climbed the stairs, a cup of tea in each hand.

'Only me,' she said again as she pushed the bedroom door open with her foot.

There was a fire in the grate and Gertie was sitting up in bed. The Oswin's house was always warm as there was a plentiful supply of coal from Mr Oswin's work. Emily handed one of the cups to Gertie. 'How are you feeling now?'

'Me leg's bleedin' killing me,' Gertie answered.

'You didn't half go a cropper. I thought you were... well, you know, dead.'

'I went dizzy when I were halfway down. Still, that won't happen no more, so that's one good thing as is come out on it.'

'What is?' Emily asked, then realised what Gertie meant and felt her colour rising as the heat filled her cheeks. 'Sorry. You've lost the baby haven't you?'

'Yes, but don't you say a word to Mam, she don't know – just thought I was having a bad month 'cause of the fall.'

Emily saw Ernest's letter on a little table beside Gertie's bed.

'What did Ernest say when you told him?'

'Never told him,' Gertie said, and sipped her tea.

Emily spoke about the exceptionally large delivery, mostly from the lads finally leaving for France, and said she hoped it wouldn't be long before Gertie was back helping her. She read out David's postcard, which simply said they were off to France and the next letter from him would be from abroad.

Saturday, 27th February 1915

This was it then – they were off to the Western Front and not one of them knew for sure if they would ever return to the country they loved and were fighting for. Volunteers all of them, but that's what you did, volunteer. No one wanted a white feather pushed through the letterbox of their home. None of them were cowards. When they were moved from Leicester to Luton they knew the time for their battalion to have its chance had come. They had been training for this day, hoping the war wouldn't end before they received their marching orders. They had enlisted to fight, and now that's exactly what they were going to do.

David thought about France and the state of the ground there. Would it be hard and unyielding, making their task of digging trenches an arduous one, or muddy and wet, so that the digging was easier but the living filthier? Were all the trenches dug already, and what did they really look like? He wondered if it was true that the rats were as big as rabbits and that he would have to eat the horses that had been killed in action. There was so much he didn't know about those foreign fields, but one thing he did know, he didn't want to die there. He shuddered and saw Ray turn to look at him and wink as if to say, 'We'll be all right, mate.'

The Leicester Boys finally arrived at Southampton just before sunset. The battalion was split into two and David went with his half to a rest camp where they slept in tents. The other half went to billets in schools and warehouses in the town. The officers were quartered in the *Flowers Hotel*, close to the docks. In the camp they were told to get some rest, as they would be embarking for Le Havre in two days' time: on Monday, 1st March.

David thought about his mother. He'd told her that he hadn't signed up to go abroad, but then they'd received the draft to make up the 1/4th Battalion, and he was on his way to France. She would not be pleased.

Chapter 27

Monday, 1st March 1915

Letters

The Southampton docks were packed with khaki. Hundreds of soldiers lined the quay standing shoulder to shoulder and stamping their feet, awaiting the order to embark. Two boats rocked in the swell of the swirling seawater and waves smacked against the harbour wall as each wave boiled over and spilt its spume. At ten o'clock the command finally came and eager men raced up the gangplanks and scrambled on board. Soldiers sat where they could, some on salt-encrusted wooden benches that had been fixed to the deck, others dropped their haversacks onto the floor and hunkered down on them. David stood by the taffrail and lit a cigarette. His eyes smarted from the smoke that was blown back into his face along with a salty sea mist. The *Queen Empress*[10] lurched and listed as the wind heightened its assault on the shore.

---

10. Private Adcock's diary, the officer's account and the official war diary all refer to the vessel as the Queen Empress although some other sources may refer to it as the Empress Queen.

'What's up, mate?' David turned to Swanny, who had staggered over to the railing and was clinging on as though his life depended on its safety.

'Bloody boats. I hate them.'

'Been on one before have you then?' David blew a stream of blue smoke into the wind; it blew back over Swanny, who glared at him and then dropped his forehead down onto the sea-soaked parapet and groaned.

The decks were crammed, but neither the *Queen Empress* nor the *City of Dunkirk* left the dock.

After about an hour, officers moved among their men calling into the howling wind, their orders carried away to sea. Clumsy soldiers were trying to stand up on the deck of the *Queen Empress*, swaying as if they were all drunk. When they heard the officers' commands they gradually staggered back towards the gangplanks and disembarked.

'Waste of bloody time that was,' Swanny grumbled.

'I thought you'd be pleased we don't have to sail on that rough sea.' David grinned and hitched his haversack onto his shoulder. Swanny didn't answer.

The march back to the rest camps was done at the double and with the wind behind them. They arrived at mid-day and poured into the mess tents.

'What the fuck's this?' Swanny complained, looking at an unrecognisable pile of meat smothered in watery gravy and served with lumpy mashed potato.

'Just be thankful you've got something warm to eat,' David told him, and spooned up some of the runny stew.

'Lose your breakfast over the side did you?' George Partridge asked. Swanny ignored him and finished his meal.

'I pity them poor buggers on the *Dunkirk*,' Ray said. 'They haven't come back and had to stay on board. They'll be sick as dogs.'

The next day the wind dropped, and in the afternoon the Leicesters marched back to the docks. The *City of Dunkirk* still hadn't sailed, and another boat, the *Golden Eagle*, had also anchored nearby. David and his battalion climbed the gangplank of the *Queen Empress* and settled down on deck once more.

Two staff officers counted the troops as they boarded the ships, and once more the decks filled with soldiers.

When darkness fell, the *Queen Empress* and *Golden Eagle* left the dock, accompanied by a torpedo boat destroyer; the cheering could probably be heard back at the rest camps. David hunkered down on his haversack and lit a cigarette.

'About bloody time.' Swanny blew out his cheeks and leaned back. Ray stood on a seat and, as he had on the train, conducted the men as if they were an orchestra.

'Let the Hun watch out, the 4th Leicesters are coming!' The men cheered even louder at his officer impersonation.

Through beams of searchlights they slipped down the Solent and into a calm channel, anticipating the adventure that lay ahead of them.

'Can I do the delivery today?' Gertie reached for her coat; although the sun was out, there was still a slight chill in the morning air.

'Perhaps tomorrow,' Emily told her.

'But it's always tomorrow. I'm fine now and I could do with some fresh air.'

'Tomorrow. I promise.' Emily put her hand on her friend's shoulder. 'Besides, if we get a shower you're not quick enough to dodge the spots.'

Gertie smiled – the smile of defeat.

'If it's a lighter load tomorrow, then you can do it,' Emily yielded, and swung the bulging sack across her shoulders to begin the day's deliveries. As usual, she headed for the Rectory, where a large proportion of the letters were destined. She rang the bell and pulled a fat bundle of letters addressed to the Reverend Avery from her postbag. Footsteps tapped on the flagstone floor and the door swung open. The curate, Reverend Evans, greeted her.

'Come, come.' He beckoned her inside.

Emily stepped over the threshold and waited to be asked into the study.

'Come, come,' Reverend Evans repeated, and ushered her into a room that held so many books they would be impossible to count; it was bathed in bright morning sunshine. Reverend Avery, who had been sitting at his desk, stood up when Emily entered the room.

'Good morning, my dear. And what have you for me today?'

'A grand delivery, Reverend,' she replied.

'Then please sit and I shall read them. Perhaps there may be some you can take on to relatives.' His smile was warm and Emily passed the letters to him. She had recognised the handwriting on one envelope and was thrilled that the vicar was going to share it with her. He methodically opened each one and laid them on top of each other, and then began reading.

> *'Our daily routine in the trenches: We are on lookout duty until daylight and then we start getting ready for breakfast at nine o'clock – bacon, bread and jam, etc. We then make our trench in good condition so that we do not have to stand in mud. In the afternoon we have a rest in our "dug out" in the trenches, and begin to get nicely rested, when over comes one of the enemy's artillery souvenirs, just to remind us that they have got a few left.'*

'Have you noted that?'

The curate completed his notes, nodded and rested his pencil.

'Would you take that to Mrs Simpson on Bath Street, please, Miss Wade? I believe she will be pleased to hear from George.' Emily took the letter and he moved on to the next one.

'Oh dear.'

Emily and the curate exchanged glances. The vicar continued reading:

> *'Just a line hoping you will do a little for me as I am fast in Germany. I was a member of the Church Lads' Brigade when I was at home and a good many boys I think are "Fighting the good fight" out here in this awful war. I should be glad if you could send me a parcel of groceries. C A Earl'*

'Please put him down for a six-shilling parcel to be sent.'

'Will that be through Lady Bective?' Reverend Evans asked. The vicar nodded and carried on. Emily wanted to ask who Lady Bective was but felt it rude to interrupt. Reverend Avery's eyes twinkled and his grin was broad. He read a short note from someone who simply signed himself: H. P.

> *'I like soldiering all right. They have been teaching us French. They call it Sunny Devon where we are, but I think it's Rainy Devon.'*

They gradually worked their way through the pile; the last letter was the one Emily had been waiting to hear:

> *'I received your parcel this morning, and was very much pleased to know that you are doing your utmost for the sailors and soldiers of the village. I hope that you get the amount for the alterations*

required for the schools. I know you will do your utmost to carry it through. E Wade.'

Reverend Evans laid down his pencil.

'Would you like to take that letter to Mr Wade?' Reverend Avery asked Emily.

'Oh, thank you, Reverend.' Emily took the letter and slipped it into her pocket. She said goodbye and made her way back into the village.

Emily had shown Ernest's letter to Gertie before taking it home to her father. There had also been one from Sydney, which Mary had left on the kitchen table.

Just a line saying I arrived quite safely. Please remember me to them all in the Church Lads' Brigade. Bill Pratt and me go to Church every Sunday morning. I am quite enjoying myself here – having the time of my life. I could not write before as I could not get any stamps. I have only 6d per week pocket money and 3d in the bank. We have good food here, so I ought to look well. If I do not, when I come home, it is not their fault.

Sydney, R. N. Barracks, Shotley.

Emily went into the front room. It had hardly been used since Christmas; only she and Henry were left now that Sydney had joined the navy. She had taken to reading and writing her letters in there, usually with Robbie lying at her feet. She opened an envelope bearing a foreign stamp and a photograph fell onto her lap when she pulled out the letter.[11]

A group of around twenty young men were standing in front of what could only be outside showers; she had heard about showers but had never seen one. 'How dreadful,' she thought, 'to have to wash out in the open where people could see you.' In front of the men was a bathtub, which

11. *See photograph 4, page 320.*

was filled with potatoes. She laughed to see George Oswin and George Partridge with potatoes in their hands; some of the other chaps, too, were holding them. Then she spotted David. His cap was, as usual, askew, and he was resting his chin on another's shoulder. They all looked happy and some were even in their shirtsleeves. One soldier had stood so far over that only half of him could be seen. 'What a shame,' she thought, 'he looks to be quite handsome,' what bit of him she could make out. She smoothed out David's letter and began to read.

Dear Emily,

We left for France going on a boat named the Queen Empress. Having a pretty good journey we landed at ~~Le Havre~~ on March 3rd where we marched to another rest camp on the top of a huge hill overlooking the sea, again being under canvas and staying there for a short period of six days. From there we marched to a railway depot and entrained in cattle trucks, 38 and 40 in each truck. The officers were in the carriages. We travelled like this for 24 hours up the country and alighted at a place named ~~Cassel~~. We slept there the night in a transport barn aside of the railway, the distance being 250 miles. We left the following day and was billeted in straw barns. The officers were in the farmhouses. It snowed and the barns were draughty, cold and damp. We saw some chaps from the Leicestershire Yeomanry; they have been here since Christmas and had plenty to say about the trenches.

Fondest love,
David x x x

Snow fell and life was bleak.

Dearest David,

I hope this postcard finds you well. I haven't heard from you in such a long time. We are all well and Henry has now enlisted, so you may see him.

With love from Emily x x x

David handed over his envelope – the field postcards had all run out and every letter had to be censored.

Dear Emily,

On ~~March 9th~~ we marched to ~~Strazeele~~ with the whole North Midland or 46th Division, a distance of 15 to 20 miles, ~~seeing aeroplanes and observation balloons on the way~~. We were received by ~~General Sir Horace Smith-Dorian~~ and he complimented us on the smart way in which the men marched, as the roads were so awfully bad. Our packs were crammed full with as much as we could carry. Everybody was tired out when we reached the town and our billets were farms again.

I have learnt some French – 'Estaminet' means the pub. We are being well fed and drinking lots of café o lay. My address is now B.E.F. France.

Last night we heard heavy firing.

Fondest Love. David x x x

The Battle at Neuve Chapelle had begun.

To my Dear Son at the Front,

I am longing to see your dear face. I am waiting patiently.

Your loving Mother. xxxx [12]

---

12. *See postcards page 323.*

The firing continued and the 1st/4th Leicestershire battalion was paraded in fighting order and told to be ready to move at an hour's notice.

Dear Emily,

We have moved to ~~Sailly sur la Lys~~, another long march on bad roads. At this place where we was put up there was a ~~15 inch Howitzer~~ that they called 'Grandmother' ~~and an armoured train chuffed up and down the track, firing at the Hun~~. There were also plenty of troops billeted in barns for two nights and we were ordered to 'stand to', for a ~~Battle at Neuve Chapelle~~. We then marched from ~~Sailly~~ to ~~Bac St. Maur~~ arriving on ~~March 14th~~ and then to ~~Steenwerck~~ on ~~March 16th~~. The barn where we sleep is made from wood and mud. It's draughty and there's not much straw for us to lie on. The lice are getting into our clothes and there are rats and mice. You wouldn't like it. The beams have got thick cobwebs hanging down and there are all sorts of farm implements lying about. But at least it gives us shelter from the cold wind. We have all been given goat-skin overcoats. They were smelly to begin with but we don't notice it now. We did some third-line trench digging, bayonet practice, and we practised throwing bombs with jam tins. We are having an altogether decent time here. We drew our first pay in France, which was 10 francs.

Fondest love. David x x x

Orders were received for the battalion to go to the trenches. On Friday, 26th March, the men marched to Armentières and, one company at a time, went into the trenches at Le Bizet for twenty-four hours to receive instructions from the 1st King's Own and the 2nd Essex Regiment.

Dear David,

I hope you like this little postcard (Mizpah) and that it finds you well.[13] *Mother has received a card from you and has sent you a cake. I have knitted you some socks.*

May the Lord watch and bless us both. Until we meet again.

With love from Emily x x x

They were taught that large periscopes were risky, how dangerous steel loopholes could be, and that smoke was a sniper's bidding.

Dear Emily,

I am sorry to have to tell you that we have had our first casualty, ~~Pte. Preston~~ was killed. I was on a fatigue party in some houses at the back of the line. The day we went in these trenches being ~~Palm Sunday, March 27th~~.

We moved again to a place in ~~Belgium named Dranouter~~, the date being ~~April 2nd~~ and again was billeted in barns (afterwards in bivouacs ~~on a big hill called Kemmel Hill~~). Here we took over our first line of trenches, having four days in and four out, regularly doing some good work in repairing them. The barn we first billeted at had been occupied by Germans. ~~We killed a German officer and buried him at the back of our line~~. We then had orders that we should be relieved by Kitchener's Army men. We took over a line of trenches in front of a wood, which was named ~~Sanctuary Wood (captured by the Canadians before we went up this part of the line~~). We weren't in these long before we took over a fresh line of trenches on ~~Hill 60,~~ having 18 days in and

13. See postcards page 324.

6 out. Our 6 days rest were in huts in a wood just behind ~~Dicks Bush~~, about 8 miles behind the firing line. I am having a good time.

I shall write again soon.

Fondest love from David xxx

> *'Men should only be in this trench 24 hours and then relieved. Ground all round is insanitary.'*
> War Diary, 4th Leicestershire Regiment.

Dear David,

I have wonderful news. Henry and Hilda were married on April 17th. He was allowed two days' leave and is now back at the training camp. She is getting quite bonny and Mother says she eats too many pies.

We have been told we can send parcels to prisoners of war, but no one can put a letter or anything written inside. We are going to get a list of things we can send from someone called Lady Bective, who is organising the sending of the parcels. How awful to be a prisoner in an enemy state. Gertie and I are collecting for them at the post office.

Rev. Evans has enlisted in the Welch Fusiliers and the Bishop has sent him his blessing and wished him a safe return to his work at home. His photograph was in the Daily Sketch!

Barrow Grammar School is forming its own cadet corps and Syston lads can join.

We are busy preparing for The Feast – there is going to be a soldiers' portrait gallery where photographs of all you lads will be on show – there are more than 200 of you.

I pray that you will come back to me safe and I miss you so much. Thank you for the photos so that I can remember what you look like.

God be with you every day.

With love from Emily x x x

Lieutenant Colonel R E Martin rode up to battalion headquarters on Kemmel Hill and, on 22nd May 1915, took over command of the 4th Leicesters.

Field Post Office, 5 June 1915
Passed by Censor No 404

3rd June 1915

Dear Emily,

I received your letter and will answer it in a few days as I am very busy at present. I hope you are quite well as I am.

With fondest love from

x x David x x

Far away, Ypres burned. On the one hundredth anniversary of the battle of Waterloo, 18th June 1915, the 4th Leicesters came out of the trenches they had made into the best on the Ypres Salient, and left the Messines Ridge.

Dear David,

What news! Henry and Hilda have had a baby boy and called him Ernest. Our Henry is a lad! He might not be able to see very well, but he had to have a shotgun wedding! He has been discharged from the 4th Leicesters on account of defective eyesight, so he is going back into the shoeing. He won't be joining you after all. Baby Ernest is being christened on the 26th September, just five months after their wedding. People in the village are tattling about them now, rather than us.

The Feast was a great success this year and nearly one hundred pounds was raised. The soldiers' portrait gallery only took 18s 6d, but the Hoopla made £1 8s 6d.

I shall send you a parcel next week.

With love from Emily Jane x x x

Chapter 28

Friday, 3rd September 1915

Trenches

'Christ! That was close.' The blast was still ringing in David's ears. 'Bugger. Forty-eight trench has been sausaged.' He wiped the sweat from his face with the back of his hand. 'It looks as if they've hit forty-seven and forty-two an' all. Ray, what can you see?'

Ray lifted a periscope and peered into the pitted abyss that passed for no man's land. He pushed the scope up and as far round as he could.

'Yep, forty-seven's definitely gone. Bugger, that's the communication trench.'

'What about forty-two?' David shouted above the deafening explosions.

'Can't quite see, but I think so.'

'Bloody hell, we're gettin' crumped.' Ray blew out a long smoky breath, which he must have been holding since the last shell had slammed into the earth and shook more sandbags into their trench. 'You'll be graftin' all night again.' He gave a mirthless, hollow laugh and returned to his periscope.

David began to lift the fallen bags. The Leicesters affected the best repairs they could, until another shell dislodged more. They all knew it would be a long night, repairing sandbag barricades only to see them demolished when the early morning shelling began again.

'Colonel! Colonel!' David turned to see a soldier running towards them – scared eyes showing white in a blackened face, tunic ripped and bloodstained. Colonel Martin dropped the bag he was about to lift and spun around. The soldier fell onto the duckboards. The colonel strode over to him and knelt down.

'You shouldn't be down 'ere, Colonel.' The soldier's voice was weak. 'It ain't safe.' Colonel Martin looked back over his shoulder and shouted:

'Get the stretcher-bearers in – now!'

'He's right, Colonel, you shouldn't be down here.' David had joined them and knelt beside the injured soldier. 'Hey, Smithy' – he could recognise Private Tom Smith now he was closer – 'what happened to you?'

'Never mind me, Bursie's gone.'

'What do you mean gone?' Although David knew the answer already – Private Edward Bursnall had been in forty-eight trench.

'Blown to fuckin' bits he was. God, I never want to see owt like that again.'

'Well,' Colonel Martin's high-pitched voice cut in above the constant noise, 'with a bit of luck you won't. We'll get you back to the field hospital, and then on the train home.'

'Blimey, mate, you've copped a Blighty, you lucky bugger,' David shouted. Tom Smith raised his head and looked down to where his arm should have been. His scared eyes latched onto Colonel Martin.

'It's all right, lad, you'll live,' Martin reassured him. 'Keep your dressing pressed tight until the stretcher gets here.' The colonel stood up, leaving David holding a second dressing to Smithy's mangled shoulder.

'What about Bursie?' Tom Smith groaned, but the colonel just shook his head. David knew that they would try to recover what was left of him, but if the shelling continued, there was no chance of them finding anything.

David gulped down his rum ration and felt it burn the back of his throat. Compared to the taste of broken sandbags, cordite and mud, it was pure nectar to him. The men picked up their tools and walked wearily out of the trenches towards the reserve railway dugouts. The sun had climbed to a decent height and it was quiet enough for them to hear birds singing from the few trees that were still left standing. The only other sounds were of the odd whizz-bang flying around.

'Bloody hell. The Boche have shelled the dugouts. Bastards!' Ray shouted when they came out of the communication trenches and saw their sanctuary shattered. 'I was lookin' forward to a few hours' kip in there.'

'We'll find somewhere.' David slapped him on the shoulder. 'Come on, I'm starving. I hope they haven't crumped the rations an' all.' The working party moved forward steadily, picking their way over the mud.

'Will you look at that?' George Partridge said, pointing to a soggy crater. 'Bloody Fritz has put a big bugger into the pond.'

'No fish for tea tonight then,' David sighed.

David had been awake for a while and was sitting outside, cleaning mud from his bayonet. Ray hunkered down next to him. Heavy firing had begun again, somewhere to the south.

'There's summat doin'.' Ray blew a stream of cigarette smoke upwards. 'Listen to them bloody bombs.

'I hope we don't have to give up our rest days and get back in the trenches to keep them buggers back.' David ducked instinctively as rifle fire crackled across no man's land.

'That's my signal,' Ray said, and picked up his rifle.

'Are you on sniping again today?' David looked surprised.

'Every bloody day until we get out for our six days' rest.' Ray threw down his cigarette.

'I don't know how you keep awake for so long. What do you reckon to them poor buggers being court-martialled today?'

'Ratcliffe and Smith?' George Oswin had joined them.

'Mmm.' David shook his head. 'Field court-martialled for falling asleep. You know what the penalty for that is?'

'They could end up afore the firing squad,' Ray called over his shoulder as he left for lookout duty.

'There were them two last month with the Fifths,' David said.

'Saddington and Squires?' George Oswin could always remember names.

'Yes, and that one with the Eighths a bit ago.'

'Fouracres, but it wasn't confirmed. Saddington got ten years in jail and Squires five.'

Harry Hamson was running towards them, ducking instinctively each time he heard rifle fire.

'What's your hurry?' David asked.

'Ratcliffe and Smith.' Harry was flushed but didn't look troubled.

'Well?'

'Ratcliffe got one year's hard labour, but Smith didn't do so well.'

A small crowd had gathered to hear the news of the field court-martial. Harry looked at each of them in turn, fuelling the suspense.

'Oh come on for fuck's sake, spit it out,' someone in the gathered group shouted.

'He got fifteen years' penal servitude.'

'Fifteen years in jail?'

Harry nodded.

'Well he'll miss all the fuckin' action,' the same soldier said and spat.

David had been looking through some field glasses, which he had found on the ground near to one of the shelled dugouts. He jumped to his feet and pointed to a figure in no man's land.

'Isn't that Swanny?' He passed the field glasses to George Oswin, who peered across burnt grass and shell holes.

'What the bloody hell is he doing?' George passed the glasses to Harry.

'I think there's someone trying to get back,' David answered.

'Oh good God, there's Jerry.' Harry pointed to the east of Swanny.

'Where?' George narrowed his eyes.

'Up at the back of him. Oh for Christ's sake,' said David, who had taken the field glasses and had seen the German too. He watched as Swanny lifted an injured man across his shoulders and began to make his way back. The German raised his Mauser.

The crack of rifle fire split the air.

The German fell to the ground.

Swanny ran as fast as he could, his burden hardly slowing him down at all.

The wounded man was a South Staffordshire signaller. His injury was fresh – probably given by the same German. David watched as the signaller was taken away, probably to a dressing station behind the lines.

Swanny sank down onto a straw bale and lit a cigarette.

'What the fuck did you think you were doing?' Ray had thundered over and was bawling at Swanny. 'You halfwit. Couldn't you see Jerry out there?'

Swanny opened his mouth to speak, but Ray continued: 'If I hadn't been there, he'd have shot you – you'd have been dead! You stupid bugger.'

Swanny looked up at Ray. David thought he was going to lash out, but he just smiled and stood up, offering his outstretched hand to Ray.

'Thanks,' was all he said. David and the others slapped Ray on his back and shoulders; at last he had stood up to Swanny, and this time Ray had the upper hand.

Eventually the hostilities died down and the 4th Leicesters took their six days' rest whilst the Germans remained on their side of no man's land.

Saturday, 2nd October 1916

'With respect, sir' – Colonel Martin was inches taller than Lieutenant General Allenby, who had paid a visit to the battalion – 'I believe it to be inadvisable to send totally untrained officers fresh from England to join battalions in the front line. It will be disastrous for the battalion and the whole offensive. How will we be able to move forward without experienced leadership? You are unnecessarily risking the lives of these men.'

'Good man, Martin.' Allenby slapped him on the back. 'You've done splendid work here and your battalion is to be congratulated. I wish you and those under your command good luck in France.' He had left the colonel with no option.

Colonel Martin stood before his battalion. He looked ill and tired, but to his men this was his usual appearance. He towered above them and his thin frame was held erect, as though starched. The early morning sun reflected off his round spectacles and his full, fair moustache twitched.

'The division is to depart Ypres and all leave is cancelled,' he addressed his men. A quiet rumble of disapproval rippled through the ranks. 'We are moving to a hotter part of the line. I cannot disclose where, but you will get to see some open fighting. We leave this afternoon. You will each carry two days' rations as the distance is a great one.' The colonel saluted and the men scattered to prepare for the great distance and the promise of open fighting.

'This is better than slogging away in the trenches.' David was actually happy to be marching through the Ypres Salient towards the railway.

'How far do you think we've come?' Ray asked.

'Well I reckon about ten or twelve miles – look, there's the depot.' David nodded towards the railway track where black smoke was belching from the stack of a waiting engine.

The train wheezed and grunted as it prepared to depart. All along its length, doors were pulled open and tightly formed ranks clambered into waiting carriages.

'Hey,' Ray called to the men in his section, 'this is all right, not a bloody cattle truck this time, and we've got proper seats. Come on!' He flopped down nearest to the window and David made himself comfortable next to him. The whistle blew.

The compartments were soon filled with blue cigarette smoke and raucous singing as the train rattled its way to Fouquereuil. It was dark when they arrived and the men alighted and began marching towards Gonnehem. Archie Phillips kept them in step as he beat his drum with a steady rhythm. Left, right, left, right, left, right. David felt his eyelids getting heavier each time his foot fell to the ground on the drummer's beat. Left right, left, right. David stumbled and pitched into the back of the man in front of him, catapulting the soldier into the next and causing a ripple of disarray in the ranks. David rubbed his eyes and, along with his fellow stumblers, fell back into the strong, regular repeated pattern Archie continued pounding out. The church clock struck one as they entered a sleeping French town.

'It's been a grand day,' David said to Ray, 'but I'm ready for me bed. We must have been marching for at least ten miles.'

'Aye, me too,' Ray replied. 'What do you reckon that place is?' He wasn't asking anyone in particular, as they could all see the large building at the end of the road, illuminated by the full moon. Gothic-style wooden doors to an old theatre stood open, welcoming the weary soldiers into its auditorium, which would be their billet for the next two nights. David dropped his heavy pack onto the floor and took in his surroundings. He was staring at a faded poster of a beautiful woman that had been proudly displayed high up in the foyer.

'Cor, she's a beauty,' Ray said. 'Who is she?'

'Sarah Bernhardt.' David laughed. 'You know, the "Divine" Sarah?'

'Aah, but this one's better.' Ray pulled David's sleeve like a child might their parent's, and they stood together guffawing with their pals at the tatty announcement that *Le Pétomane* had performed there in January 1914. The caricature of a man in a red cape, black trousers, white cravat and a pair of white gloves, showed cherubs holding up his coattails whilst musical notes depicted melodies being issued from his backside.

The men retired to their new billet still chuckling.

A sea of steel glistened as the 4th Leicesters stood at ease; their bayonets had all been sharpened.

'What the fuck's that?' Bob Swann asked when he was handed a grotesque mask and told to pull it over his head.

'That's your bloody life saver,' Corporal Green shouted. 'You lucky lot are among the first to be issued with these new gas helmets. Now get them on.'

'I can't breathe,' Harry Hamson spluttered.

'You won't fuckin' breathe without 'em if Fritz sends gas our way,' snapped Green. 'Right you lot.' The corporal was strutting up and down in front of his section – ten men with monstrous heads. 'Take them off and keep them safe. The rest of your time here will be spent in training to attack the Hun's trenches so you can make us proud, Fighting Tigers.'

'Yes, Corporal!' the chorus came and the men fell out.

'Well, mate, at least we've had some decent grub,' Ray said, wiping his mouth with the back of his hand.

'Aah, I reckon we're about to move on soon though.' David swallowed his Pusser's Rum and lit a cigarette. 'Stuart-Wortley's here. I've seen him with Martin.' He blew a stream of smoke into the air. They sat quietly for a few minutes then David nudged Ray.

'Look out! Corporal's coming over – we'll know what's to do soon enough,' he said, and stubbed out his cigarette.

'Atten... shun!' Corporal Green barked at the men who were resting after tea. There was a rush as they scrambled to their feet, hastily drinking rum rations and throwing down cigarettes. The whole division came together and stood in columns, waiting for the officers. Major General Stuart-Wortley spoke first:

'This division is to retake the Hohenzollern Redoubt. Much is now required of you, and you will leave behind the caddish sort of fighting of trench warfare and experience the joy and glory of going over the top. Your CO will brief you all. Good luck and give them hell.' He saluted Colonel Martin, who then spoke:

'The division is to take four lines of trenches, the redoubt and the village of Haisnes. Tomorrow, 8th October, I shall travel by motor lorry into Vermelles with the other commanding officers and we shall visit the K trenches, where, by means of periscopes, we shall view the redoubt, the Dump and Fosse 8. You will practise attacking by throwing live Mills bombs and be instructed on how to reverse the parapet of a captured trench. Be in readiness, men.'

After the reconnaissance of the K trenches, the officers returned to heavy shelling as the Guards division tried to hold fast and push the Germans back. The deafening bombardments carried on all afternoon and into the night. Colonel Martin gave the order to be ready but not fall in. His men waited. At eleven fifteen the state of readiness was cancelled – the attack had been repulsed by the Guards. The Leicesters, who were preparing to take their place, cheered when they heard the news, but their high spirits were soon dampened when the colonel told them that the Grenadier Guards had suffered great losses.

David stood at ease with the other Tigers in the late-morning sunshine; their bayonets glistened.

'The body of Christ given for you. The blood of Christ given for you.'

'Amen.' The soldiers and officers acknowledged the sacrament they had been given and together they mumbled The Lord's Prayer, pulling themselves to attention for the Creed. An emotionally charged rendition of 'The Strife is O'er, the Battle Done' ended the service at mid-day and left an eerie quietness over the battalion. Even the birds had stopped singing. Most of the soldiers spent the afternoon writing a letter home. At a quarter past five in the afternoon, General Haking, the corps commander from divisional headquarters, gave his address: 'Full preparations have been made for the offensive. The bombardment will be so terrific and the gas so dense that you will meet with little opposition in taking the objective.' His speech was one of assurance and encouragement. 'You will leave here at 0900 hours tomorrow. Good luck and I'll see you all in Haisnes.'

'Better polish the bayonet again before we get some kip then,' Ray said as the men fell out and left the parade. David wondered if thrusting a bayonet into human flesh would feel much different from when they had practised on straw bodies.

Gertie had been gone for over two hours. Although the post office had been busy, Emily had found time to write a letter to David, and another to Ernest. She placed them with the others that villagers had brought in for sending to their sons and husbands; they were all stamped 'B.E.F. France'. The doorbell jangled and Emily's heart sank.

'Good morning, Mrs Walker-Holmes.' She forced a smile – this was an irritation she could well do without.

'I want you to put this notice up.'

Emily took the paper and read it:

'*Wanted – £30 at once or 600 shillings so that we can send each of our boys a Christmas present.*' Under the heading was a list of people the money could be given to, including the school's headmaster, the vicar and Mrs Walker-Holmes.

'But isn't it a little early to be thinking about Christmas?' As soon as Emily had spoken she wished she hadn't.

Mrs Walker-Holmes glared. 'It will take time to collect the required amount, then the parcels will have to be wrapped and shipped. So, no, it certainly isn't too early. Now get on with it.'

'How is William?' Emily enquired.

'He is well, thank you. He has served his country like a true hero.'

'When will he come home?'

Mrs Walker-Holmes took a deep breath and narrowed her eyes. 'When he is recovered.'

'Where is he now?'

'At a place they call Saint Dunstan's. Not that it's any of your business.'

'Will he need more surgery?'

Before Mrs Walker-Holmes could answer, the door opened and Hilda stumbled in carrying baby Ernest. Mrs Walker-Holmes looked at Emily's sister-in-law as if she had a contagious disease and, without another word, turned and left. Emily and Hilda listened at the door as she told whoever was outside how dreadful that family was; first one carrying on with her brother and then the other giving birth to a bastard child. They should be ashamed.

Hilda and Emily were still laughing when Gertie finally returned.

There had been the usual scramble for letters and parcels. David took his and moved away so that he could read it with some privacy.

> *Dear David,*
>
> *Thank you for the photograph of you with your army friends. The dog at the front looks just like Robbie.*[14] *You all look quite serious, even George Partridge, standing tall behind the officer. Annie Partridge had a little boy. She has called him William Eric and he was christened on September 7th. It was a lovely service, tell George, although they did sing a wrong hymn, but the Vicar said it was just as appropriate. George can be the proud father when he gets back. I showed the photograph to Gertie so she could see her brother, George, sitting on the front row. Is Bob Swann there too? The police were looking for him. We had a letter from Sydney – all he ever talks about is the Church Lads' Brigade. We now have a Girls' Sandbag Brigade. There are 234 names on the Roll of Honour nowadays, so you will see lots of familiar faces.*

---

14. See photograph 5, page 321.

When will you be home on leave? Surely it must be soon. I haven't seen you for over six months.

I pray that God will bring you gladly back to me.

With fondest love. From Emily Jane x x x

'What you smilin' at?' Harry Hamson asked David.

'Nowt. Just a letter.'

'From Emily?'

'Yes, and she's signed it from Emily Jane – I thought that privilege was only for Ernest.'

'When do you reckon we'll attack?' Ray had joined them.

'Tomorrow by all accounts, that's the thirteenth.' David pushed his letter into his pocket.

'Yeah, but surely not in broad daylight.'

'Apparently, General Haking said the artillery would bomb them first, then gas 'em, and we'd just walk in and take it.'

'Seems as if we're off.' Ray was looking across the field where they had rested. David followed his gaze. He could see that the 12th Battalion had fallen in and were beginning to march. Colonel Martin took up command of the 4th Leicesters and they too made ready, fell in, and marched towards Vermelles.

Chapter 29

Tuesday, 12th October 1915

Tigers

Dusk fell and the men of the 46th North Midland Division marched from Sailly-Labourse into Vermelles. The three-mile journey took almost two hours as the column snaked and stumbled over rough roads. The soldiers at the front couldn't see those at the end of the crocodile when they turned and looked back. They carried their overcoats rolled up on their backs and were dressed in fighting order. Each man marched with around seventy pounds of equipment; his gas hood, wire cutters, one hundred rounds of ammunition, bayonet and entrenching tool, water bottle, mess tin, small haversack and large pack that was heavy with rations.

'Aaaagh! Bastard!' David looked round and saw Bob Swann slip, try to recover his footing and then trip head first into a ditch. George Oswin stepped forward and stretched out his hand to help him out but fell in on top of him. The mud squelched and sucked as they tried to pull themselves free. The stench was sickening; Ray was retching and covered his nose with his hand as he joined in with David in an attempt to pull them from a roadside, equine graveyard. Swanny pressed his foot against the swollen belly of a dead horse, its feet pointed skywards – dark, decaying rods of hair and bone. The bloated stomach burst with a dull, squelching thud and Swanny slipped back, up to his knees in rotted entrails. David pinched his nose and looked to George Oswin, who had managed to drag himself out, pulling on a rifle that had been held out to him by a soldier from the Lincolns. He wiped his hands on his tunic, shook hands with his rescuer and rejoined the ranks.

'For fuck's sake get me out.' Swanny retched and spat.

'Get away from the 'oss,' Harry Hamson told him.

'Move aside o' that tree stump,' David called, and Swanny stumbled past the horse he had just exploded and stood between it and the next, which stared at him with unseeing eyes, whites showing, reflecting the terror it had faced before going down.

All the time soldiers marched past, covering their noses as they went by. Still the end of the column of men couldn't be seen.

'Grab this,' David said, and pushed his rifle butt towards Swanny, who tried to grasp it, but his mud-and-guts-coated hands slipped from it.

'Wipe your bleedin' hands on yer tunic, you damn fool.' David tried again. Swanny gripped the rifle and managed to lurch his way out of the ditch, using what remained of the tree stump as a lever instead of horseflesh.

The stench remained with them as they rejoined the column of marching men and made their way towards the town.

It was dark when they finally reached Vermelles.

'This place looks as bad as Wipers,' George Partridge said as he looked around. The church was still standing proud at the top of a small rise and they could just make out a chateau. Buildings were smashed, and lattices of roof timbers teetered on walls that could barely hold on. Piles of stones flanked the streets. There were more dead horses, upturned carts, and doors set in stonework that led nowhere.

'God, this is awful,' Ray said, checking the telescopic sights on his rifle. 'All that rubble, hardly a building left standing, even the big hall has been hit. This must be what Hell's like.'

Hundreds of men took up stores and, after some time, headed for the front-line trenches. Somehow, Swanny had managed to exchange his stinking tunic for a cleaner one and was wrapping less-soiled puttees around his legs. These had obviously been given to him because no one could bear the smell of decaying flesh, which clung to him like a miasmic shroud.

Rations for the next day were issued and the battalion fell in and marched along an uneven track, past the reserve trenches, past the second and third line, and made their way to the front.

'So, this is the hotter part we were promised,' David said as they drew nearer. It was almost mid-day when they finally made their way along the communication trenches. Moving in the opposite direction were the Grenadier Guards; they were leaving after fierce hand-to-hand fighting. Their tunics were covered in dust and blood. Filthy faces wore haunted looks, white eyes staring from blackened sockets. The Guards were exhausted and welcomed their replacements with weary gratitude. Some had bloodstained bandages wrapped around their heads and arms, but still they had carried on in their dogged attempt to push the Germans back.

The next day, the 137th Brigade were going to attack to the right, cross the Big Willie trench and Dump trench, take Slag Alley and occupy Fosse Alley. David and his pals were in the 138th Brigade to the left of them. They were to clear the Hohenzollern Redoubt.

They moved into the trenches like a relay team, ready to take up the baton and run with it.

'These are bloody good trenches.' Harry Hamson was taking in his surroundings. 'Cut deep in chalk they are.'

'No more repairing fuckin' sandbags like we had to at Kemmel,' George Partridge commented, as they moved in and sat down along the fire step and where they could on the floor of the trench.

'I reckon it'll take until early tomorrow morning for the whole of the division to fully occupy these trenches,' David said, and wiped the sweat from his brow. He could still smell the scent of death on his hands.

Ray was standing on the fire step, his head just below the parapet. He'd strapped a periscope to his Lee Enfield and wire ran from its trigger to a second trigger positioned below on a rifle-shaped piece of wood that steadied the firearm and rested on his shoulder. Every so often his rifle would crack and a strategically delivered bullet would find its way to a German who had let himself be seen by the sniper's keen eye.

The trench had yards of piping snaking up its wall and out over the parapet. Each pipe was connected to a cylinder that lay in the bottom of the trench. Over three thousand gas cylinders skirted the walls – the division's canisters of preservation.

'So this is what we're going to smoke 'em with,' Harry said, and sat down on one of the canisters.

'Yeah,' said David, 'but we can't call it "gas", we have to call it "the accessory" according to the special order that came round.'

'Or what?' said Swanny.

'Or severe penalties would be imposed,' David answered.

'You just said it.' Swanny bent his head and lit a cigarette.

'So I did,' David agreed, 'so I did.'

David had tried to sleep, but sleep hadn't come. He took Emily Jane's photograph from his pocket. His thumb gently brushed across her smiling face and he prayed he would see her again soon. He looked around at the others. Some were writing notes home, most were smoking and a few played cards. Hardly any were sleeping. Someone further down the trench was playing a mouth organ; the sound of deep humming accompanied the tune, which David recognised as the 'Londonderry Air'. George Oswin, who had been leaning on his pack next to David, said: 'Did you hear about the London Irish Rifles, who had been here in these trenches for the first attack last month?'

David shook his head.

'They did a grand job, and the London Irish's football captain, a chap called Edwards, had a ball tied to his backpack. They went over the top, fixed bayonets and got ready to charge. They'd sent gas, or, rather, the accessory, over first, just like we're going to. Anyroad, Edwards took the ball and kicked it towards Fritz. The ground was better than it is now, flat wi' some grass, just like a great big football pitch. They kept kickin' the ball fo'rads and, they say, that when it were kicked into Jerry's trench our lads shouted "goal!" Now they're being called "The Footballers of Loos".'

'I hope we can do as good a job tomorrow,' David said pulling a crumpled packet of Black Cat cigarettes from his tunic pocket. He smiled at George and held out the pack. 'Are you gonna do the same then, you being our skipper back home?'

'Not on your nelly, mate.' George leaned forward and slid a cigarette from the packet he was being offered. Harry Hamson had squeezed down the trench, past Ray, and leaned back against the wall next to Ray's legs.

'Give us a fag would ya?' Harry nodded at the packet and David extended his arm across to meet Harry's outstretched hand.

There was another crack, and the smell of cordite drifted down into the trench from Ray's rifle. Above them, shells lit up the sky like shooting stars.

Ray remained as still as a cat stalking a mouse.

'Give us a light then, mate.' Harry stood with a cigarette between his finger and thumb waiting for someone else to provide the lucifers.

David tapped his pockets and shook his head.

'What's the use of a fag wi'out a light?' Harry sounded unusually tetchy.

George stretched his leg out as far as he could and fished around in his trouser pocket. He extracted a box of Swan Vestas and sat back again. He struck a match on the box, but it wouldn't light. He tried another, and another, until phosphorus popped and flamed. After lighting his own cigarette he held the match to David, who leaned over and lit up. Harry pushed himself from the cold, damp chalk wall and leaned in towards the match.

'Bleedin' hell!' George called out as he watched Harry stagger and fall to the floor. The whistle of a bullet, followed by a dull slurping pop, told David that Fritz had sniped them.

Ray jumped down. 'Get up, you stupid beggar!' He kicked Harry, who groaned and pushed himself upright. 'Haven't you learnt anything?' Ray's face was flushed and his eyes glinted wildly. Another star shell burst above them. 'It takes three seconds to light three cigarettes, and three seconds for Fritz to see the flame and get you in his sights. Never, ever, be the third man or you'll be a dead man. It's too much of a risk, you stupid sod.'

Harry blew out his cheeks and rubbed his side where Ray's boot had struck and knocked him to the ground.

Ray climbed back onto the fire step, placed the rifle and periscope against his shoulder and resumed his vigil. The Leicester Boys sat in pensive silence.

'Londonderry Air' was still playing, and it reminded David of Emily; she loved that tune in all its guises. He re-read the postcard he'd just written to her and stood up. Picking his way over legs and packs, he made his way to where letters and cards were being deposited for sending back home. He had wished he had written a letter, but a postcard was all he could manage. Leaving the card with a teetering pile of others, he made his way back along the trench, on the way passing a group of men who were chatting around a brazier. David thought how futile their efforts to prise lice from their clothing and pop them over a flame was. He scratched his side and then the back of his neck. The little blighters were everywhere, and no amount of chatting would rid their clothes of them. David was looking forward to having a bath once they had taken the redoubt and were in Haisnes. The thought of a washed body and clean clothes cheered him along, especially no more chatting for a few days afterwards.

He made his way back along the trench to his makeshift bed, where a young man had found a place in the trench and was sitting on one of the gas canisters opposite to where David sat down. The young soldier was carving a piece of wood that looked as though it had once been part of one of the now destroyed trees. He had scraped off the blackened parts and was deftly sculpting the pale timber into a small animal shape. David moved across and sat down next to him on the canister; it felt unsympathetically cold through his trousers. He had seen the soldier at work when they'd been digging trenches and had been impressed by the way he turned the ground with his spade.

'What is it you're carving?' David asked.

'A tiger.'

'I once had a wooden tiger,' David told him. 'Father carved it for my birthday when I was a child.'

'Bet you never thought you'd be a Fighting Tiger then, did you?'

'No. Not then.'

They sat in silence for a moment and David pulled out his cigarettes. He offered one to the soldier, who shook his head.

'You were skilled with your spade when we dug trenches,' David said.

'I'm used to working the land.'

'How's that then?'

'I worked on the Belvoir Estate.'

'What, at the castle?'

'Yes. I loved that job, working in the gardens. Made me proud it did.'

'Why did you enlist then?'

'John Manners.'

'Who?'

'The duke's son. He's a captain with the 4th Leicesters, a pal of Stuart-Wortley's an' all.'

'I ain't seen him.'

'No, he keeps getting sent back home. He's got some illness, appendix or summat. He was sent back with the same thing in July, when we were fighting at Hooge.'

'So he'll miss the action tomorrow.'

'Aye, he will.'

David stood up and shook the young man's hand.

'Better try to rest. We've a big day ahead of us.' The Belvoir gardener nodded and David turned back to his earlier position and sat down, watching the whittling of the wood and listening to the mouth organ as it played 'To the Colour'. From a distance, a bugle played 'Taps', but no cigarettes were extinguished and their glow defiantly decorated the trench until sunrise.

Colonel Martin walked up and down all night; he didn't speak, just nodded to each of his men, who nodded back.

Chapter 30

Wednesday, 13th October 1915

Hohenzollern

A subdued sunrise greeted Loos.

'Tea?' Ray called. David rose and took his mug over. Second Lieutenant Harvey joined them. Ray lifted a blackened pot from a fire he had made in a recess in the trench wall and poured out steaming drinks.

'Cheers.' They raised their cups to the second lieutenant, who sipped his metallic brew. David smelt petrol fumes in the vapour. They had to drink the tea without milk, but there was sugar, so they heaped some in to soften the bitter taste.

'How old are you, Lieutenant?' Ray asked, leaning back against the chalky wall.

'Nineteen.'

'Sweetheart?'

Rob Harvey smiled. 'Yes, she writes every week.'

'What's her name?' Ray asked him.

'Joan. God I miss her.'

'Your father's a colonel ain't he?' David asked.

'That's right.' Rob Harvey didn't elaborate and turned to David. 'You had one of Patch's pups didn't you?'

'Yes, sir.' David grinned. 'Gave it to my fiancé at Christmas.'

'Good.' Harvey nodded.

'She called it Robbie,' David told the junior officer, who was also the brigade's acting adjutant and intelligence officer.

Harvey laughed and patted David on his shoulder.

'An excellent name. I'm looking forward to seeing Patch again when this is all over and we go back home.'

'And Joan?' Ray raised his eyebrows.

'And Joan,' Rob Harvey agreed.

They finished their tea and Second Lieutenant Harvey returned to his dugout to prepare for the afternoon's attack.

David and Ray sat on the fire step and began cleaning their rifles. Swanny was sitting close by and lit a cigarette. He lifted his rifle and pointed it across at George Partridge.

'You'd better shove them ears under your Brodie[15], mate, or Jerry'll see you coming.'

'Piss off,' George told him.

'Wish we were playing football instead.' George Oswin looked pensive.

'Nah,' Swanny scoffed, 'you can't get rid of the opposition with a ball like you can with a bayonet like this gleaming beauty.' He held up the shining blade for them to see.

'Bugger!' Harry Hamson snatched his finger to his lips.

'What've you done?' David asked.

'Cut me sen on the bayonet's edge.'

'Trying to get out of it?' Swanny said, and grinned at him.

'Not likely, besides, I would be for it then if they thought I'd done it on purpose.'

They all laughed and carried on with their cleaning.

---

15. Metal helmet.

At noon, they were told to *stand to* and the promised bombardment began. Fifty-four heavy and eighty-six field howitzers pumped and pounded shells onto German trenches approaching Fosse 8, The Quarries, Chalk Pit Wood and the Hohenzollern Redoubt. Around three hundred field guns joined in. Whumping and thudding pulsated through no man's land and shook the trench walls.

'I hope they blast that barbed wire out,' Ray shouted. He was looking through a periscope, always ready to dispatch a careless Hun.

'Should do. We were promised a terrific bombardment, and by the sound of that lot, the artillery lads are doing their bit,' David yelled back.

The rum ration was brought up the line and generous tots given out.

'One for the road,' George Partridge joked.

'Or two.' David felt the warming liquor flow down into his stomach.

The battering of the Boche was causing adrenaline to course through the soldiers' veins. David looked up; the once blue sky had been smothered. It was grey, bloated and French. Then the bombardment lessened and the men looked at each other.

'What's goin' on?' Ray asked.

'Well, not the bleedin' biggest bombardment of the war like we were told it would be by the sound of things,' Harry Hamson replied.

'Them guns are giving short measure,' David groaned. 'Let's just hope they've done their job and that's why it's not as strong.'

After an hour, the order came for them to put on their smoke helmets, roll up their overcoats and waterproof sheets and strap them to their backs.

David heard a noise close by, like a dog when it's on the trail of something tasty. He looked to his left, and a few feet away someone was huddled on the ground, rocking and whimpering. David pushed his way through and put his hand on the soldier's shoulder. A young lad with frightened, bulging eyes stared up at him. David hunkered down beside the boy and offered him a cigarette, which was taken in a hand that shook. He helped the boy to his feet and gave him an encouraging pat on the back.

Gas and smoke were released from the canisters; the projectors protruded well over the parapet and a prevailing wind blew it between the Hohenzollern Redoubt and the road that ran from Vermelles to Auchy. The conditions were ideal for sweeping the smoke across to the German trenches; everyone hoped that, as promised by Haking, the Germans in the trenches opposite would either be suffocated or run for their lives.

'Let's get at 'em.' George Partridge was animated and kept stamping his feet like a restless horse.

The artillery continued to shell the German trenches and thick smoke crept over no man's land.

'Why don't we use a few sandbags to make steps, so that when it's time we can get over the parapet easier?' Harry Hamson suggested. The men set to work on a jumping-off step and sang their marching song:

We are the Leicester Boys. We are the Leicester Boys.
We know our manners. We spend our tanners.
We are respected wherever we go.
When you see us on parade, open the windows wide,
All the girls begin to cry, 'I tiddly. I tiddly, I ti, ti.'
We are the Leicester Boys.[16]

---

16. Marching song of the 4th Leicesters. Author unknown.

They all cheered and poured more sand onto their step.

Second Lieutenant Harvey asked what they were doing, and when they told him he tapped his watch.

'Ten minutes, boys.' At that moment the gas and smoke stopped. The men in the trench recoiled as German snipers began spattering the edge of the parapet with precision.

'How the fuck can they see us?' Swanny shouted.

'Fix bayonets!'

The snapping of a thousand blades chattered along the trench.

Ray jumped down and pulled off his smoke helmet. The others too pulled theirs off and exchanged them for Brodies. This wasn't what they had been expecting. The smoke should have blocked any view of the British front line.

The trenches were thronged with men; ladders were in position.

'Five minutes to go, and then the best of luck.' Rob Harvey had his watch in one hand and a whistle in the other. David thought he detected a slight shaking of the junior officer's hand.

The barrage had lifted completely. A distant whistle blew. Cheers went up, and to the right the Staffords went over and began their attack to take Slag Alley and Fosse Alley. Seconds later, the firmament exploded with shellfire and the remorseless firing of accurately positioned machine guns. Streams of bullets cascaded across no man's land and cut down the Staffords like scythes sweeping a cornfield, hitting every officer and man as they tried to advance.

Five minutes later it was the turn of the Fighting Tigers and at five past two Second Lieutenant Robert Harvey blew his whistle. Among a succession of 'Terriers', as the Territorial Forces were known, David followed Corporal Joseph Green onto the step and up the ladder. They jumped over the parapet, followed by Harry Hamson. What David saw took his breath away; it was contradictory to what he had been told to expect. Smoke hadn't formed a safety blanket; the wind had been too strong and blown it away, settling in shell holes instead of reaching the German trenches. To the left the Lincolns were advancing, and to the right Maxims were spitting round after round of bullets towards them. The noise was ear-splitting and the smell of smoke lingered in fuggy air.

Colonel Martin sprang to the parapet and shouted:

'*En avant, mes braves!*' And he helped his men with a machine gun and bags of bombs. The continuous stream of men went up and over towards their objective. None faltered.

David and the others of the battalion advanced. As men fell down, wounded or killed, more from behind took their place. The sky had darkened and a vast black cloud hung in the air, as if the devil had cast his cloak over them.

Bodies were strewn all about on the ground to the right. Some were burning, as what was left of the grass caught alight and cruel fingers of fire reached out and overwhelmed them. Their screams were dreadful, and David hoped the poor buggers would die quickly; some were already dead when the flames claimed them.

David moved steadily forward towards the first trench. The German machine guns at The Dump and Mad Point doubled their fire, and their artillery put down a barrage, responsive to the earlier British assault. Before they'd advanced many yards, David saw the Belvoir gardener fall like a puppet who'd had his strings cut. He glanced around quickly; Harry Hamson had been just behind him, and George Oswin too, but he couldn't see them in the melee. Bob Swann was making progress to his left, but there was no sign of George Partridge. He knew Ray would be guarding their advance.

'We're too exposed,' David called to Lieutenant Harvey. 'There's no fuckin' smoke cover.'

Rob Harvey was lifted off the ground by bullets; he arced in the air and rolled into an old firing trench.

The Germans continued firing; bullets fell like rain, puckering the ground and bringing down wave after wave of the advancing soldiers. Colonel Martin was shot in the leg and tumbled backwards into the jumping-off trench.

Men were dropping in swathes, mercilessly butchered. Whole regiments were obliterated and officers sacrificed as they led their men into indefensible positions.

David and those who were still attacking reached their objective. There were four Germans in the first dugout. The Tigers attacked, and two Leicester privates, who David thought were called Brown and Johns, threw in Mills bombs.

When the smoke began to clear one of them shouted: 'Come on, down these steps,' and they climbed down to the next dugout, which had been expertly cut under the ground. They looked around quickly, and seeing only dead Germans, they turned to leave. David noticed one of the 'dead' Germans move and extended his arm to warn the others. Bayonets slashed and scored.

They stepped on lifeless bodies piled on top of each other, some face down, some face up, all killed by the direct hits of shell blasts and trench mortars. Once they were satisfied that the first trench was taken, they moved on to the next. David saw a serjeant major with the Leicesters fighting with three German soldiers. They desperately tried to hold their ground, but the serjeant major's bayonet was swift and they fell; their blood flowed, coating the floor of the trench. The 4th Leicesters pressed on and stormed the second-line trench, bayonets flashing, slapping and crunching into their targets. Tunics turned from feldgrau to red as blood spattered and stained them. Grenades were thrown round the dog-legs of the trench until every German there had been killed.

David leaned against the trench wall and looked back over the young men who were lying in heaps along its floor. Men like him, serving in a foreign country only to lose their fight. He wondered if they had sweethearts at home waiting for news from them.

'Come on!' They were being called to move forward towards the third German trench and a captain called Faire led the battalion onwards. Machine guns positioned in Fosse 8 rattled on relentlessly and bullets came like streams of water from hosepipes. David could hear them cutting through the grass, what was left of it, as they showered down. Men plunged to the ground all around him. David had to step over the bodies of those who had become his friends since arriving in France and push on; hundreds of boots slogging through hell for King and country. David pressed on. He could see the redoubt. The earth was pounding, jarring his head and shoulders. The loud explosions of mortars, the roar of guns and the horrible shrieks and screams of men wounded and dying were the most awful sounds he had ever heard in his life. In front, Corporal Green fell and David tripped over him, sprawling headlong onto the blackened earth. The corporal was staring and David thought he might still be alive. He put his hand on Joe Green's shoulder, but the staring eyes didn't flicker. He closed his own eyes for a second and heard the terrible cries of dying men all around – it tormented him far more than the screams of shells. He got to his knees and began to push himself up when something slammed into him. It didn't feel like a bullet though, more like a hefty blow from something big and hard, like a cricket bat. It knocked him backwards. An explosion deafened him and he felt something like a balloon bursting just below his shoulder blade. He groaned and tried to get up, but his right arm couldn't support him. He looked down; there was a slash of scarlet, like a huge rose bursting open, at the top of his chest between his armpit and breastbone.

A body slapped into the ground next to him, surprised eyes staring as the boy's blood trickled into them from a dark cavity in his forehead. David knew he had to get back somehow or he would be taken prisoner, or worse still – killed. He pulled off the kit he had been carrying and left it on the battlefield. With only his rifle to carry, he began to crawl, pulling himself along with his one good arm and pushing his feet against the mud. There were hardly any clumps of grass for him to cling to and his fingers dug into the earth. A foot came down in front of his face. The rattle of rifle fire was all around and the foot went no further; the running soldier fell down next to him, his Brodie, which resembled a colander, was dislodged, revealing the soldier's blasted skull as a mass of blood and brains. David retched and pressed his face against the mud and sparse, wet grass. He prayed that if he had to die on this godforsaken field, then let it be quick; he didn't want to go like some of the men lying around him, mangled and smashed and in unbearable agony. Whizz bangs and shells were bursting in their hundreds and he dragged himself forward wondering if the next shell would have his name on. All around, men were falling like skittles being bowled over. Some fell in crumpled heaps, others would shout, throwing their hands in the air and totter forward a pace or two before falling face downwards, never to arise again. A shell dropped close by and its fumes choked David; earth flew into his face, his eyes, his mouth; he was drowning in a sea of silt. He had to get back.

With tightly clenched teeth, he pushed and pulled against the cold earth, keeping as low to the ground as he could, moving between the dead and dying. He was parched with thirst; he wished he hadn't left his water bottle behind with the rest of his kit. The next body he crawled past, he looked to see if they had water, but the bottle was riddled with bullet holes. He just wanted to lie down and sleep, but he slogged on; crossing back over no man's land had seemed like a lifetime. The smell of blood and dead bodies was nauseating. At last he could see the parapet of the jumping-off trench, and when he was within a couple of furlongs, he scrambled to his feet and ran to its sanctuary, slipping in mud that was mingled with blood and bullets. A rifle was firing over his head, a protective arc of sniping. He slithered down the trench wall and collapsed onto the floor. The noise from the shells and relentless machine-gun fire pounded his eardrums and his head began to swim.

'It's all right, mate, I've got you.' Through the clamour he heard Ray's familiar voice. He was trying to peel off David's tunic and the pain was excruciating. He pulled David's field dressing from the tunic pocket and gradually eased his friend's arm from its constraints. He fixed the dressing to David's chest and held a water bottle to his lips, which were caked in mud and blood. David drank with greedy gulps, not noticing the taste of petrol. He just needed to quench his raging thirst.

Ray pulled out his own field dressing and pressed it against David's mutilated back, in an attempt to staunch the flow of blood.

A shell exploded, sending soil and shrapnel cascading into the trench.

'We need to get out of here,' Ray shouted above the incessant din, and he helped David to his feet.

'Have you seen any of the others?' David asked.

'It's like needles in haystacks,' Ray answered.

Unsteadily, the two men headed towards the reserve trenches. Stretcher-bearers passed them as they hurried to the dressing stations with more wounded. As they approached 'Barts Alley' they saw a familiar figure directing operations from the floor of the trench. Colonel Martin, who was obviously in great pain from a knee wound, was also reading the Bible to Rob Harvey, mortally wounded and being comforted by the colonel in his final moments. Each time a stretcher or walking wounded passed, the colonel flashed his pocket lamp and gave words of encouragement and praise to his men.

They staggered on, David leaning heavily on Ray, until they reached a dressing station where a doctor was patching up soldiers who had managed to make it back. He handed Ray a dressing and told him to wrap it tightly round his bleeding hand and go back to his battalion. His was only a flesh wound. David hadn't noticed that Ray, too, was injured.

'You'll be all right now,' Ray said as he was wrapping the lint around his left hand.

'Sorry, Ray, I hadn't seen your wound. You gave me your dressing an' all.'

'It's nowt.' Ray had finished winding. 'Good job it weren't the trigger finger though.'

'I dunno. You might have got some leave.'

'I doubt it. Probably latrine duty.'

They both gave a mirthless laugh, and David watched Ray until he was out of sight as he headed back to his post on the front line.

A captain from the Medical Corps chatted idly to David, who sat patiently whilst his dressings were changed. Droplets of sweat had formed on his brow with the intensity of the pain.

'Drink this, Private.' The medic pushed a tin cup into David's right hand. He tipped the contents into his mouth and brandy burned his throat as it trickled down. He was then sent on his way along a communication trench, feeling comforted by the warming spirit. He dragged his weary body along with other walking wounded, passing heaps of dead bodies that had been piled up ready to take out for burial. After about half an hour they came to the chateau in Vermelles. Hundreds of men stood in line waiting to have their wounds tended. David slumped to the floor, weak from blood loss. He was pulled to his feet by one of the stretcher-bearers nearby and led away into the chateau; blood was flowing freely down his back.

The chateau walls trembled as the bombardment continued. David slid to the ground and lay down on the cold floor. The pain in his shoulder and back was worse than anything he had ever experienced; even worse than that awful initial agony of those times when he had accidentally hit his thumb with a hammer when he'd missed the nail he'd been aiming for. He felt light-headed and hot. Sweat mingled with his blood, and the coolness of the stone against his back was actually quite comforting. Then blackness descended.

Chapter 31

Thursday, 14th October 1915

Fallout

Swanny and Ray were sitting together on a pile of spent shells in an old quarry. The morning mist had settled all about them. Both men had the same haunted look as the other one hundred and eighty-six who had made it through the previous day's Armageddon. Their uniforms were caked in mud and blood and none had washed or shaved for three days. The men hadn't eaten for almost twenty-four hours and their stomachs growled and clenched in protest. At sunrise, the quartermaster serjeants brought rations of bully beef and hard biscuits, but the food was momentarily ignored because a flagon, marked SRD, was being passed around. Exhausted and despondent, each man in turn hooked a filthy finger through the handle and tipped the container with his arm until a stream of thick, dark liquor poured down his throat.

Swanny took a large draught and wiped his mouth with the back of his hand. He spat mud from his cracked lips and passed the flagon to Ray.

A German Picklehaube lay in the mud and Swanny kicked it as if he was trying to score a goal. It was someone's trophy – a grisly souvenir. It hardly moved; its spike fastened it to the hostile ground.

'What a fuckin' waste!' Swanny kicked at the helmet again. 'All them wasted lives! All that fuckin' wasted effort – and for what? A few trenches in farming land. Not even a hundred yards taken from the fuckin' Boche.'

Ray laid a steadying hand on Swanny's arm and offered him a cigarette. Swanny took one and sat down again on the shell cases. Stretcher-bearers were still moving past to fetch and carry whoever they could reach. Those that couldn't be saved would either perish on the field or be taken prisoner. A stretcher came past bearing a soldier crying for his mother – his tunic was riddled with bullet holes and his face was a pulpy mess on one side.

Swanny put his head in his hands and cried with him.

Roll call was taken; the names called out formed a tragic epitaph. When one of the battalion didn't answer, their pals would say: 'Gone west,' or 'Over the hill.'

Having survived the last twenty-four hours on the odd biscuit and cigarettes, the Leicester Tigers finally ate their rations.

Shelling continued as the German Army tried to reclaim the redoubt. The Sherwood Foresters relieved the Leicestershire battalions, who made their way back to Lancashire trench between the railway and Vermelles. They slept for several hours before being taken to a rest camp in Hesdigneul.

David had lain on the floor for two hours, drifting in and out of consciousness. His dressings were changed again whilst he waited with hundreds of others for Red Cross ambulances to take them to field hospitals. Eventually his turn came and he was helped on board. The driver wore a cap with a red band that said *Salvation Army*. He looked as tired as David felt. An officer slapped the driver on the back and said: 'Are you taking them to heaven?'

The Salvationist climbed into the ambulance's cab before leaning out towards the officer who had just made the jibe.

'No,' the driver said, 'I'm taking them away from hell.'

The vehicle bumped over rough roads, heading north, and every so often swerved to avoid shell holes. It took over two hours to complete the seven-mile journey; wounded men cried out when they were pitched this way and that against each other. Eventually, and well behind the firing line, they arrived at an old building that was being used as the Béthune Field Hospital.

Girls with the Volunteer Aid Detachment and more Salvationists brought them food and water whilst they waited for a doctor. The water didn't taste of petrol and the bread and cheese didn't taste of anything, but David was too hungry and thirsty to care.

David caught his breath and clenched both fists when the dressing was prised from his chest. The bullet hole was clean and about the size of a farthing. After re-dressing the wound he was turned over and work began on his back. He could feel the doctor pulling and then pushing at his injury, and pain wrapped around him and squeezed his stomach, threatening to expel the food from inside. He was then helped to where those who had been treated were lying down, and throughout the night and the following morning his dressings were changed every two hours. The blood still flowed freely. He felt weak, and the black cloud above him kept descending and smothering his consciousness.

David was awakened by shouting.

'We have to get out!' The nurses and VADs moved swiftly among the sleeping soldiers. 'We're being attacked and the shells are getting closer. Quickly!'

A German bombardment had begun.

Those who could struggled to their feet; David was too weak and wondered how many more minutes of life were left in him. He mentally said goodbye to Emily and those he loved before he was lifted onto a stretcher and taken down a filthy cloister nearer an entrance to the cellars. Rows of badly wounded men were left on the floor to await being carried down to safety in the basement. David closed his eyes and thought Ray had been wrong and that this must be what hell was like; across his eyelids rode four black horsemen.

The spaces between the stretchers were packed with dead pigeons and tin helmets.

'What a place!'

It was cold; it was noisy; it was crowded and it stank of stale sweat and blood.

'Anywhere must be better than this godforsaken ginnel!' David thought.

He was wrong.

He felt himself being lifted and looked up at the stretcher-bearer.

'What's all this with the pigeons?' he asked.

'They've all died o' shellshock, and it might be catching,' came the sarcastic reply.

He had only been carried a yard or two when a grip-handle snapped off the stretcher with a pitiless jolt. He screamed as pain lashed through him and, try as he might, he couldn't halt the tears. He could bear it no more, and as they descended the tight stairwell into the cellar, the darkness deepened.

David woke with a start and immediately reached out to his left side to check for his rifle, but the exertion was too much and he slumped back down again. He tilted his head and tried to take in his surroundings. A flickering oil lamp, which appeared to be hovering at shoulder height in a dark recess, offered a pale orange glow to the gloom where the doctor who had patched him up earlier was bending over an unsteady table. Beneath him the cellar floor lurched rhythmically in step with the relentless pounding outside. David closed his eyes. His head throbbed in time with the falling shells and he felt as though every cell in his battered body was screaming in a bid to burst through his skin. He forced his eyes open again and squinted in an effort to focus on what was happening around him. His gaze was drawn back to the feeble flame spilling from the lamp, which dangled from the low ceiling above the makeshift operating table. He watched it waver and tremble as it strained to give light to the murky treatment area. David tried to see who was on the table being patched up. He couldn't identify the patient but knew the poor bastard would never walk again – if he survived. It had been a while since David had been the one on the same table receiving his treatment, and the doctor had worked hard to stem the flow of blood that poured from the bullet's exit wound in David's back; the sticky straw where he was now lying told him he hadn't been completely successful.

The steady whumping of shells thundered down onto the village, accompanied by groans of injured men as they waited for treatment, or release. David watched the nurses and VADs as they moved deftly among the wounded, and the doctor, working in the dimness as quickly as he could to seal wounds, put back falling entrails and covered torn faces. There was a rank smell of unwashed bodies overlaid with the metallic stench of blood, and in some cases guts, which stuck to mud-caked clothing and flesh. David felt sick. He closed his eyes and lay back. He felt a bloody dampness beneath him but he was too exhausted to move to a drier patch. At the same time as unconsciousness came, his pain went.

When David regained awareness he watched a new batch of walking wounded stumble down the stairs; each man was labelled 'WW' as if he belonged to the walking club for those who didn't play school sports. The men walked indifferently into the gloomy cellar; vibrations of destruction rocked the stairs and the walls shook out of harmony. No small patch of this cellar had sympathy with anything else. However, the men showed mutual concern. They helped one another along; hands wrapped in bloodstained bandages guided those with bound eyes and others impaired by broken and shattered limbs. They all coughed and wheezed, lungs straining to suck in another draught of stagnant air. These men had become accustomed to the army's love of exaggeration; they accepted their official classification; their injuries were not life-threatening. They assembled in an area on the far side of the doctor's table where they would try to rest before their next journey, either to another field hospital or back to their regiments, and then, once again, the front line.

An authoritative voice boomed over the groans.

'Well, well.' It was the company serjeant major David had seen fighting with the three Germans; he was standing near the lamp beside the rickety treatment table.

David stirred and tried to sit up, but the pain, which seared through his body, rendered him helpless. He strained to hear what was being said to the doctor, but all he could make out was:

'Top hole!' and he wondered what the hell was 'top hole' about this desperate bloodbath?

'Well, well!' The voice was closer this time, repeating the phrase as the CSM moved through the broken bodies, his swagger stick tucked under his right arm.

David tried to sit up again.

'At ease!' the CSM instructed. David wished he would fuck off.

The CSM looked the men over.

'Well done, chaps. A splendid dash!' And that being his valediction, he saluted and swaggered towards the stairs.

David closed his eyes and listened to the shells that were relentlessly blasting into what was left of some distant building. A nurse stopped and knelt beside him. The stains that clung to her clothes were different shades of blood: dark-brown patches overspread with bright scarlet. She lifted the dressing that covered the entry wound just below his collarbone. Taking his dog tag in her other hand, she leaned closer.

'Hello, Private 3488.'

'3458!' his own sandpaper of a voice replied, correcting her.

'3458,' she affirmed, raising her voice so she could be heard above the guns, the coughing and the grunts.

'Emily!' he murmured. Her voice was not that of a stranger; his confused condition forced it to be familiar.

'Emily,' was all he said; it was full of memories and affection.

He opened his eyes again and a pretty face swam before him, the blurred and shaking image dancing with each throb and jolt.

He felt her cool hand on his forehead and his cracked lips stretched feebly upwards.

'What's your name?' she asked. He raised his head slightly and looked at her more intently; he frowned and then slumped back onto the thin scattering of straw.

'I thought you were Emily.'

'Can you sit up for me?' she coaxed. 'Who's Emily? Is that your wife?'

David shook his head. 'Not yet.' The corners of his mouth embraced a loving smile.

'Come on, please try to sit up. I need to dress your back. Now, what's your name?'

'Adcock.' David's answer was more a grunt. He pushed himself up. It felt as though his muscles were on fire, and he beat the ground with the flat of his hand. Then his fist clenched, dragging mud from the floor under his broken nails, his other arm rigid, holding him upright. He flinched and moaned as she pulled the blood-soaked dressing from gaping, mangled flesh. She would have seen the sharp edges of his splintered ribs and the jagged vertebrae of his backbone bulging through torn muscles. Blood poured afresh from the wound and she quickly pushed a clean dressing into the ragged hollow and bound it in place as best she could. Pulling some of the stained, damp straw away, she replaced it with a marginally fresher handful or two.

'Try to rest.'

'Can I have a drink?' David croaked.

The nurse looked around and stepped away. David thought she hadn't heard him and let his head drop onto the straw. He was cold and began to shiver. He lay there in just his torn shirt, trousers and puttees with his boots still on.

David drifted between grotesque reality and savage frightening dreams. He didn't know how long he had slept for, but he was awakened by the same kind voice.

'Private Adcock, wake up, I have water for you.' She held a blood-caked water bottle to his lips. He opened his mouth and she tilted it until the water ran over his tongue. He felt the soothing liquid slide down his throat. Some ran out onto his chin and dribbled down his neck; it put out the flames of his thirst and was better than any ale he had ever drunk in The Bell.

'Thank you.' He rasped his gratitude and she smiled as if he were the only soldier in her care. He lay back and closed his eyes once more, bathing in the memory of the water. He felt something being placed across his body and looked down to see a tunic peppered with bullet holes being laid over him. He knew that whoever it had belonged to wouldn't need it now, but was grateful for the warmth it offered. He watched the nurse move down the line of wounded men, treating each one as if he was the most important.

The crowded cellar shook less as the shelling began to subside.

A few more lamps had been found and lit.

The line of men waiting for the doctor shortened.

David awoke from a fitful sleep.

He reached out to his left side to check for his rifle again, but the exertion was too much and he slumped back.

A VAD worked her way down the line and stopped beside David. She knelt and gently turned him onto his right side so that she could dress his wound. Unlike the nurse who had attended to him earlier, she didn't speak. Nor did she spend long unpacking and repacking the mess that used to be his back; she then quickly moved on to the next young man needing her attention, who David recognised as their drummer, Archie Phillips.

The shells gradually stopped.

David continued to shiver and shake uncontrollably. He thought it must have been getting on for dawn as the barrage had lifted. He tried to sit up, but the pain wrapped around his torso and squeezed his stomach. Again he felt nauseous. His throat began to tighten and his tongue worked rapidly as its muscles caused it to hit the roof of his mouth. His stomach clenched in an effort to expel its contents. The intense pain burned; he felt as though he was encased in flames. His head swam and a black curtain descended, smothering his brain and covering his eyes as he once more drifted into unconsciousness.

The first convoy of ambulances had left and the cellar now only held those with severe injuries who needed transporting to another hospital or to await a train that would return them to England. Some, who had been there earlier, had been patched up and sent back to their battalions, others were already on their way to Lille.

Along the far wall, and scattered across the floor of the cellar, another battalion had been formed. Row upon row of lifeless bodies lay beside each other, and on top of each rested a wooden cross. The stretcher-bearers, who had brought them in the night before, would later help to carry them out to a burial ground where a chaplain would collect their belongings together for sending back home before he said a few words of prayer at their interment.

A young VAD was tending those who were clinging on to life. The stretcher-bearers lifted a man who had been sleeping next but one to David and carried him away to the waiting ambulance. She nudged David.

'Come on, Private, time to go.' He didn't move. She tapped his shoulder and bent down and called to him again, her mouth only inches from his ear.

The stretcher-bearers returned and moved down the cellar. They passed the doctor who was sitting beside the bloodstained table; he was holding his head in his hands, desperately in need of sleep. The air was fetid, and they coughed when the heavy stench filled their lungs. They approached the VAD who was retying a dressing around a soldier's face; he was able to walk out to the ambulance, unaided.

'Is this the last?' one of them asked, nodding towards the man lying next to David. The VAD nodded. They moved forward and lifted the conscious man who was moaning loudly.

'Me legs,' he shouted, and his arm dangled helplessly over the side of the stretcher as they headed towards the stairs and fresher air, leaving David where he was. The VAD bent down. She pulled the torn tunic to cover him and shook her head. Picking up the blood-spattered water bottle, which lay empty beside David, she followed the stretcher-bearers out of the cellar.

She never looked back.

Chapter 32

Friday, 15th October 1915

Desertion

He was cold, so cold, so achingly bloody cold. David imagined he was awake, but his eyes were closed. He was exhausted, too exhausted to open them; the lids were pressed together as if cemented. He had heard once, couldn't remember when, that in some places they put coins on your eyes when you die. Had he died? Is that why his eyes were so heavy? With his right hand, he reached up towards his face and a wave of hot pain stabbed him under his collarbone. The kind of pain he supposed that someone who had been bayoneted would experience. He hadn't been bayoneted. He knew that much. No, he had been shot by a Jerry machine gun. Maxims they called them. Maxim verses Vickers. Vickers verses Maxim. A duel for supremacy stormed his consciousness. This time, the Maxim had won, had beaten him. The bullet'd had his number on it. He opened his mouth to cry out, but no sound came. He was having one of those nightmares where he was shouting loudly but had no voice. His throat felt as if he had been gargling with broken glass, tongue wooden and sticking to the roof of his mouth. Forcing his arm further upwards, his fingers touched a cheekbone. That was OK, intact, just slightly sticky. He pushed his hand further to feel for the coin on his right eye. There was no coin.

'Thank Christ for that,' he managed to mutter. He spread his fingers across to his left eye. No coin. He blew a stream of relief through swollen lips. In the knowledge that there were no coins, he forced his eyelids apart. He was staring upwards, but everywhere was pitch-black; he was encased in an envelope of darkness. Quietness hung heavily over him. That can't be right. There were shells, a bombardment; it was the stillness now that was hurting his ears. He turned his head to his right, but everything was as black as the Earl of Hell's waistcoat, just like in the coalhouse at home. His mind swam and a mental picture took shape of the time when Whattoff had locked him in that coalhouse when he was seven. It had been so dark in there that he hadn't been able to see his hand in front of his nose. He'd banged on the door until his knuckles hurt, but no one had come to let him out. The dark cubbyhole had been his prison and it stank of the coal that filled it and made him cough. Even when he had called to his brother that he needed to pee, his pleas were ignored, and when David thought he would never be found he cried and his bladder had released a hot stream down his legs. David didn't need to pee now. In fact, he couldn't remember the last time he had. 'You don't need to pee when you're dead,' he thought.

A feeling like a thousand needles sticking into his skin swept up his body.

'Oh my God, I'm in a coffin,' he said aloud. That was why it was so dark; he was encased in a wooden box. But he couldn't be dead. They were going to bury him alive! He was sweating and a hot panic boiled in his veins. He had to get out. He gradually raised his arm, and screwing up his eyes, he reached upwards, pushing through the pain.

He would force the lid from the coffin. But there was no lid. Fingers waved in a blind abyss. The dark tomb was not that of a wooden overcoat; it was bigger, damper, colder. Irrational ideas gave way to pragmatism and more rational understanding. Those who had gone west, o'er the hill, for the long sleep, dead, weren't buried in coffins out here – they were wrapped in blankets, faceless, and lowered into the unforgiving ground. Thoughts of men dying swam in concentric circles behind his closed lids, whirlpools of fear and confusion. Snapshots of comrades falling face down in the mud, backwards with blood blooming like rose petals from wounds, sideways as machine-gun fire swept across their path. Then an image of a mass burial pit manifested and his breathing quickened.

'Jesus Christ, no, not that!'

He reached sideways with his right arm, stretching through the pain as far as he could, and felt nothing but relief. Relief that he wasn't in a mass grave lying beside another soldier whose life had been snuffed out, relief that he couldn't feel the muddy side of his own clay tomb.

From his struggles, David knew that his right arm was still there, and working. He tried to move his left. He wiggled his fingers. They worked. Lifting his elbow slightly away from his body, he screamed as a pain like a tiger sinking its teeth into his back coursed through his shoulder, his side, his arm, his neck, his head. It was as if an electric shock was surging along the nerve endings; even his teeth ached. He let his arm rest back down again and gradually the agony eased to a dull, persistent throbbing. He was tired, dog-tired. He drifted off to sleep once more; too worn out to keep trying further movement.

When he woke up he became aware of something resting on his upper body. He wasn't sure if the feeling had been there before or not. It was painful to do, but he pressed his chin towards his chest and opened one eye in an attempt to find out what was there. The blackout was still absolute, and even with both eyes open, visibility was impossible. His head fell back onto a thin cushion of damp straw and he closed his eyes once more.

'Oh, God,' he croaked; realisation had slapped him in the face. The pressure was from a wooden cross with his name on, just like the ones lined up in the cellar the day before.

Fuck! He was still in the cellar.

'No!' He moaned. 'No! No! No!' A teardrop pressed through his closed lids, ran down his face and dribbled into his ear. Sobs caught in his throat and he wept tears of helpless despair, until sleep closed in once more.

He didn't know how long he had slept for, shifting between mangled, mutilated reality and mordant, frightening dreams, but when he awoke, a pale white light was piercing the gloom in front of him. He thought this must be what people referred to as the light at the end of the tunnel, the light you saw when you died and went to heaven. The shaft slid down a wall and tapered away into a shape that reminded David of a bayonet. He couldn't see or feel his rifle and he still wasn't able to make out what it was that he could sense pressing down onto him. He pushed his right arm against his side and little by little raised it onto his chest. There was no cross. As his hand moved slowly over his torso he felt something round and metal, then, a few inches away, another one – buttons. The thing lying across him was a tunic, and there was something in the pocket that rested on David's breastbone. It must have been the previous owner's Bible or pay-book. Bible probably; pay-books weren't that heavy. He wished it had been a full water bottle so that he could quench a thirst that was making his head pound from dehydration. He wondered if his own tunic was being used to keep another wounded man warm and if that soldier would find Emily's photograph in the breast pocket.

'Emily! Oh Emily!' Her name lingered on his dry lips. He couldn't bear to think of her. Instead, he concentrated on the light that had become stronger and the shaft wider. It was daylight, and as darkness receded, David was, at last, able to make out his surroundings. A black shape scuttled across the floor, followed by another. Rats were feasting on blood-soaked straw and pieces of flesh that had once belonged to someone who had lain with him in the malodorous basement. He managed to look across to where the dead had been lined up; only a few remained. Painfully, he strained to see as far as he could in all directions. Bile rose in his gullet as a slow, but very real, understanding gripped him. The cellar was empty. Only he remained. Everyone else had been taken to their next destination, whether it was a field hospital or a cemetery. He opened his parched mouth as wide as he could and yelled, bawled, screamed, for help.

'Please! Somebody! Help me! Don't leave me here! Please! Help!' He listened for any movement, the sound of someone, anyone, coming to rescue him, but could hear nothing more than the scratching of rats. He shouted again and again until he felt as though he had been calling out for hours rather than the few minutes that passed before his voice had rasped into silence.

This godforsaken, stinking, putrid, damp, dark, subterranean shit-hole was his burial pit. Consciousness left him.

With the memory of his boyhood's Saturday penny, everything in his cellar was spent.

Chapter 33

Wednesday, 20th October 1915

Corollary

Silence. It surrounded her like a shroud. Emily sat beside the fire in the tiny post office, head in hands. Once again the morning's post hadn't brought her the news she wanted, or that she didn't want. She tried so hard to carry on, just as Mary was doing, but she was weak – 'no backbone' Mary had said.

Outside, the morning crawled past like a salted snail, and stillness veiled the streets. Black-edged telegrams adorned windowsills; it wasn't supposed to be like this, to feel like this. This wasn't what they were promised!

Emily slid from her stool as if she was sliding into an ice bath. On the counter were the parish magazines ready for distribution. Emily felt only apathy; she would deliver them that afternoon, as it was half-day closing. She pulled a postcard from her pocket and stared at the picture; it was of a soldier holding a rifle.[17]

---

17. See postcards, page 326.

The inscription was '*Pour le devoir. For duty's sake.*' She turned the postcard over. Tears welled up and escaped, sliding down her cheeks like raindrops on a windowpane. Her tears were of sadness and utter disappointment.

> *Field Post Office, 12 October 1915*
> *Passed by Censor No 404 J E Barker*
> *Dear Emily,*
> *Just a post card to say I have got my parcel. We are in the trenches now and it keeps raining. It was fine the first two or three days in. I will write a letter as soon as I get out as it's too wet now so you can look out for one in a day or two's time. I got your letter with the parcel. I thought it best to send this instead of keeping you waiting.*
> *Fondest love from David xxx*

The doorbell jangled and Mrs Walker-Holmes walked in. Emily quickly dried her tears with a silk handkerchief that Ernest had sent from France and pushed it back into her pocket, along with the postcard.

'We need to do more recruiting.' The older woman slapped a poster onto the counter. That woman was beyond belief. Emily just stared at her and shook her head.

'That brother-in-law of yours ought to enlist.'

'Whattoff is in a protected industry,' Emily countered. 'He's a foreman at the shoe factory making boots for the troops. He's doing his bit!' Emily knew Whattoff had received a number of white feathers.

'The country needs more men.'

Emily thought that Mrs Walker-Holmes resembled a turkey with her neck flushed and eyes bulging.

'Have you seen the hospitals?' Emily asked. 'They are full of men in blue uniforms looking pale and solemn. And the streets are full of women wearing black.'

'Well, it has to be seen through.'

Emily fought back a new threat of tears – she was damned if she was going to let this awful woman see her cry.

'Goodbye, Mrs Walker-Holmes. And as you haven't asked, no I haven't heard anything more of my fiancé.' She knew the reference would annoy the blasted woman.

'Just put the poster up,' Mrs Walker-Holmes snapped, and turned away. Emily stepped forward and held the door open, then took the poster and threw it onto the fire. Perhaps she did have a backbone after all.

Emily picked up a parish magazine and sat down again. She opened it and began to read. The main concern appeared to be the condition of the church roof, then a few cheerful messages from serving soldiers and sailors. A new section had been added:

R.I.P.
'Greater love hath no man than that he lay down his life for his friends.'

Emily would continue to read the monthly magazines, but it would be a long time before there would be any good news.

SYSTON PAROCHIAL MAGAZINE[18]
NOVEMBER 1915
R. I. P.

'Greater love hath no man than that he lay down his life for his friends.'

GEORGE OSWIN – Killed in action, October 13th 1915. Member of the Institute and Formerly Captain of the Football Club and one of the most regular boys in Mr. Pain's Bible Class. One of his last acts before leaving the village was to make his communion at the Parish Church.

Dear Mr Oswin,

I am sending you these few belongings of your dear son George. I feel it my duty to let you know of his death. He died a brave soldier on making the attack on October 13th 1915.

(Extract from a letter from George's comrade.)

DECEMBER 1915

3 Brookside, Syston
Nov 17th, 1915

Dear Vicar,

I am now writing to thank you for your kindness to us in our great trouble; it was very good of you to put it in the magazine. We had official news come on November 13th that our dear son was killed in action on October 13th.

Well, he has died an honourable death and also he has given his life for his King and country. We always tried to think he would come back, brave as he went away – so brave he always used to say he should do his best when he was in it to win it. We are sure he did his best.

---

18. The magazine entries are written exactly as they were in the parish magazines including capitalisation and punctuation.

Well, though we have heard our dear son was buried comfortably, we hope to meet again where partings are no more.

Mr. and Mrs. Oswin

P.S. Will you kindly accept this small amount towards our Church roof as it was George's last wish that the Church over there would not be destroyed.

GEORGE OSWIN,

Killed in action, October 13th, 1915. Captain of the Football Club, and one of the most regular boys in Mr Pain's Bible Class.

JANUARY 1916

HARRY HAMSON, whom we announced as 'reported missing' in last month's issue, has now been officially reported 'killed in action' on October 13th, 1915. Our sympathy goes forth to his widowed mother and relatives and we trust that the sense that the boy did his duty will be a consoling thought to them in their sorrow.

R.I.P.
PRIVATE HARRY HAMSON,
killed in action, October 13th, 1915,
Hohenzollern Redoubt.

APRIL 1916

We have to put on record the name of another of our men who has laid down his life for his country, and whose death has not been recorded in the Parish Magazine, viz, Private GEORGE E. PARTRIDGE, son of Mrs Partridge, Wilby Place, aged 26 years. He was in the 4th Leicesters and was killed on October 13th, 1915, at the Hohenzollern Redoubt.

Private G. E. Partridge was formerly a member of our Church Sunday School and a member of the Football Club. He leaves a widow and two children.

Private G.E. Partridge
11th Leicesters.
Killed, October 13th, 1915.

AUGUST 1917

LANCE CORPORAL WHATTOFF ADCOCK (2nd South Staffords) Missing, 13th November 1916, now reported killed in action.

Private WHATTOFF ADCOCK.
(2nd South Staffords)
Missing, November 13th, 1916,
now reported killed.

JANUARY 1918

ERNEST WADE, killed in action, 1 October 1917, Age 23.

ERNEST WADE,
Killed in action, Oct. 1, 1917.
Age 23.

Chapter 34

Monday, 27th December 1920

Epilogue

David awoke with a jolt. Someone was crying out; a scream ripped through his semi-conscious mind and he pressed his palms over his ears to shut out the demons that invaded and threatened his sanity. Sweat oozed from his pores and ran down his forehead. He pushed himself up; a pain shot through him, just under his shoulder blade, and he slumped back down again into darkness.

He was clawing his way through an ocean of rank, slimy mud mixed with putrid blood. He reached out and grasped at a rock the size of a football. It rolled away; the rock was a head, and the face of Harry Hamson stared at him through unseeing eyes. Machine guns rattled and his body began to shake. George Oswin was shouting to him from across a burning field, and George Partridge fell to the ground, stood up, fell again. David stumbled along, tripping over bodies, trying to find a way out. The dark walls of a trench closed in. The nightmare had returned.

Another scream. He awoke, rubbed his eyes and blew out his cheeks. The terror of seeing such slaughter and then being left alone in a dark, stagnant cellar had invaded his subconscious once again. He thought he had been forsaken and left to die that night when he woke up and found that all the other wounded had gone; he had been abandoned on the cellar floor with rows of dead soldiers. The stretcher-bearers had taken quite a fright when they returned to move those who had perished to their freshly dug graves and David had asked them for water. That had been five years ago, and still it haunted him.

He wiped the beads of sweat from his forehead with a starched white handkerchief, and then pushed it back into his trouser pocket.

'David!' It was his mother's, voice.

He jumped up from his chair beside the fire. Robbie yelped; David had trodden on the dog's tail. Robbie had been sleeping on the hearthrug and he too sprang to his feet.

David sank back down again and reached for a cup of tea that he had been drinking before he fell asleep. As he stretched forward, his hand shook and he clenched his fist to stop the tremor caused by the earlier turbulent dream.

'David!' Mary called again from upstairs.

'Is everything all right?' David called back.

'Everything's fine, but we could do with some more coal on this fire, and young Raymond needs his tea.'

David put down the teacup, which rattled in its saucer, and stood up. He lifted the coal scuttle and climbed the stairs. He could hear his mother scolding her grandson:

'Ernest Raymond Adcock, will you keep away from that fire – and don't throw your socks on it!'

David pushed open the bedroom door and felt the warmth from inside wash over him. A wooden tiger clattered loudly across the floorboards towards him, followed by Raymond, who toddled over to his father, bare-footed and laughing at the tiger he had just thrown. David put down the coal scuttle and patted his son's head.

Mary was flushed, and tendrils of her silver hair had escaped their pins. Smiling widely, she wiped her hands on her pinafore and beckoned David over.

David walked across to the bed. The sight that greeted him banished the fear and trembling he had just relived – until the next time.

'Now then, Emily Jane,' he said, 'what have we here?'

Emily looked exhausted but happy, cradling their newborn sleeping baby who was wrapped in a grey blanket. Looking down at his wife and child, David, after a moment said:

'What'll we call this 'un then?'

'David.' Emily smiled up at her husband and then closed her eyes to sleep.

''Bout time,' he answered, and lit his pipe.

David Adcock with his wife, Emily, and sons
Ernest Raymond (right) and David (left).

Afterword

Seeking Tangible Realities

From the working class came the perfect foot soldiers: deferent, fatalistic men who expected little from life and for whom the army often meant an improvement in living standards. This flood of recruits seemed to justify the British faith in muddling through.[19]

Gerard J. De Groot

Private 3458 David Adcock was my grandfather, and my grandmother was Emily Jane Wade. Both his, and my father's, valediction when leaving was invariably: 'Don't be late in the morning.' Part one, 'Foreshadowing of Youth' was written from conversations I had with my late father, also David Adcock, and part two, 'Heroism in the Abstract' from original diaries, letters and postcards, as well as handed-down memories. The letters in the novel are written as the originals were with, perhaps, unusual use of some words and capitalisation. Words that are crossed through denote censorship.

---

19. *Gerard J. De Groot, Blighty: British Society in the Era of the Great War (Harlow: Longman, 1996), p. 31.*

'Heroism in the Abstract' is part of a PhD thesis in creative writing that examines a lacuna in Great War fiction, the analytical element of which is evidenced in the novel's composition, thus placing the creative component in its literary and historical context.

When consulting archival information I was not just looking at military history relating to the Great War, nor was I looking at social history, but I sought an element of realistic inspiration for the novel. Through the use of these documents I was seeking to use historical events as the basis for a convincing fictional narrative. I approached the research as a creative writer, not as a social or military historian, with an alertness to creating an accessible, factually sound account whilst observing what a creative writer is looking for as distinct from what a historian wants.

This novel is the first to deal with the events at Loos on 13th October 1915 and it paints a picture of life on the home front and Western Front not yet dealt with in fiction. The narrative transcends the narrow genre of 'war fiction', deals authentically with the lives of actual combatants, their families and communities, and tells how the war affected their future.

The opening quotation here is from Chapter Three, 'To Die Young', in Gerard J De Groot's 1996 book *Blighty*, which considers the historical context that my novel explores through fictional reconstruction.[20] My research has used unique private sources together with some published accounts to weave together truth and fiction to illuminate

20. *'On 1 May 1914, the regular army was nearly 11,000 men short of the size prescribed by the army order of 1907, proof of the population's lack of enthusiasm for military service. Four months later, after the outbreak of war, the army was swamped by a flood of recruits too large to be processed. When Britain was forced to improvise an army, her population responded with alacrity. The men who came forward proved, superficially at least, the perfect raw material for an army.' De Groot, p. 31.*

what has become a forgotten battle, fought by men from a town often overlooked in considerations of the Great War: Leicester. The rationale behind the research and resultant novel is to share the knowledge gained from historical investigations by placing it in an accessible form. The novel, *Don't Be Late in the Morning*, is a work of fiction, but it is founded upon a detailed reading of military history, official documents and, most significantly, unpublished primary sources, which reveal the human and personal cost of the conflict. In combining these different types of writing, my aim has been less to reveal the potentially disputatious relationship between different modes of historiography than to explore how the dialogue between public and private history on one hand and creative invention on the other can produce new ways of understanding the past.

My intention is to show the reader what it is that I have done to create a novel from my original research topic, a project initially entitled: *The Forgotten Battle: The Battle of Loos, and its Effects on the Soldiers on the Western Front and Civilians on the Home Front*. The research question, however, has also become an ethical one.

To blend together carefully researched facts and compelling fiction necessitates much consideration where moral responsibility is concerned. A decision I made when I was given Private David Adcock's diary was, rather than to publish a soldier's diary in its unaltered form, to take it forward, fill in the gaps with meticulously researched facts together with fiction, and create a novel.

I found that hardly anything had been written about the Battle of Loos other than the first offensive, which began on the 25th September 1915. The second offensive, sometimes called *The Battle of the Hohenzollern Redoubt*, has been overlooked, and my decision to research not only this particular battle, but how those affected by it could be portrayed in a novel, was the catalyst for my decision to undertake a PhD and write the novel from the diary, together with letters and postcards, about a hitherto unwritten part of the Great War.

Some of the original sources that I have either been allowed to borrow, or in the case of the diaries, postcards and letters, I own, are unique and unpublished. I was also allowed to borrow a full set of Syston's Parish Magazines from 1910–1920 from a private owner. These are probably the only surviving copies of the publication and represent an invaluable, indeed unique, resource. Michael Doyle, author of *Their Name Liveth For Evermore*, gave me digitised photographs of the regimental diaries for the Leicestershire Regiment from 1914–1918.[21] The historian of the Leicestershire Regiment, Richard Lane, lent me a scrapbook of newspaper cuttings kept by the father of Second Lieutenant G E F Russell, who served with the 1/4th Battalion of the Leicestershire Regiment and was killed in action on 13th October 1915. From these documents I was able to show that the war fought by people in Leicestershire, particularly the village of Syston, is significantly different from that of the well-documented tales from The Somme and Passchendaele.

Another area of research is the effect on women, who enjoyed new responsibilities and freedoms, together with the concomitant fears and grief always present in wartime.

I have found that research in creative writing can be achieved through some more unconventional methods, such as oral enquiry and witnessing, as well as traditionally formal critical strategies of archival study and literature reviews.

21. Doyle, Michael, Their Name Liveth for Evermore: The Great War Roll of Honour for Leicestershire and Rutland (Billingborough: Michael Doyle, 2009).

A creative writing PhD is demanding, intellectually and emotionally, both in its creation and its defence. Using real people and their previously unpublished accounts naturally generates an emotional connection to the creative work, especially when those people were engaged in such terrible historical events.

The representation of people and physical conditions have to be judged discerningly, and there is an ethical and moral responsibility involved first in slightly altering the historical record in order to fit the needs of the narrative, and second, when using characters based upon real people to tell the story. I also had to consider the question of ethical accountability in representing those individuals. There is no accepted procedure of doing this when the events themselves are deeply dramatic and emotional.

An author cannot allow the subject matter to speak for itself, and there is always a case for judging very accurately how to represent it without being complacent. These are some of the hurdles I had to overcome.

The reader of *Don't Be Late in the Morning*, unlike its characters, knows that the progress of the war would not improve. The novel shows how the Battle of Loos was an important forerunner to the atrocities to come later, when other devastating but more well-known battles were fought in Picardy, in the Somme and Ancre Valleys, and at Passchendaele.

This demonstrates how possible it is to bring something innovative about the conflict into literature, escaping the stereotypical attitudes of earlier novels, which depicted desolation and devastation rather than excitement and purpose. An important way in which a fresh perspective would be offered is by recognising that in 1915 attitudes towards the war were still relatively idealistic and hopeful, and people were, on the whole, less cynical. The Somme offensive had not happened and the belief that it would not be a long war was still noticeably evident.

My intention is that writing a novel using original, previously unseen documents will rightfully establish the second offensive of the Battle of Loos in literature as one of the recognised battles rather than a forgotten one.

Photographs and Postcards

1. Syston boys' school
David Adcock – 2nd row, 4th from left

2. In the mess hut

3. Outside the mess hut
David Adcock – seated, front row, first left

4. Showers and potatoes
David Adcock – standing in the middle

5. With the dog
David Adcock – seated, 2nd right

Leicestershire regiment mobilising
by kind permission of Richard Lane,
Historian to the Leicestershire Regiment

Afterwards at the hospital
David Adcock – back row, 2nd left

Postcard 1. Emily's birthday

Postcard 2. Mary's postcard to David

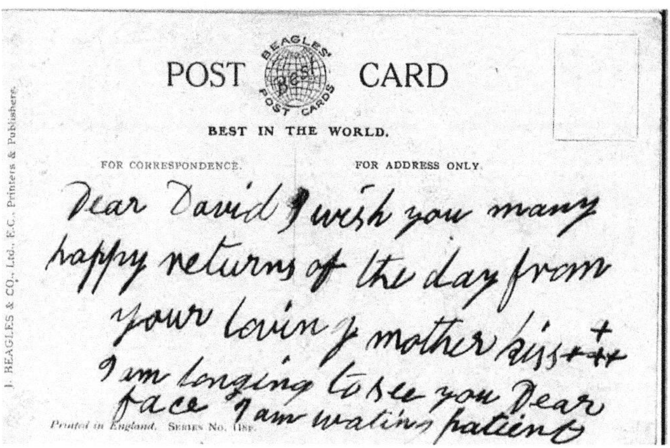

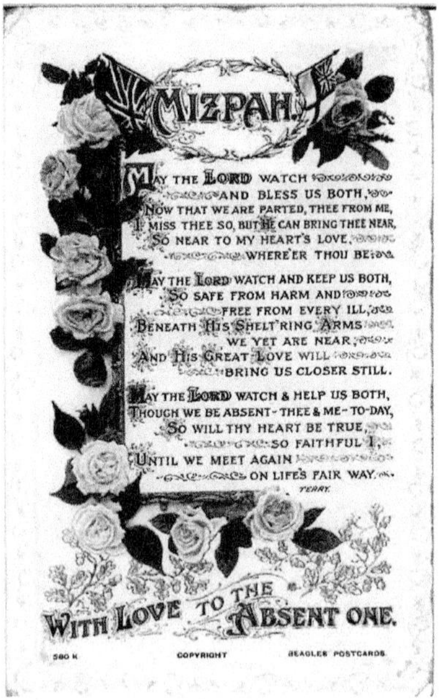

From Emily to David

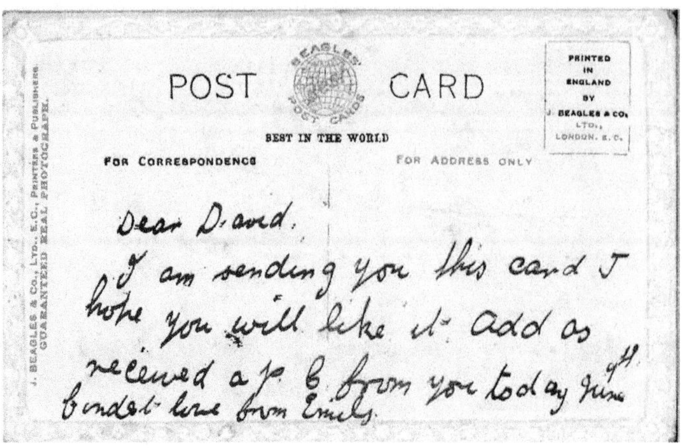

Dear David.
I am sending you this card I hope you will like it. Add as received a p.c. from you today June 9th
Fondest love from Emily.

From David to Emily

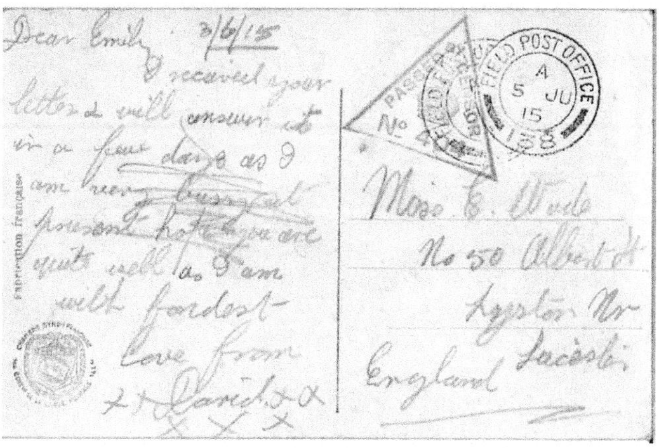
Dear Emily 3/6/15
I received your letter & will answer it in a few days as I am very busy at present hope you are quite well as I am with fondest love from
xx David xx
xxx

Miss E. Wade
No 50 Albert St
Lygston Nr
Leicester
England

PASSED BY CENSOR No 4
FIELD POST OFFICE A 5 JU 15 138

From David to Emily

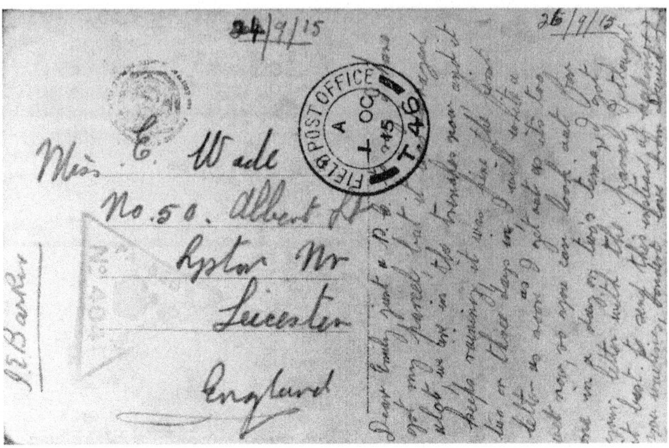

Bibliography

Primary Sources

Unpublished Documents

The diary, letters, postcards and photographs of David Adcock and Emily Jane Wade are unpublished and are the property of the Adcock family and their descendants.

The scrapbook of newspaper cuttings compiled by Mr Russell is the property of the Royal Leicestershire Regiment.

Archival Sources

War Diaries of the 1/4th Battalion of the Leicestershire Regiment, February 1915 – November 1915, Private Collection, Michael Doyle, Billingborough.

Published Primary Sources

Parish Magazines of St Peter and St Paul, Syston, January 1914-December 1914

Parish Magazines of St Peter and St Paul, Syston, January 1915-December 1915

Parish Magazines of St Peter and St Paul, Syston, January 1916-December 1916

Parish Magazines of St Peter and St Paul, Syston, January 1917-December 1917

Parish Magazines of St Peter and St Paul, Syston, January 1918-December 1918

Parish Magazines of St Peter and St Paul, Syston, January 1919-December 1919

Parish Magazines of St Peter and St Paul, Syston, January 1920-December 1920

Parish Magazines of St Peter and St Paul, Syston, January 1921-March 1921

Secondary Sources

Armitage, F. P., C.B.E., Leicester 1914-1918, The War-Time Story of a Midland Town (Leicester: Edgar Backus, 1933)

Ashworth, Tony, *Trench Warfare 1914-1918: The Live and Let Live System* (London: Macmillan, 1980)

Bailey, Catherine, *The Secret Rooms* (London: Viking, 2012)

Barker, Derek, Foulds, Dorothy, Gamble, Dennis and Young, Ray, *Syston Past*, (Leicester: Clipper, 2003)

Beazley, Ben, *Four Years Remembered; Leicester During the Great War* (Derby: Breedon, 1999)

Blaxland, Susan, *Syston War Memorial Project* (Syston: Blaxland, 2009)

Brittain, Vera, *Testament of Youth* (London: Virago, 2004)

Cullen, Jim, *Essaying the Past: How to Read, Write and Think About History* (Chichester: Wiley-Blackwell, 2009)

De Groot, Gerard. J., *Blighty, British Society in the Era of the Great War* (Harlow: Longman, 1996)

De Groot, Jerome, *The Historical Novel* (London: Routledge, 2010)

Doyle, Michael, *Their Name Liveth for Evermore: The Great War Roll of Honour for Leicestershire and Rutland* (Billingborough, Michael Doyle, 2009)

Doyle, Peter, *The British Soldier of the First World War* (Oxford: Shire, 2011)

Dunn, Captain J. C., *The War the Infantry Knew* (London: Abacus, 1938)

Feilding, Rowland, Ed. Jonathan Walker, *War Letters to a Wife* (Staplehurst: Spellmount, 2001)

Fussell, Paul, *The Great War and Modern Memory* (Oxford: Oxford University Press, 1975)

Garner, Tim and Young, Ray, *Syston Past, Volume II* (Leicester: Clipper, 2006)

Graves, Robert, *Goodbye to All That*, (Harmondsworth: Penguin, 1960)

Hanley, Lynne, *Writing War: Fiction, Gender and Memory* (Massachusetts: The University of Massachusettes, 1991)

Herman, Judith Lewis, *Trauma and Recovery* (New York: Basic Books, 1997)

Hills, John David, *The Fifth Leicestershire – A Record of the 1/5th Battalion The Leicestershire Regiment, - T.F., During the War, 1914–1919* (Loughborough: Echo Press, 1919)

Hincks, John, *Ramsay MacDonald: The Leicester Years (1906–1918)* (Leicester: John Hincks, 1996)

Hiscock, Eric, *The Bells of Hell Go Ting-A-Ling-A-Ling* (London: Arlington, 1976)

Jenkins, Robin, *Leicestershire at War* (Stroud: Sutton Publishing Ltd., 1998)

Lloyd, Nick, *Loos 1915* (Stroud: Tempus, 2006)

Macdonald, Lyn, 1915*: The Death of Innocence* (London: Penguin, 1997)

Marquand, David, *Ramsay MacDonald* (London: Cape, 1977)

Middlebrook, Martin, T*he North Midland Territorials Go To War; Captain Staniland's Journey* (Barnsley: Pen and Sword, 2003)

Milne, John, *Footprints of the 1/4th Leicestershire Regiment, August 1914 to November 1918* (Leicester: Edgar Backus, 1935)

Neaman, Elliot, *A Dubious Past* (London: University of California Press, 1999)

Oram, Gerard, *Death Sentences Passed by Military Courts of the British Army 1914-1924* (London: Francis Boutle, 1998)

Parfitt, George, *Fiction of the First World War: A Study* (London: Faber and Faber, 1988)

Peaple, Simon, *Mud, Blood and Determination: The History of the 46th (North Midland) Division in the Great War* (Solihull: Helion, 2015)

Pegler, Martin, *British Tommy 1914-18* (Oxford: Osprey, 1996)

— *Soldiers' Songs and Slang of the Great War* (Oxford: Osprey, 2014)

Putkowski, Julian and Sykes, Julian, *Shot at Dawn – Executions in World War One by Authority of the British Army Act* (Barnsley: Pen and Sword, 1989)

Rawson, Andrew, *Battleground Europe, Loos 1915, Hohenzollern Redoubt* (Barnsley: Pen and Sword, 2003)

Richardson, Matthew, *The Tigers: 6th, 7th, 8th & 9th (Service) Battalions of the Leicestershire Regiment* (Barnsley: Pen and Sword, 2000)

— *Fighting Tigers: Epic Actions of the Royal Leicestershire Regiment* (Barnsley: Pen and Sword, 2002)

The Cambridge Companion to: *The Literature of the First World War*, Ed. Vincent Sherry (Cambridge: Cambridge University Press, 2005)

The War Office, *Infantry Training 1914* (London: Authority of His Majesty's Stationery Office, 1914)

Tighe, Carl, *Writing and Responsibility* (Abingdon: Routledge, 2005)

Tiltman, H. Hessell, *James Ramsay MacDonald, Labour's Man of Destiny* (London: Waverley, 1929)

Warner, Philip, *The Battle of Loos* (Barnsley: Pen and Sword, 2009)

Webb, Jen, *Researching Creative Writing* (Newmarket: Frontinus, 2015)

Wombell, Paul, *Battle Passchendaele 1917, Evidence of War's Reality* (London: Travelling Light, 1981)

Wylly, Colonel H.C., *History of the 1st and 2nd Battalions, The Leicestershire Regiment in the Great War* (Aldershot: Gale and Polden, 1928)

Young, Ray, *Syston Past, Volume III* (Leicester: Clipper, 2010)

— *Syston Past, Volume IV* (Leicester: Clipper, 2013)

Journals

Robert Lee, 'Rethinking History: Blurring the Edges' in *Rethinking History*, 14 (2010), 91-118.

Electronic Resources

AFS Enterprises Limited, Leicester City Football Club Match Record: 1915 <http://www.11v11.com/teams/leicester-city/tab/matches/season/1915> [accessed 11 September 2013]

[Anon.], 'Hohenzollern Redoubt and its Capture: British Gas Attack a Fine Struggle of Bombs and Barricades', *Manchester Guardian*, 23 October 1915, p. 10, in *ProQuest Historical Newspapers: The Guardian (1821-2003) and The Observer (1791-2003)* <http://search.proquest.com/hnpguardianobserver> [accessed 11 May 2013]

[Anon] 'Victorian Medicine' *Use of Laudanum and the Treatment of the Sick* <http://freepages.family.rootsweb.ancestry.com/~treevecwll/vicmed.htm> [accessed 6 April 2013]

Cecil Adams, 'Cecil's Storehouse of Human Knowledge', in *The Straight Dope* <http://www.straightdope.com/columns/read/363/did-a-french-vaudeville- star-once-specialize-in-trained-flatulence> [accessed 28 July 2011]

Dan Snow, 'BBC News Magazine', in *10 Big Myths about World War One Debunked* <http://www.bbc.co.uk/news/magazine-25776836> [accessed 24 February 2014]

J. Douglas Bremner, 'Traumatic Stress: Effects on the Brain' in *Dialogues in clinical Neuorsciences*, 8:4 Dec 2006, pp. 445-661. < http://www.dialogues-cns.com/publication/traumatic-stress-effects-on-the-brain> [accessed 15 August 2014]

Peter J. W. Folkers *Pierre's Photo Impressions of the Western Front*, <http://pierreswesternfront.punt.nl/content/2010/08/loos-en-gohelle>[accessed 01 October 2013]

Imperial War Museum: <http://collections.iwm.org.uk> [accessed 14 July 2011]

Loretta M. Alirangues, 'Funerary Practices in the Victorian Era' in *Morbid Outlook* <http://www.morbidoutlook.com/nonfiction/articles/2003_04_vicdeath.html> [accessed 2 July 2012]

Michael Duffy, 'Weapons of War - Grenades', in *First World War* <http://www.firstworldwar.com/weaponry/grenades.htm> [accessed 13 July 2013]

'The National Archives British Army WWI Service Records, 1914-1920 Record for Ernest Wade', in *Ancestry* <http://www.ancestry.co.uk> [accessed 14 July 2011]

Peter Leese, 'Men of War: Masculinity and the First World War in Britain; The Secret Battle: Emotional Survival in the Great War' in *Cultural and Social History*, Volume 7, Number 3 (September 2010), pp. 406-408, <http://ejournals.ebsco.com/direct.asp?ArticleID=4B2C8AF6759F4D813E14> [accessed 23 May 2012]

The Met Office, Monthly Weather Report, 1910s, in *Met Office Publications Archive* <http://www.metoffice.gov.uk/archive/monthly-weather-report-1910s> [accessed 19 March 2012]

Time and Date, Calendar for Year: 1894 – 1920, <http://www.timeanddate.com/calendar/?year> [accessed 01/10/2011]

Military History Online <http://www.militaryhistoryonline.com/wwi/articles/britishtacticalchanges.aspx> [accessed 01/11/2013]

Acknowledgements

I would like to thank my late father, David Adcock, for giving me my grandfather's diary, photographs, letters and postcards and for recounting both his, and my grandparents' memories.

Thank you, Richard Sheehan, for your amazing editing of the manuscript and to Sarah Houldcroft of Goldcrest Books for making it happen.

I would also like to extend my thanks to weapons expert Martin Pegler (the Oracle) and his wife, Kate, for their friendship and sharing of expertise especially when on the battlefields; Michael Doyle for his support and for letting me have his copies of the Regimental Diaries; Susan Blaxland for sharing her research on the Syston Roll of Honour; Susan Gamble for kindly allowing me to borrow the Syston Parish Magazines, Historian to the Leicestershire Regiment Richard Lane, Colonel Brian Smith, my PhD supervisors, Dr Kerry Featherstone and Dr Nicholas Freeman for their guidance, enthusiasm, patience and support and other members of the academic and library staff at Loughborough University who have helped in various ways.

Last, but really first, thank you to my husband, [also] David, who has patiently supported me throughout, and driven me around the battlefields of France and Belgium, and to Mel Plehov, my daughter, for her encouragement and belief that I could achieve this.

About the author

Dr Karen Ette graduated from Loughborough University with an MA in creative writing and a PhD in contemporary and modern English, creative writing, which focused on Great War literature. She has lectured on creative writing and is currently a lay chaplain at Loughborough University. Previously she worked in educational administration for many years and published a guidebook for students on how to complete UCAS applications.

A writer with Ruler's Wit (www.rulerswit.co.uk), she has published work with them in *Spring Tales, Summer Tales, Autumn Tales and Winter Tales*. She has also written several Christmas books including A *Second Christmas Truce?, The Advent Calendar Recipe Book,* and *On Clouds of Words*. Articles have been contributed to: *Your*

Cat, The Racing Pigeon, The Tiger (the magazine of the Leicestershire and Rutland Western Front Association) and Stand To! (the journal of the Western Front Association). She is also a member of the Leicester Writers' Club and the Association of Christian Writers.

As well as being a writer she is a freelance proofreader and copy-editor having trained with the Publishing Training Centre (PTC) and is a member of the Society for Editors and Proofreaders. She has been a judge for the BBC's 500 Words competition since it began.

Dr Ette lives in Leicestershire and her passion is cricket. She can always be found at the County Ground, Grace Road, whenever there is a match being played and where she has been a member since junior membership was just twenty-five pence.

Contact the author

Dr Karen Ette's website is:
www.the-writers-secret-helper.com

She writes two blogs – one which is travel and food based: www.fancypanscafe.com and the other is centred on WW1: www.battlefieldsandbeyond.com.

Other books by Karen Ette

The Advent Calendar Recipe Book
Your UCAS Application
A Second Christmas Truce?

Writing with Rulers Wit
Spring Tales
Summer Tales
Autumn Tales
Winter Tales
The Green Man's Dark Secret

PhD Thesis
Heroism in the Abstract

Printed in Great Britain
by Amazon

50369633R00200